Bigby Bear

By PHILIPPE COUDRAY

BiG

Philippe Coudray
Story & Art

•

Miceal Ogriefa
Translator

•

Fabrice Sapolsky
& **Alex Donoghue**
US Edition Editors

Amanda Lucido
Assistant Editor

Vincent Henry
Original Edition Editor

Jerry Frissen
Senior Art Director

Fabrice Giger
Publisher

Rights & Licensing - licensing@humanoids.com
Press & Social Media - pr@humanoids.com

BIGBY BEAR, BOOK ONE. This title is a publication of Humanoids, Inc. 8033 Sunset Blvd. #628, Los Angeles, CA 90046.
Copyright © 2019 Humanoids, Inc., Los Angeles (USA). All rights reserved. Humanoids and its logos are ® and © 2019 Humanoids, Inc.
Library of Congress Control Number: 2018954822

B&G is an imprint of Humanoids, Inc.

First published in France under the title *L'Ours Barnabé* Copyright © 2012–2018 La Boîte à Bulles and Philippe Coudray. All rights reserved.
All characters, the distinctive likenesses thereof and all related indicia are trademarks of La Boîte à Bulles Sarl and/or of Philippe Coudray.

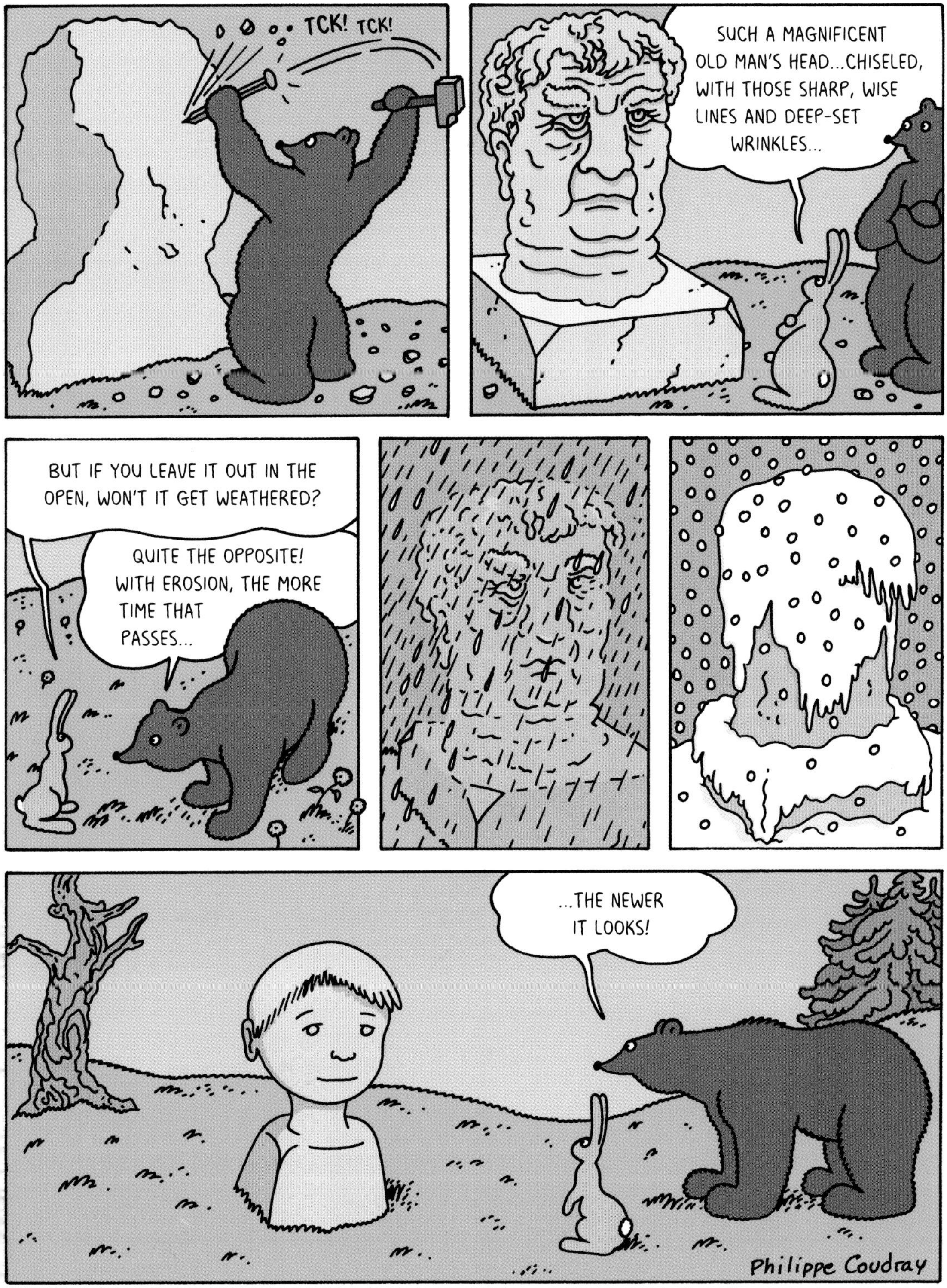
TCK! TCK!
SUCH A MAGNIFICENT OLD MAN'S HEAD...CHISELED, WITH THOSE SHARP, WISE LINES AND DEEP-SET WRINKLES...
BUT IF YOU LEAVE IT OUT IN THE OPEN, WON'T IT GET WEATHERED?
QUITE THE OPPOSITE! WITH EROSION, THE MORE TIME THAT PASSES...
...THE NEWER IT LOOKS!
Philippe Coudray

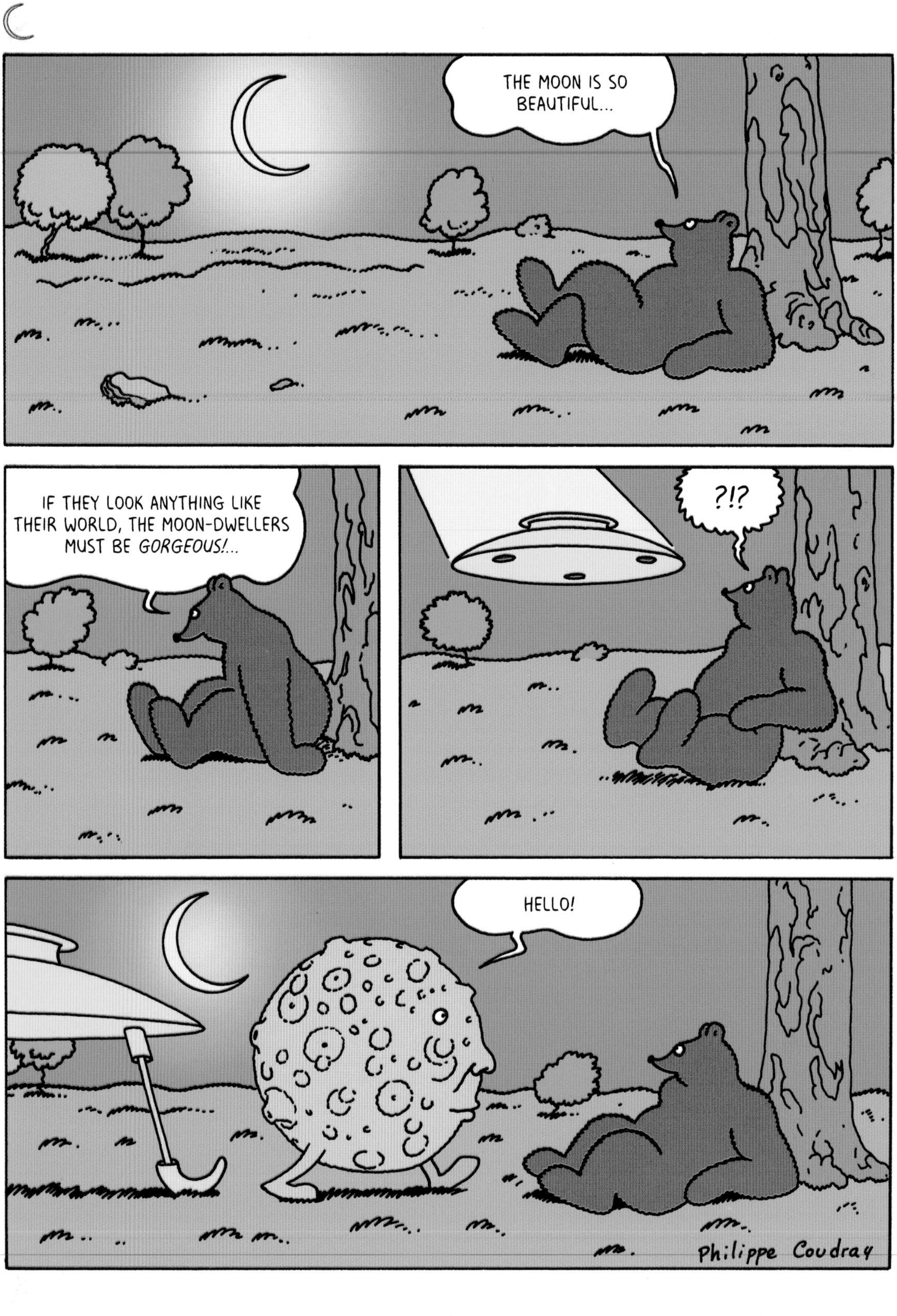
THE MOON IS SO BEAUTIFUL...
IF THEY LOOK ANYTHING LIKE THEIR WORLD, THE MOON-DWELLERS MUST BE *GORGEOUS!*...
?!?
HELLO!
Philippe Coudray

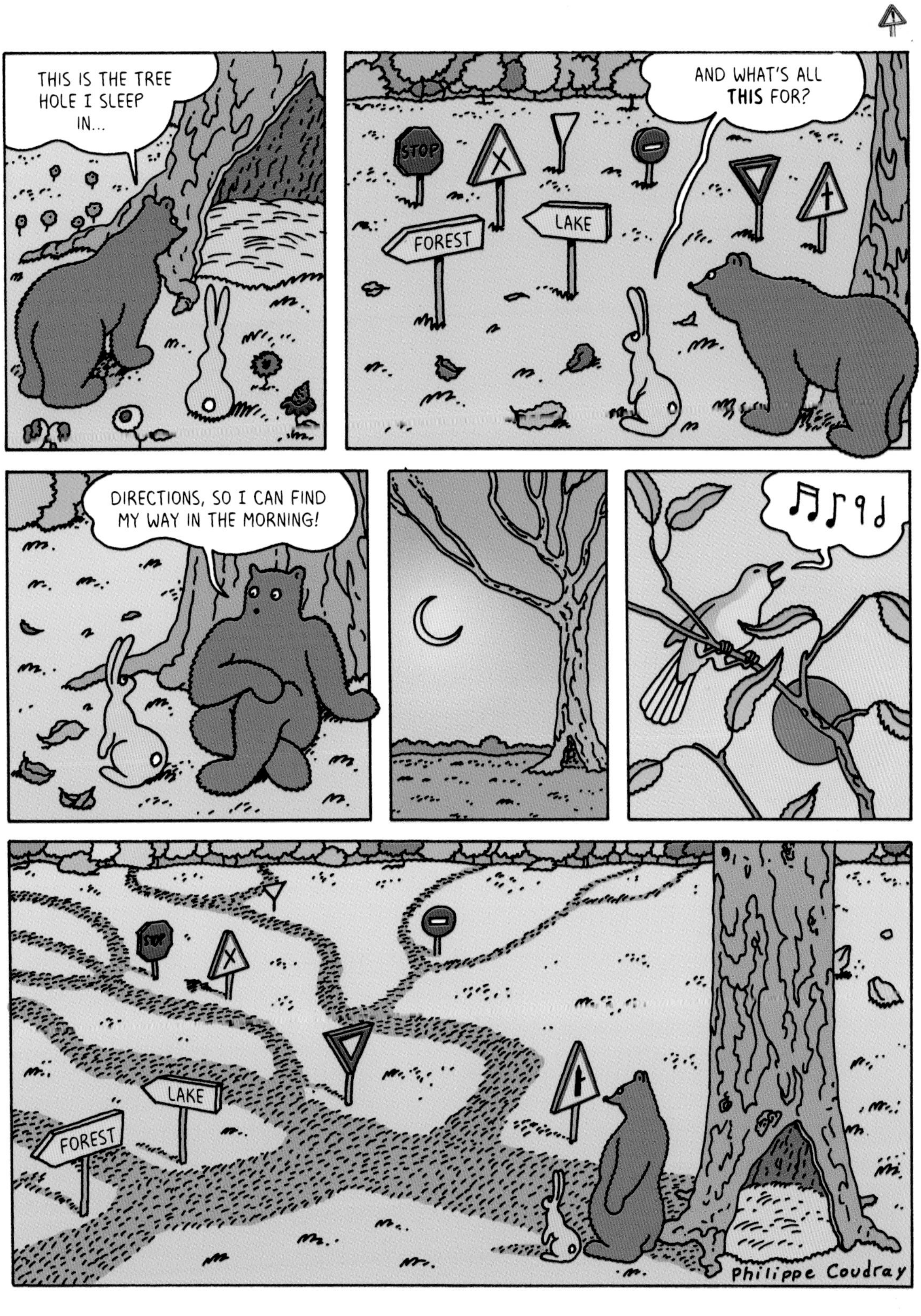
THIS IS THE TREE HOLE I SLEEP IN...
AND WHAT'S ALL **THIS** FOR?
STOP
FOREST
LAKE
DIRECTIONS, SO I CAN FIND MY WAY IN THE MORNING!
STOP
LAKE
FOREST
Philippe Coudray

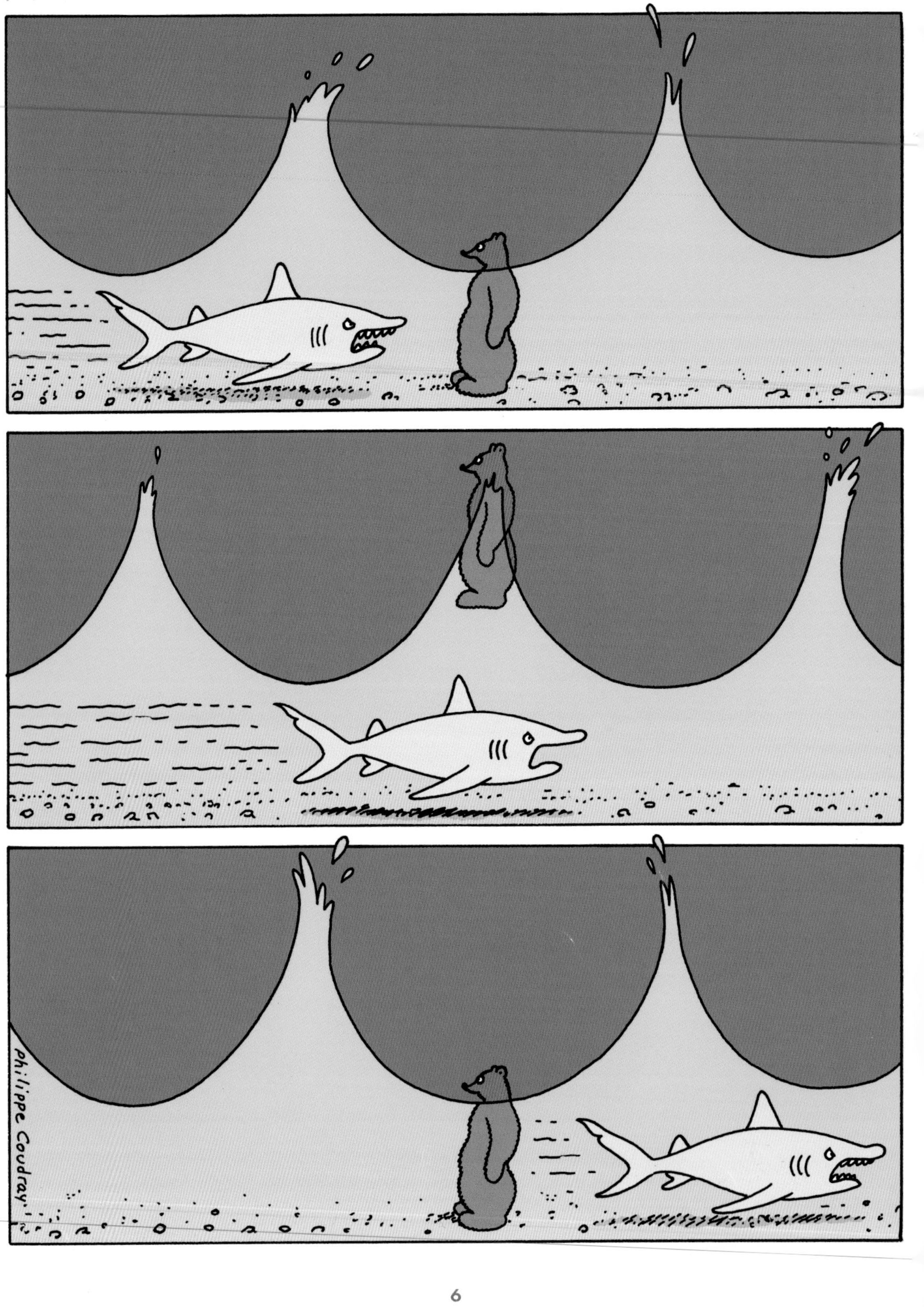
Philippe Coudray

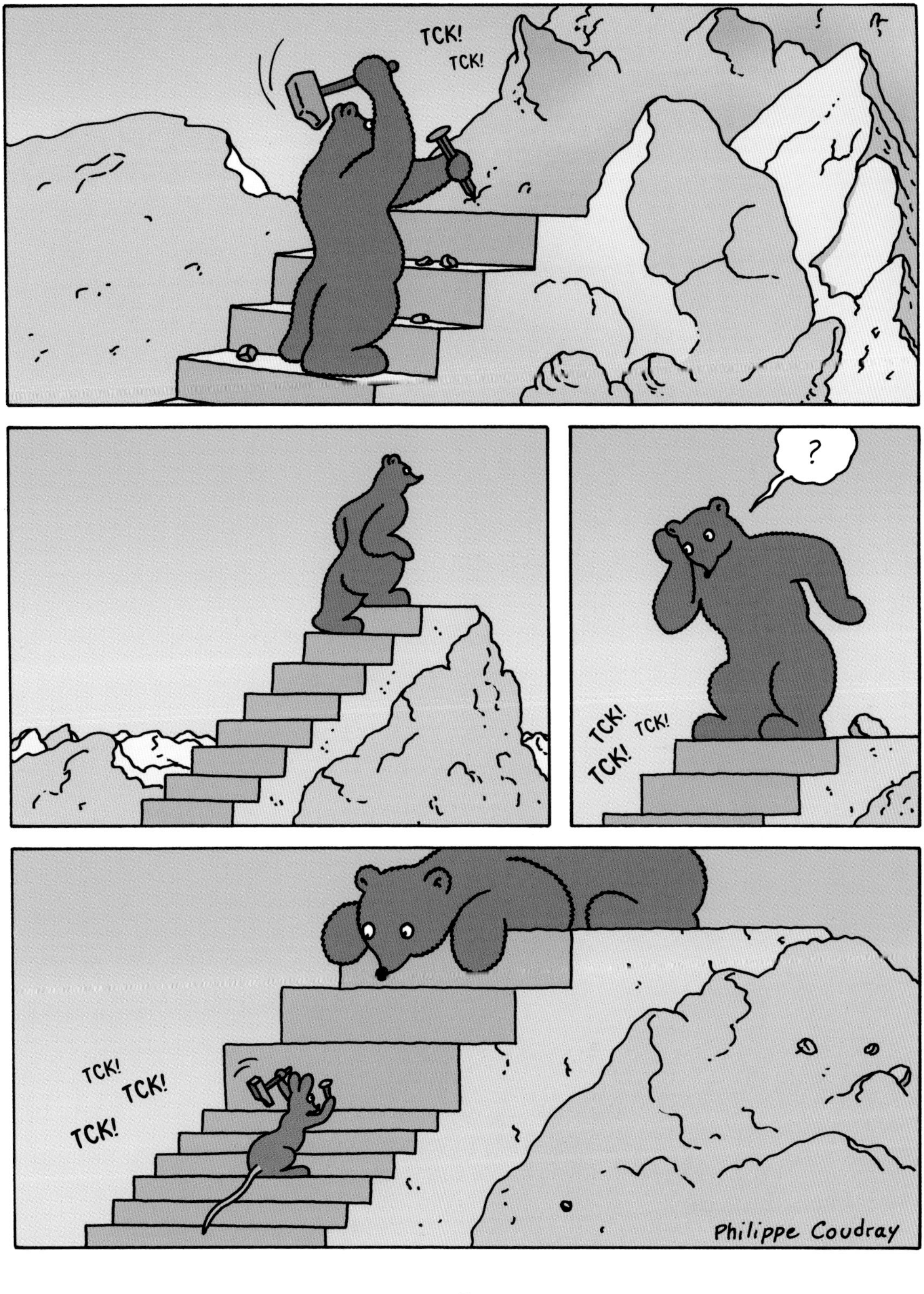

TCK!
TCK!
?
TCK!
TCK!
TCK!
TCK!
TCK!
TCK!
Philippe Coudray

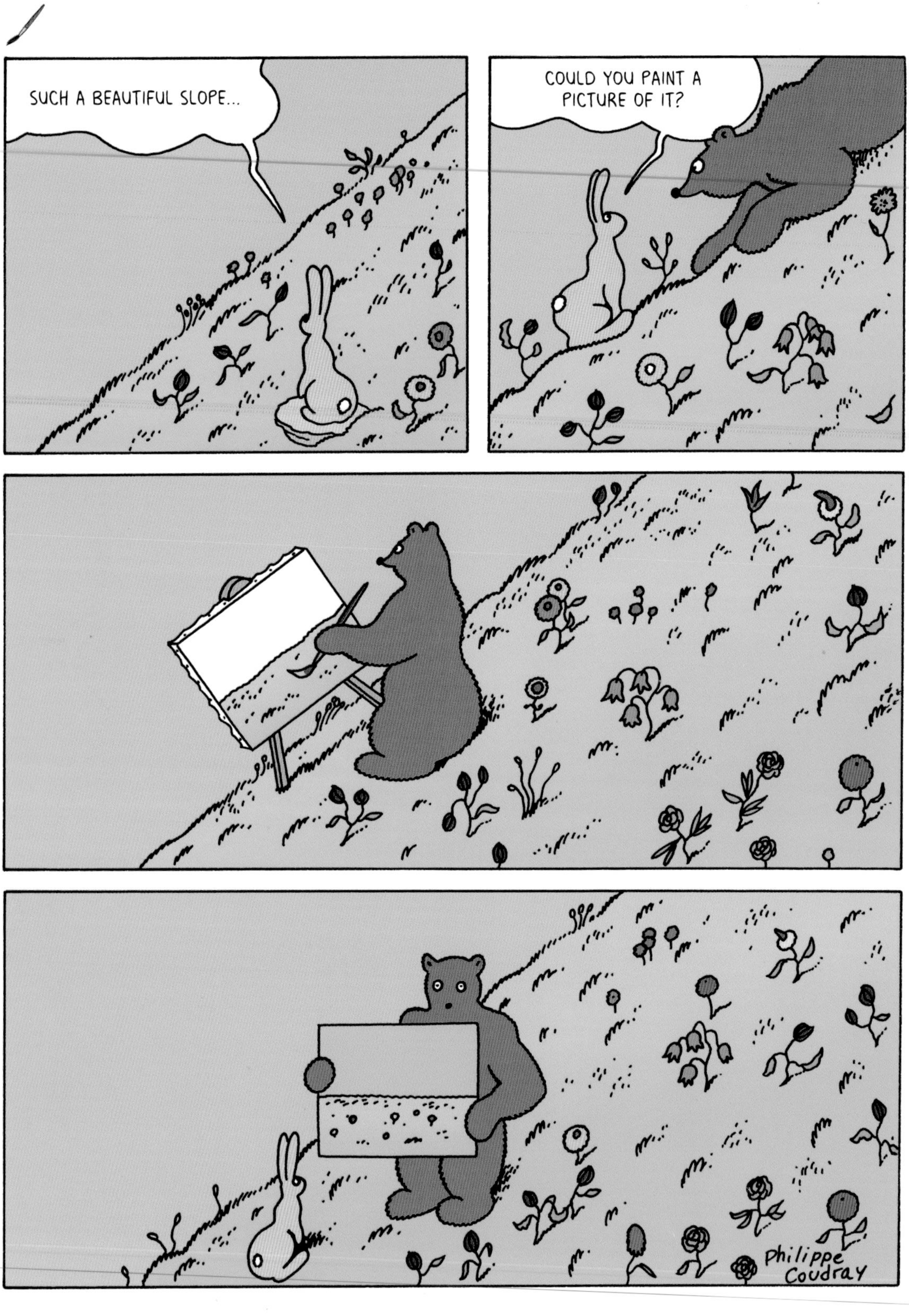
SUCH A BEAUTIFUL SLOPE...
COULD YOU PAINT A PICTURE OF IT?
Philippe Coudray

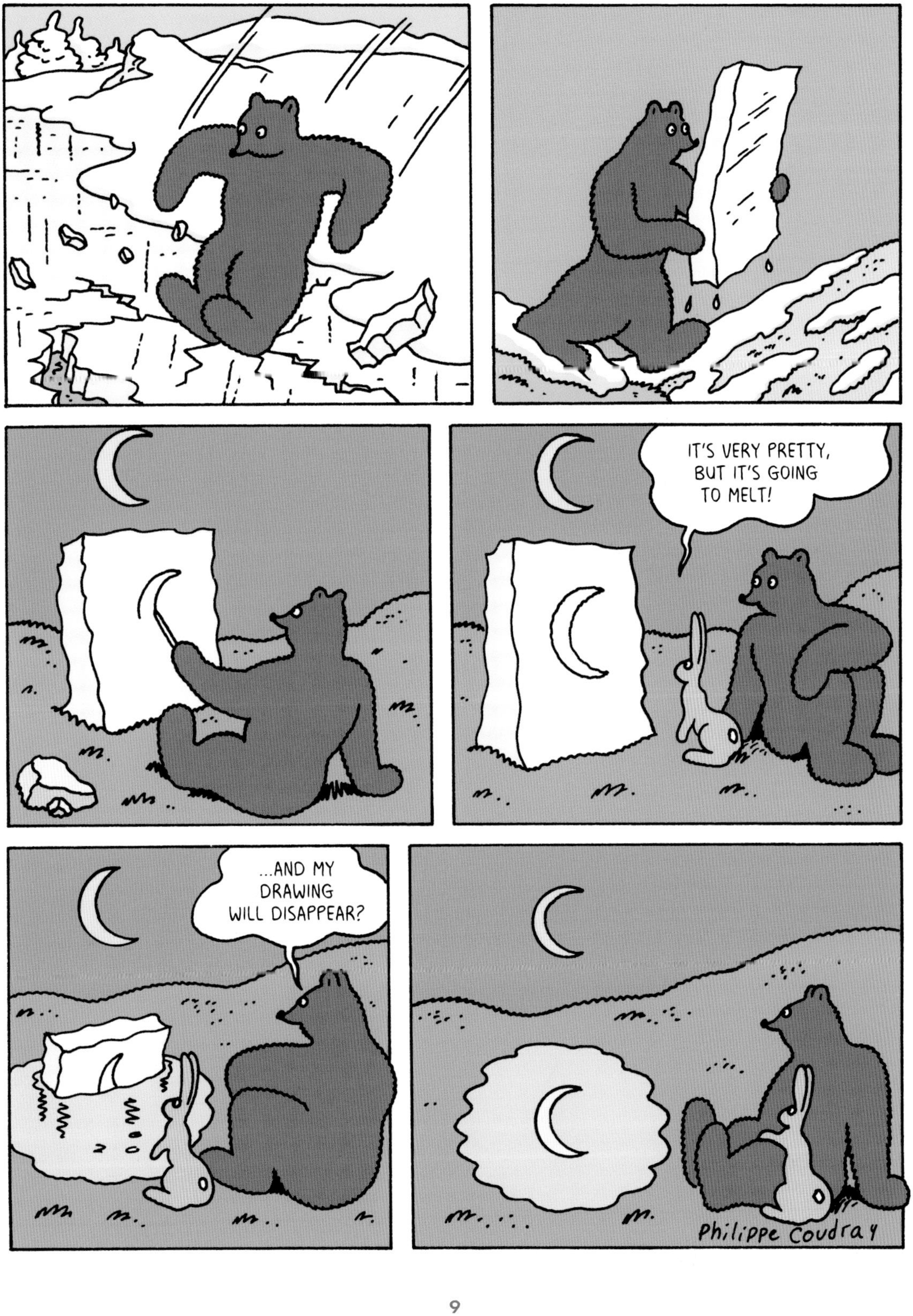
IT'S VERY PRETTY, BUT IT'S GOING TO MELT!
...AND MY DRAWING WILL DISAPPEAR?
Philippe Coudray

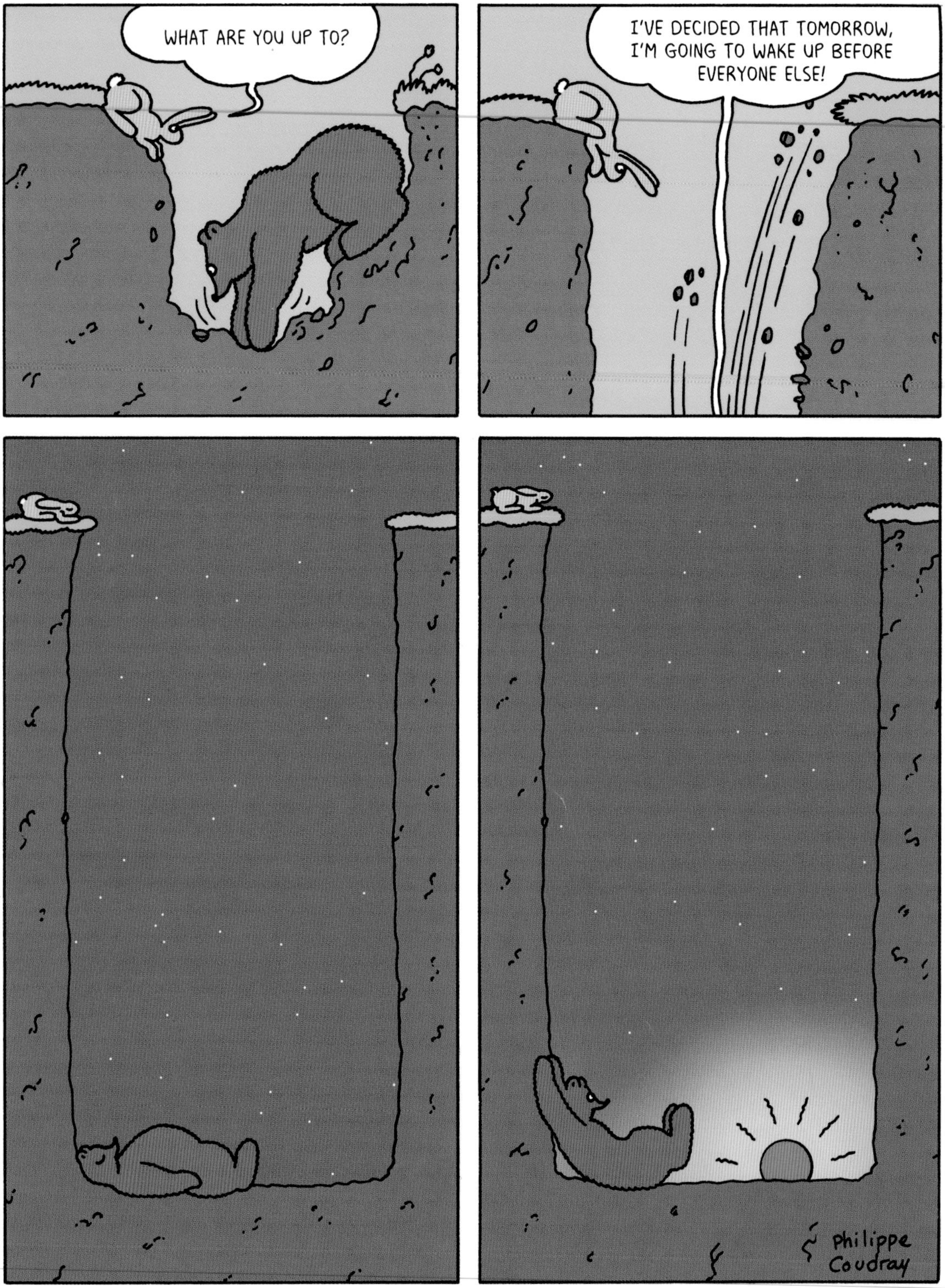
WHAT ARE YOU UP TO?
I'VE DECIDED THAT TOMORROW, I'M GOING TO WAKE UP BEFORE EVERYONE ELSE!
Philippe Coudray

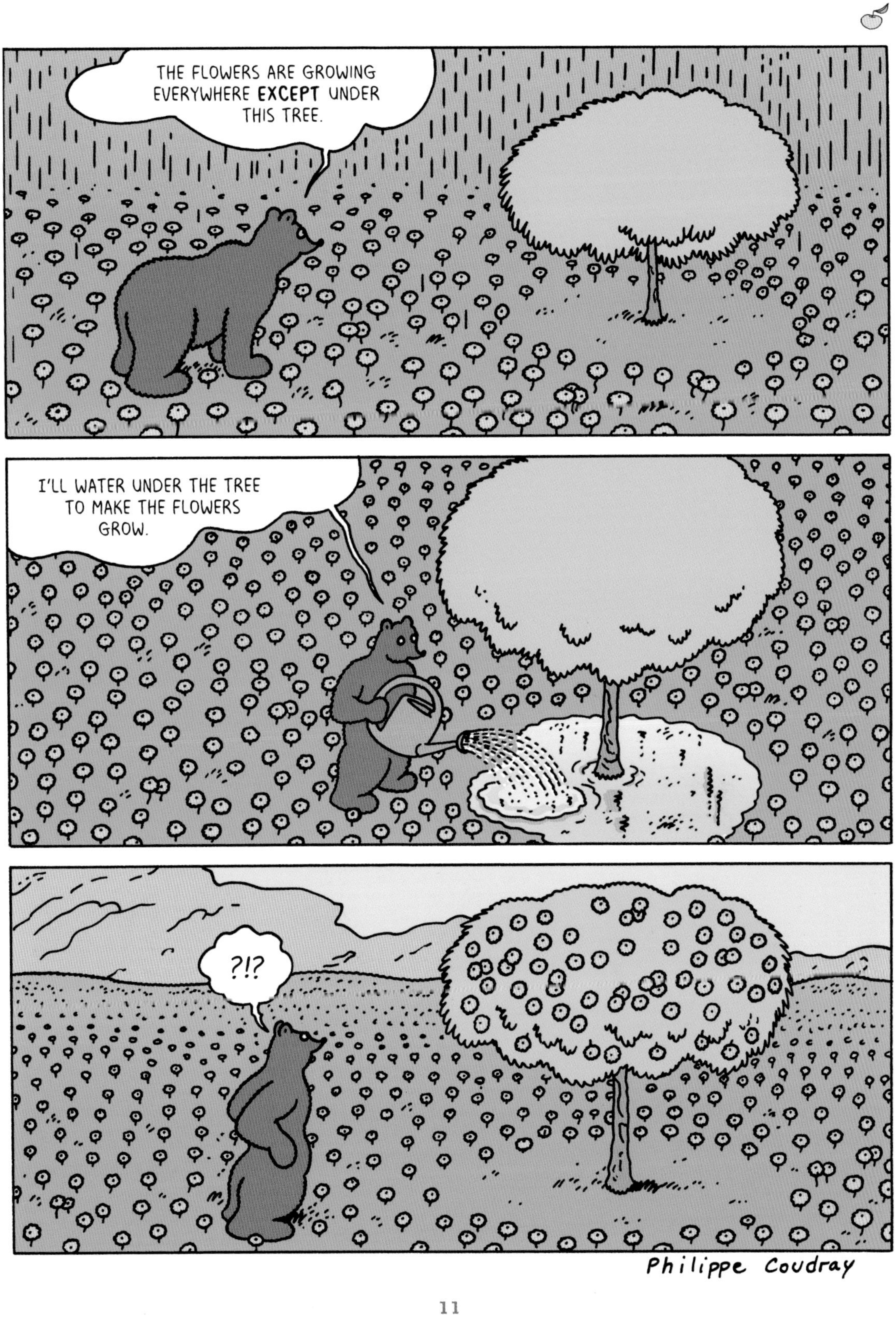
THE FLOWERS ARE GROWING EVERYWHERE **EXCEPT** UNDER THIS TREE.
I'LL WATER UNDER THE TREE TO MAKE THE FLOWERS GROW.
?!?
Philippe Coudray

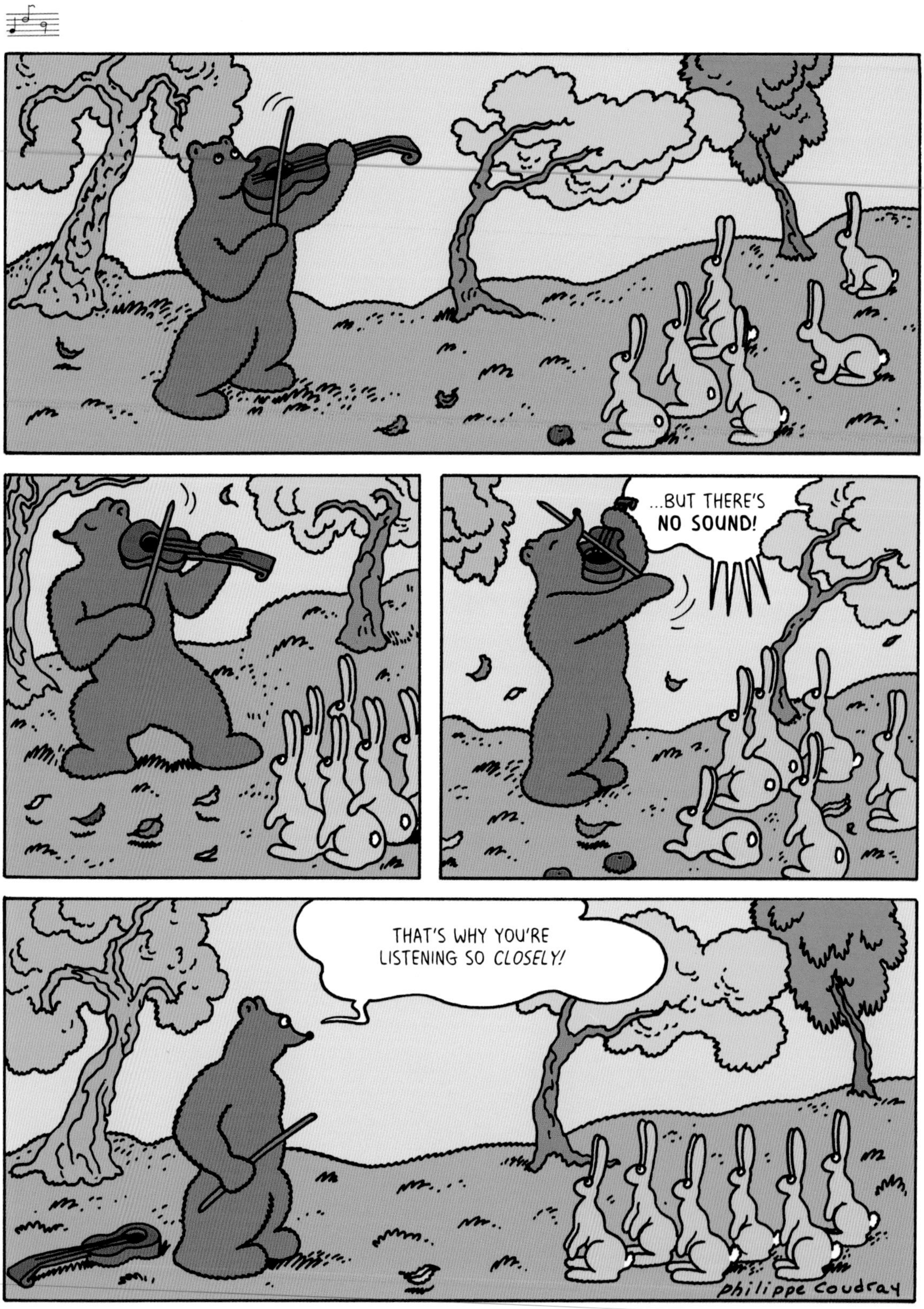
...BUT THERE'S **NO SOUND!**
THAT'S WHY YOU'RE LISTENING SO *CLOSELY!*
philippe coudray

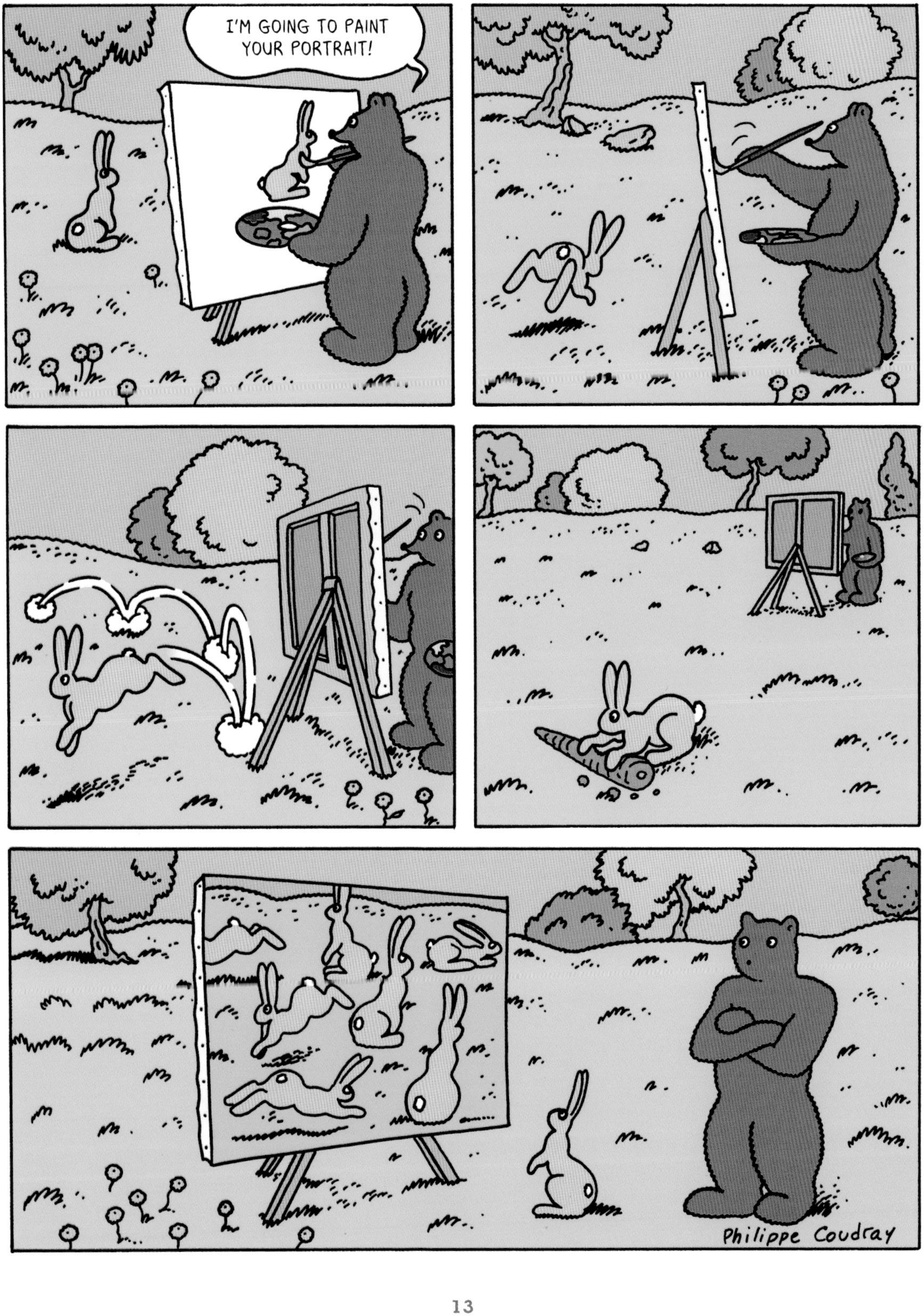
I'M GOING TO PAINT YOUR PORTRAIT!
Philippe Coudray

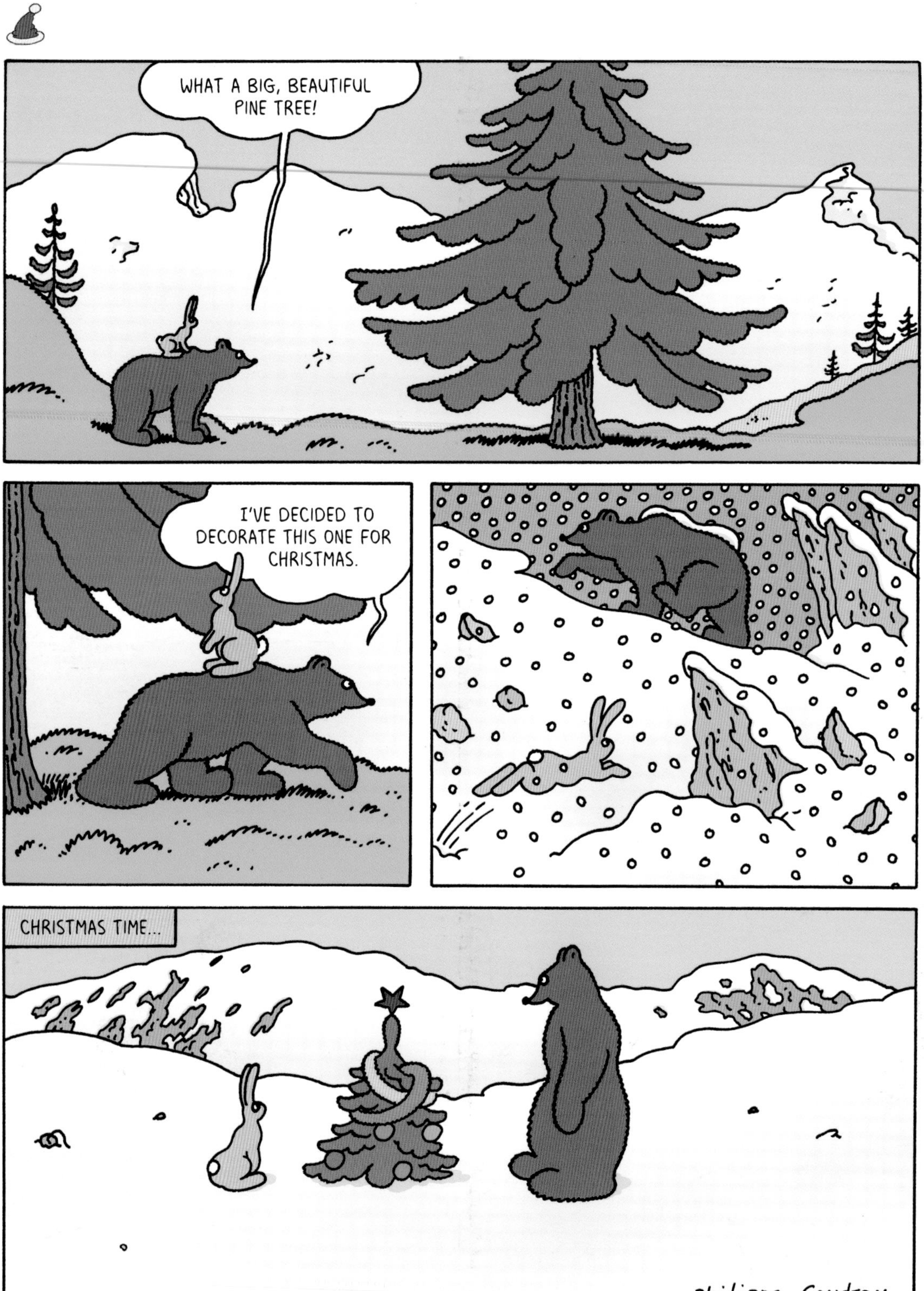
WHAT A BIG, BEAUTIFUL PINE TREE!
I'VE DECIDED TO DECORATE THIS ONE FOR CHRISTMAS.
CHRISTMAS TIME...
Philippe Coudray

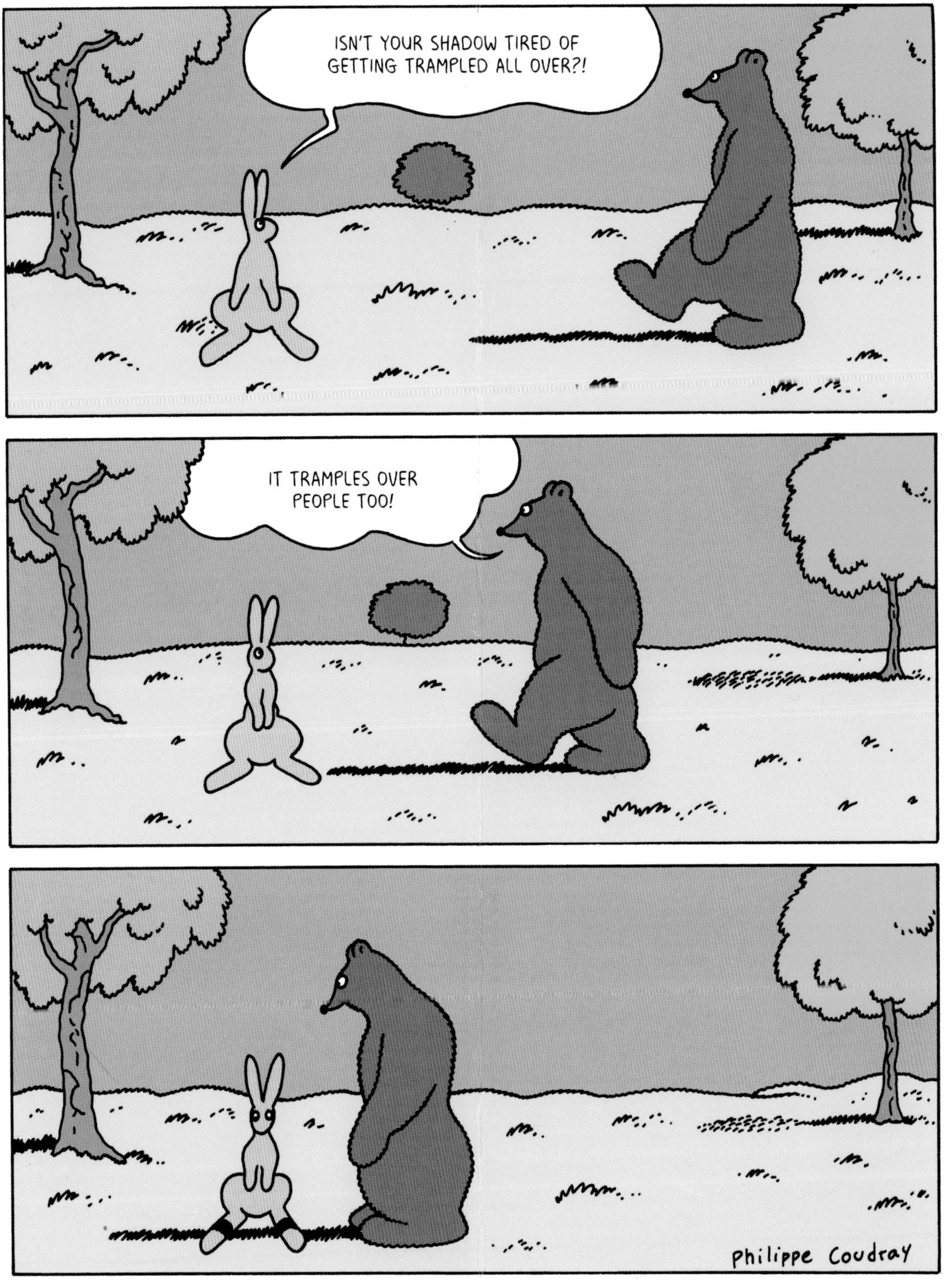
ISN'T YOUR SHADOW TIRED OF GETTING TRAMPLED ALL OVER?!
IT TRAMPLES OVER PEOPLE TOO!
Philippe Coudray

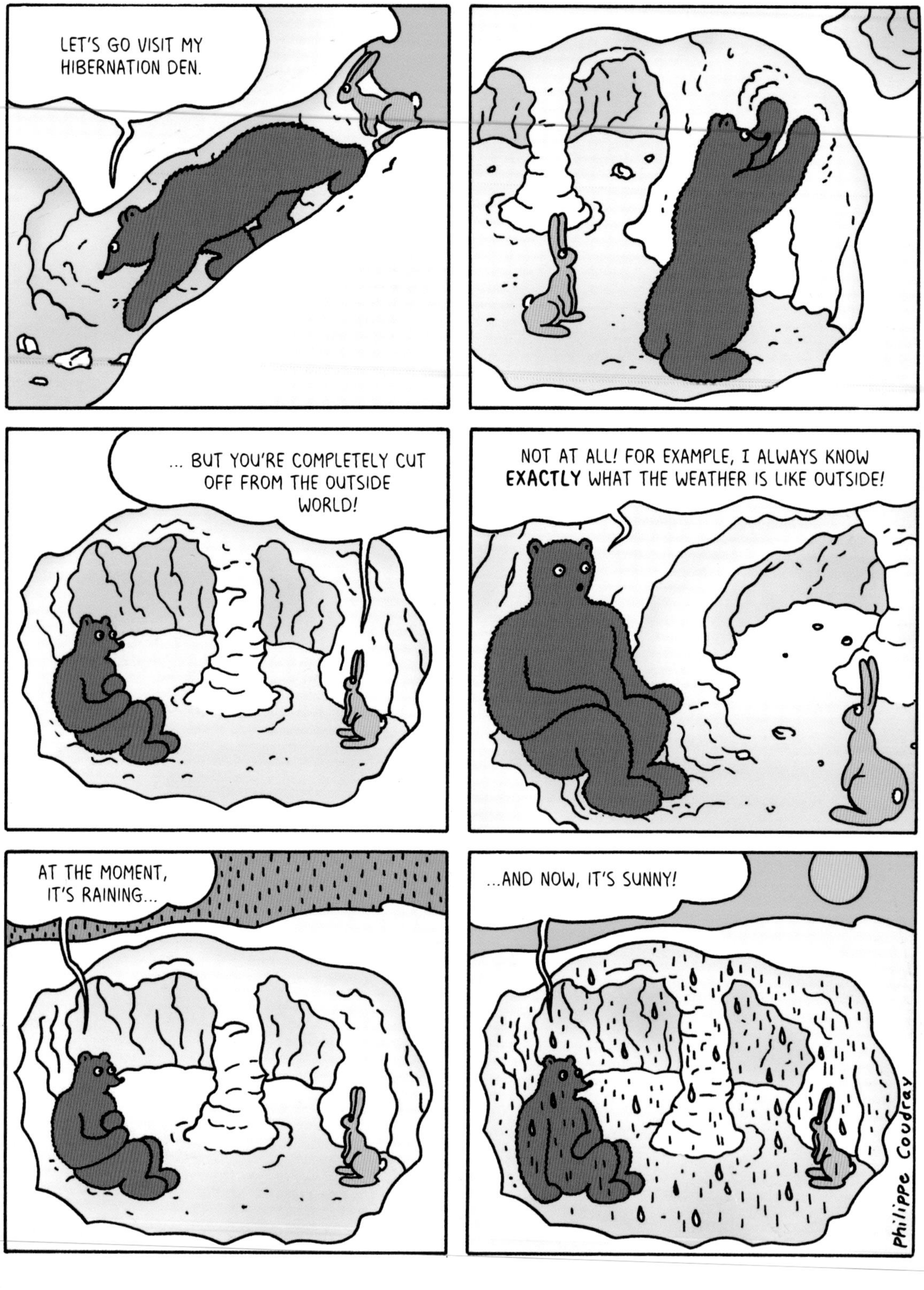
LET'S GO VISIT MY HIBERNATION DEN.
... BUT YOU'RE COMPLETELY CUT OFF FROM THE OUTSIDE WORLD!
NOT AT ALL! FOR EXAMPLE, I ALWAYS KNOW **EXACTLY** WHAT THE WEATHER IS LIKE OUTSIDE!
AT THE MOMENT, IT'S RAINING...
...AND NOW, IT'S SUNNY!
Philippe Coudray

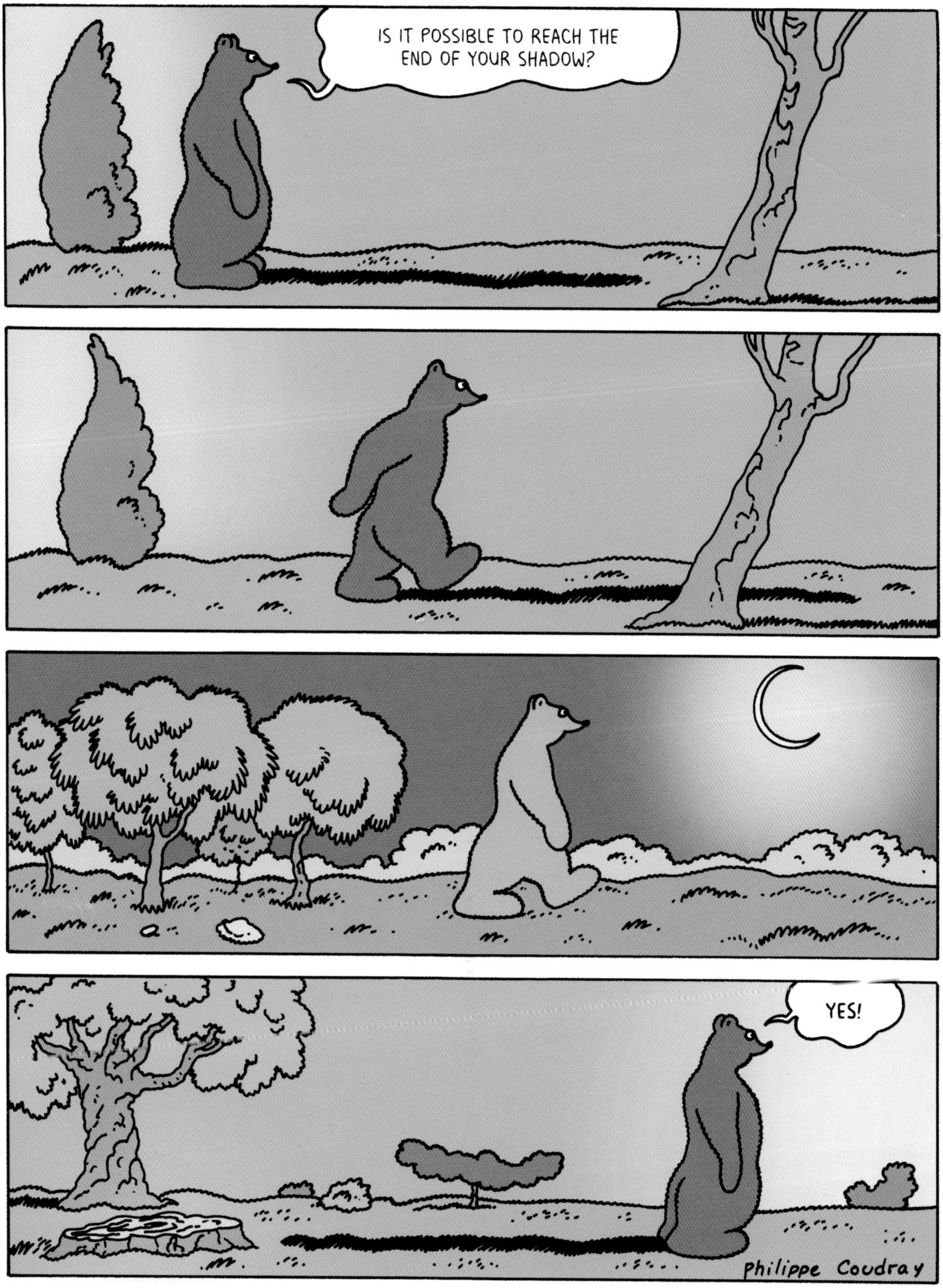
IS IT POSSIBLE TO REACH THE END OF YOUR SHADOW?
YES!
Philippe Coudray

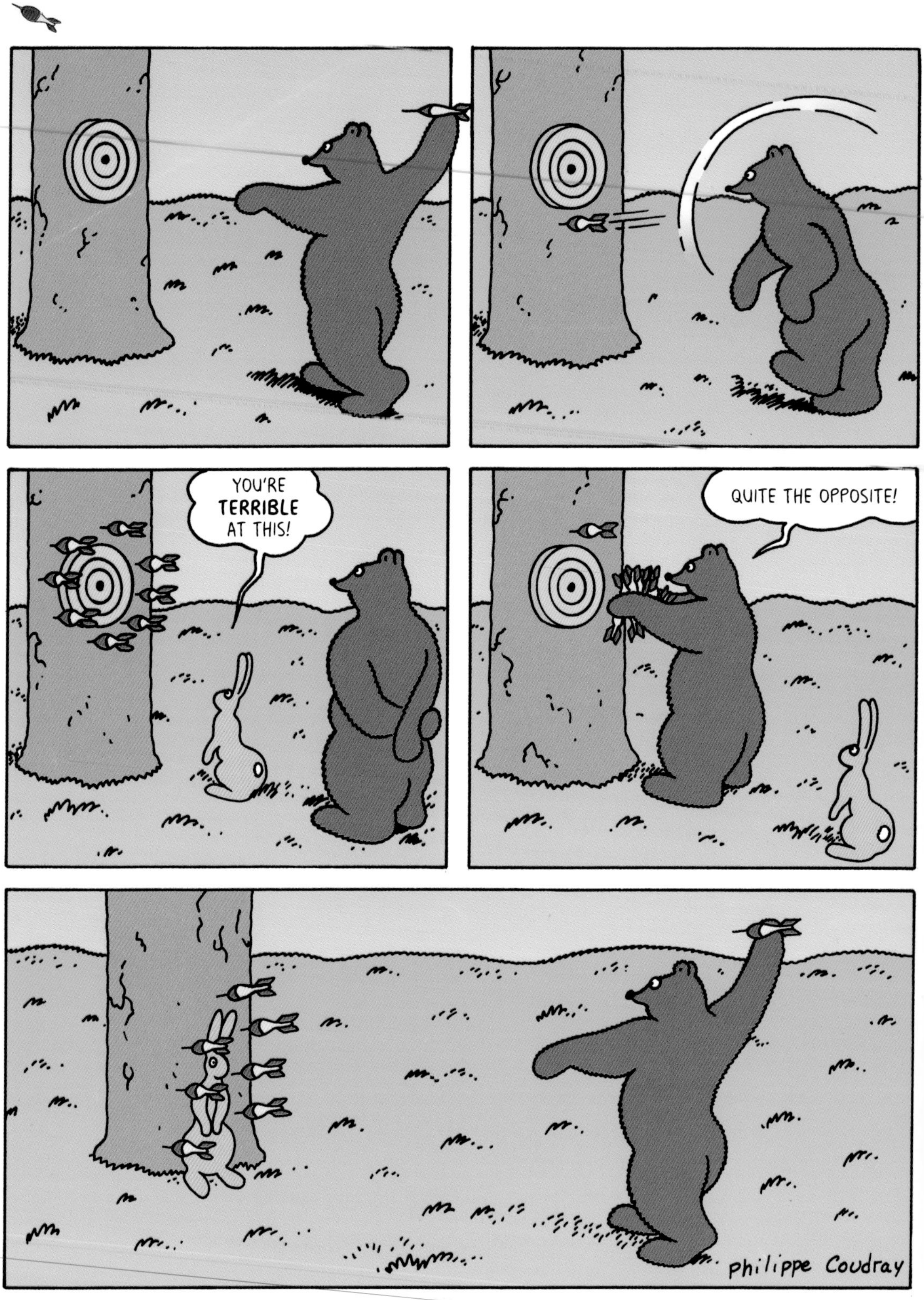
YOU'RE **TERRIBLE** AT THIS!
QUITE THE OPPOSITE!
Philippe Coudray

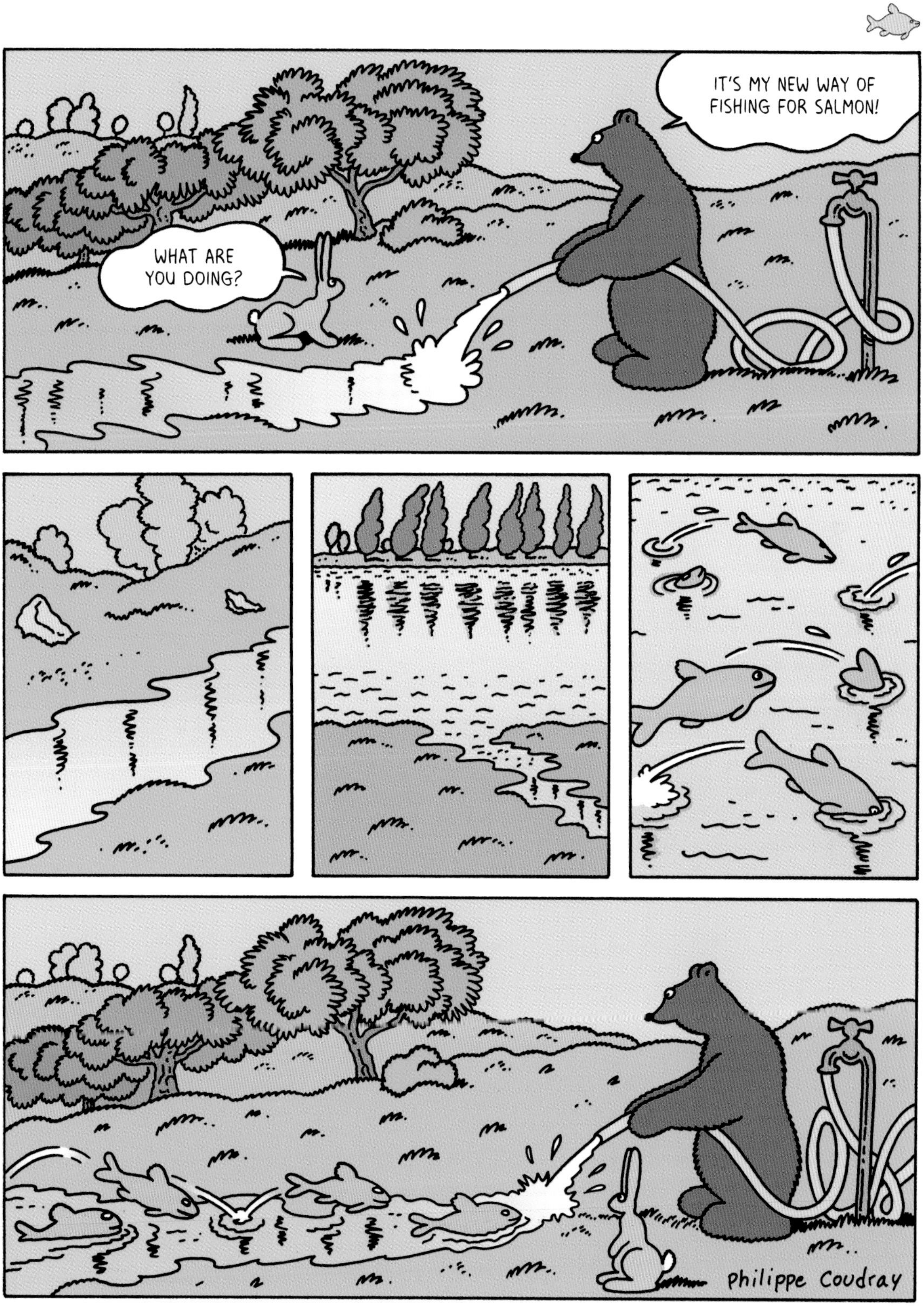
IT'S MY NEW WAY OF FISHING FOR SALMON!
WHAT ARE YOU DOING?
Philippe Coudray

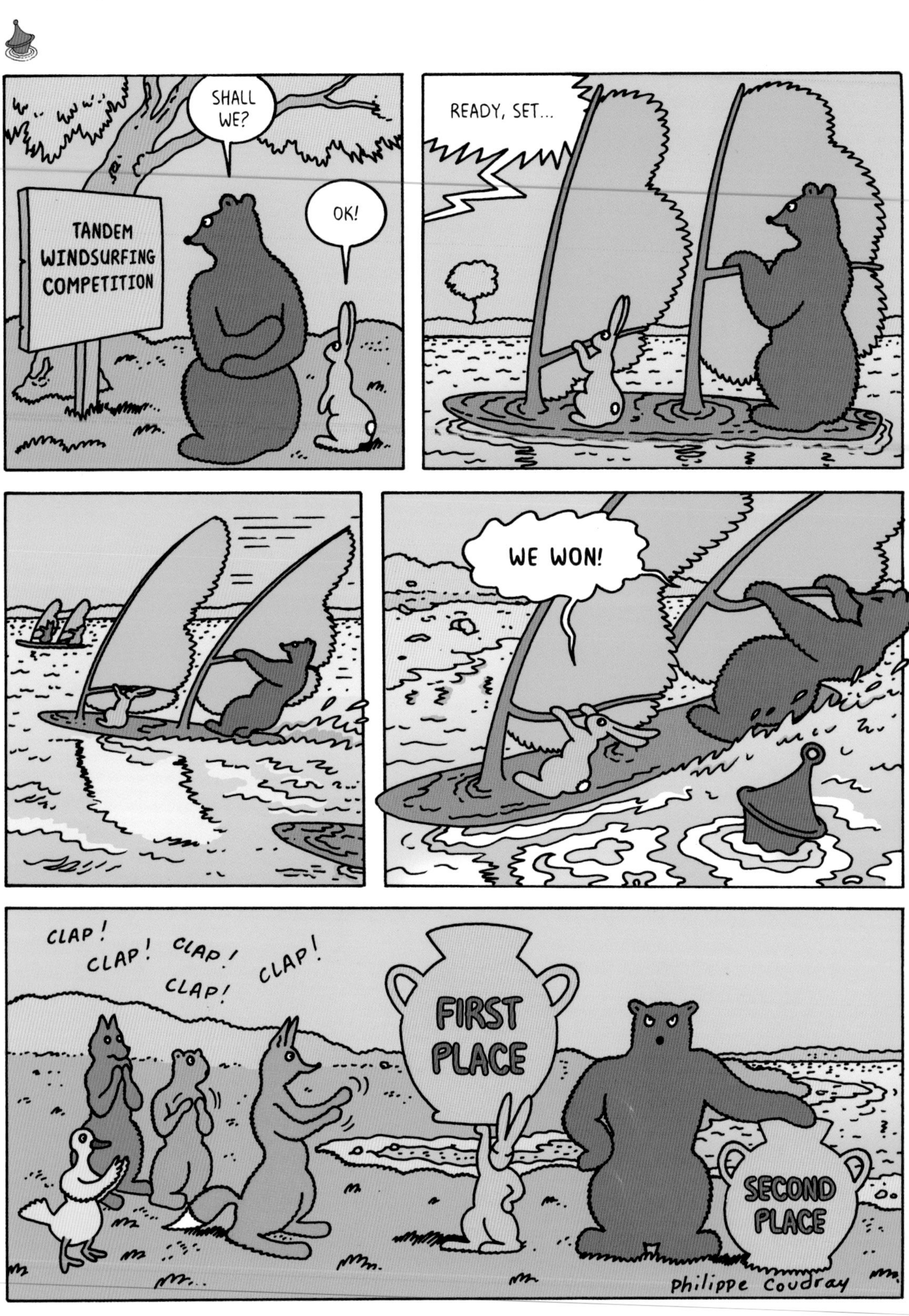
SHALL WE?
OK!
TANDEM WINDSURFING COMPETITION
READY, SET...
WE WON!
CLAP!
CLAP!
CLAP!
CLAP!
CLAP!
FIRST PLACE
SECOND PLACE
Philippe Coudray

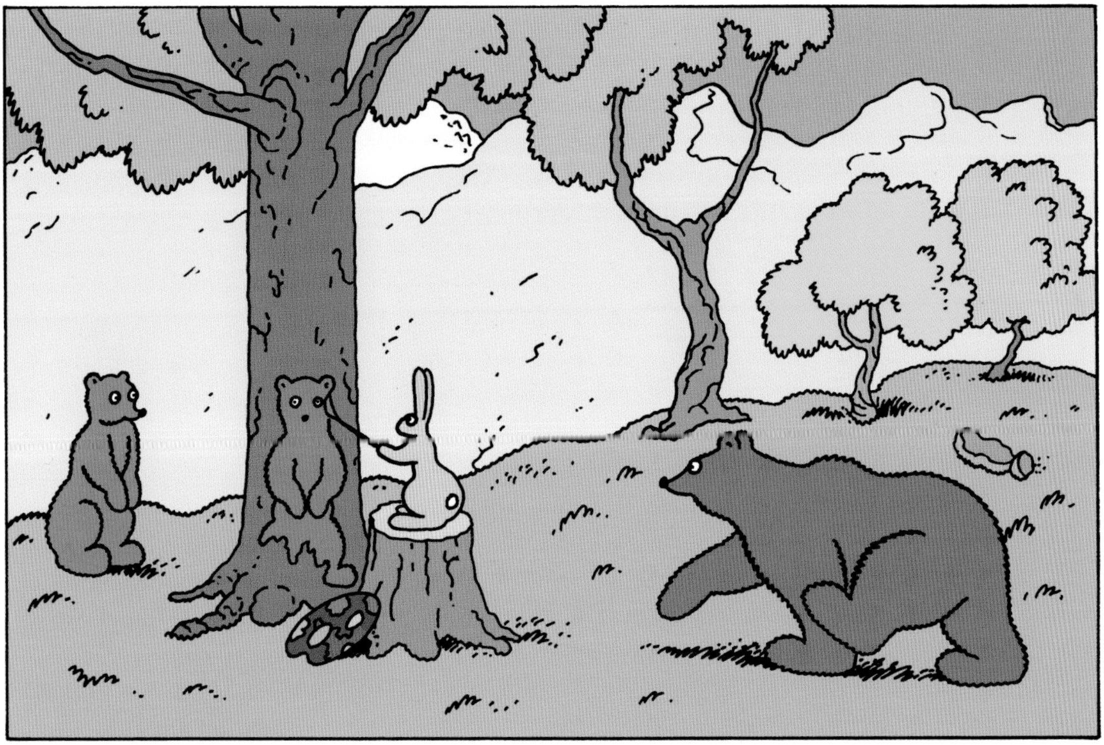

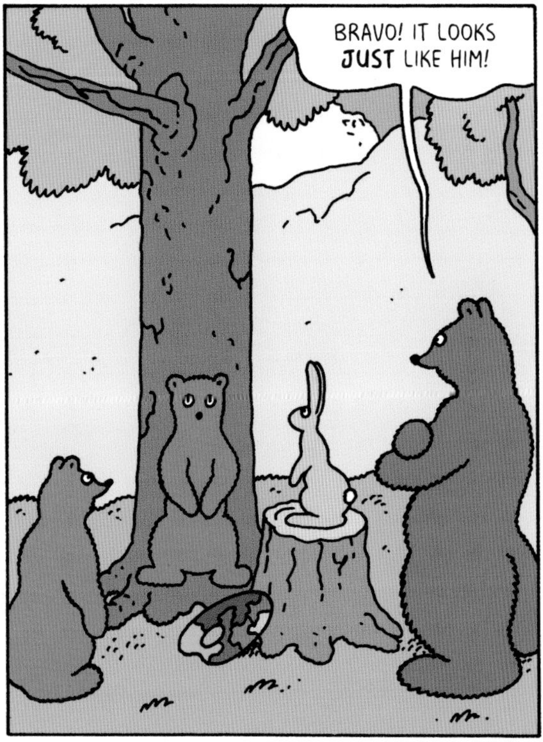
BRAVO! IT LOOKS **JUST** LIKE HIM!

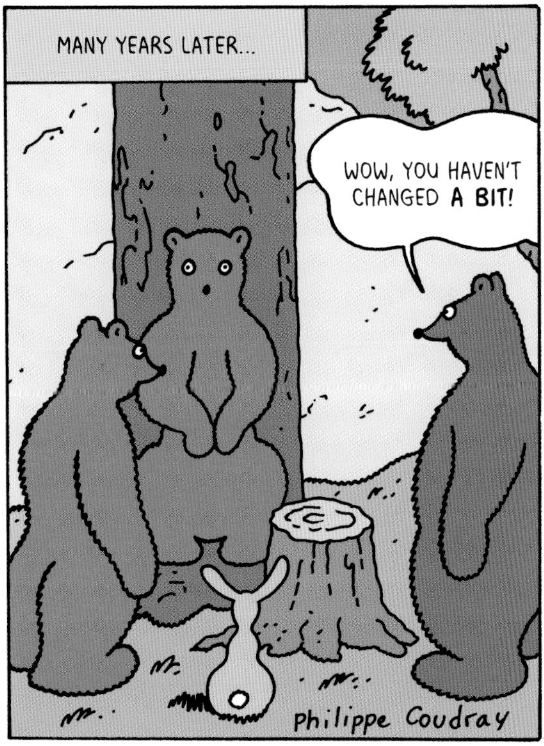
MANY YEARS LATER...
WOW, YOU HAVEN'T CHANGED **A BIT**!
Philippe Coudray

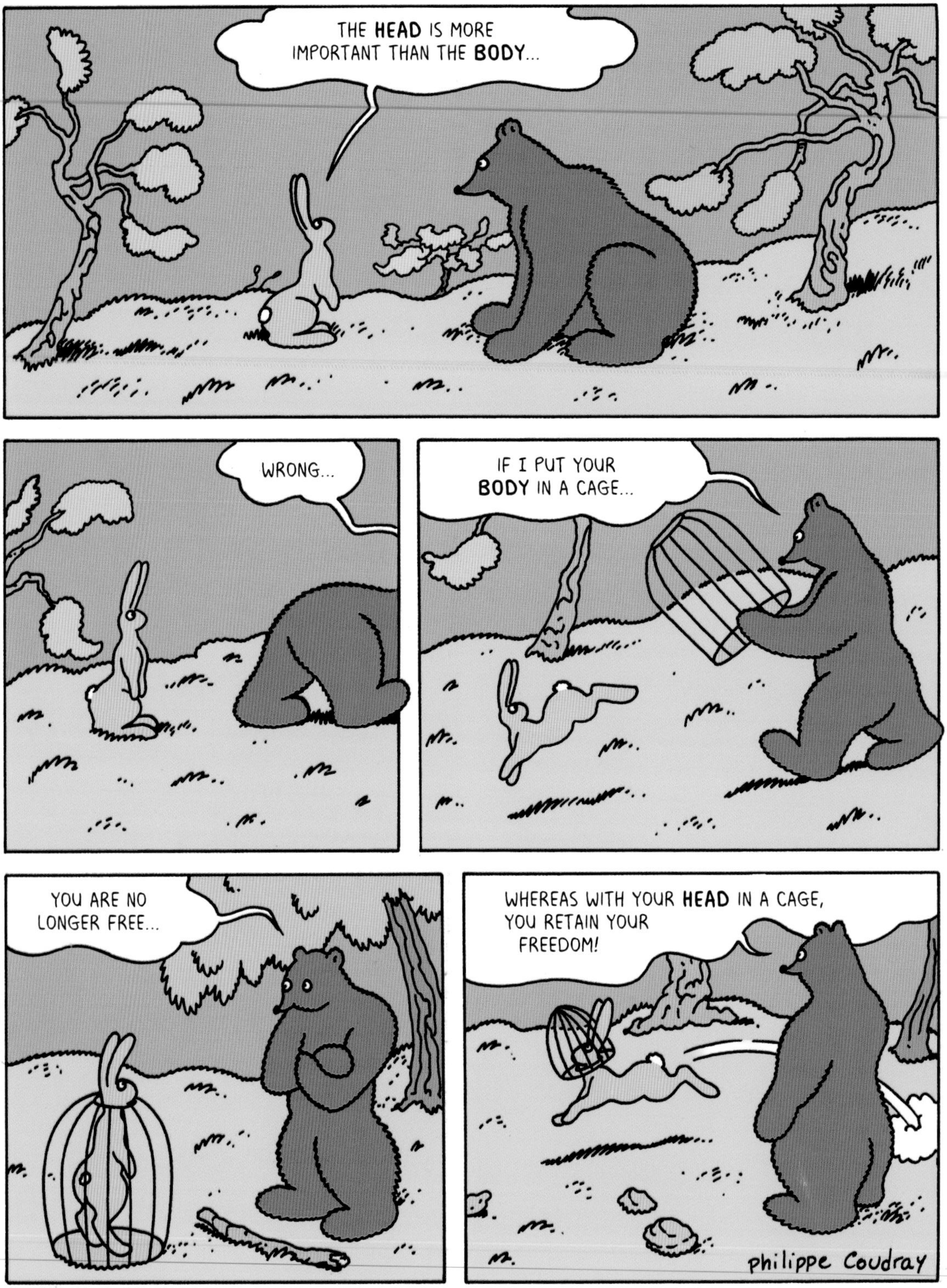
THE **HEAD** IS MORE IMPORTANT THAN THE **BODY**...
WRONG...
IF I PUT YOUR **BODY** IN A CAGE...
YOU ARE NO LONGER FREE...
WHEREAS WITH YOUR **HEAD** IN A CAGE, YOU RETAIN YOUR FREEDOM!
philippe Coudray

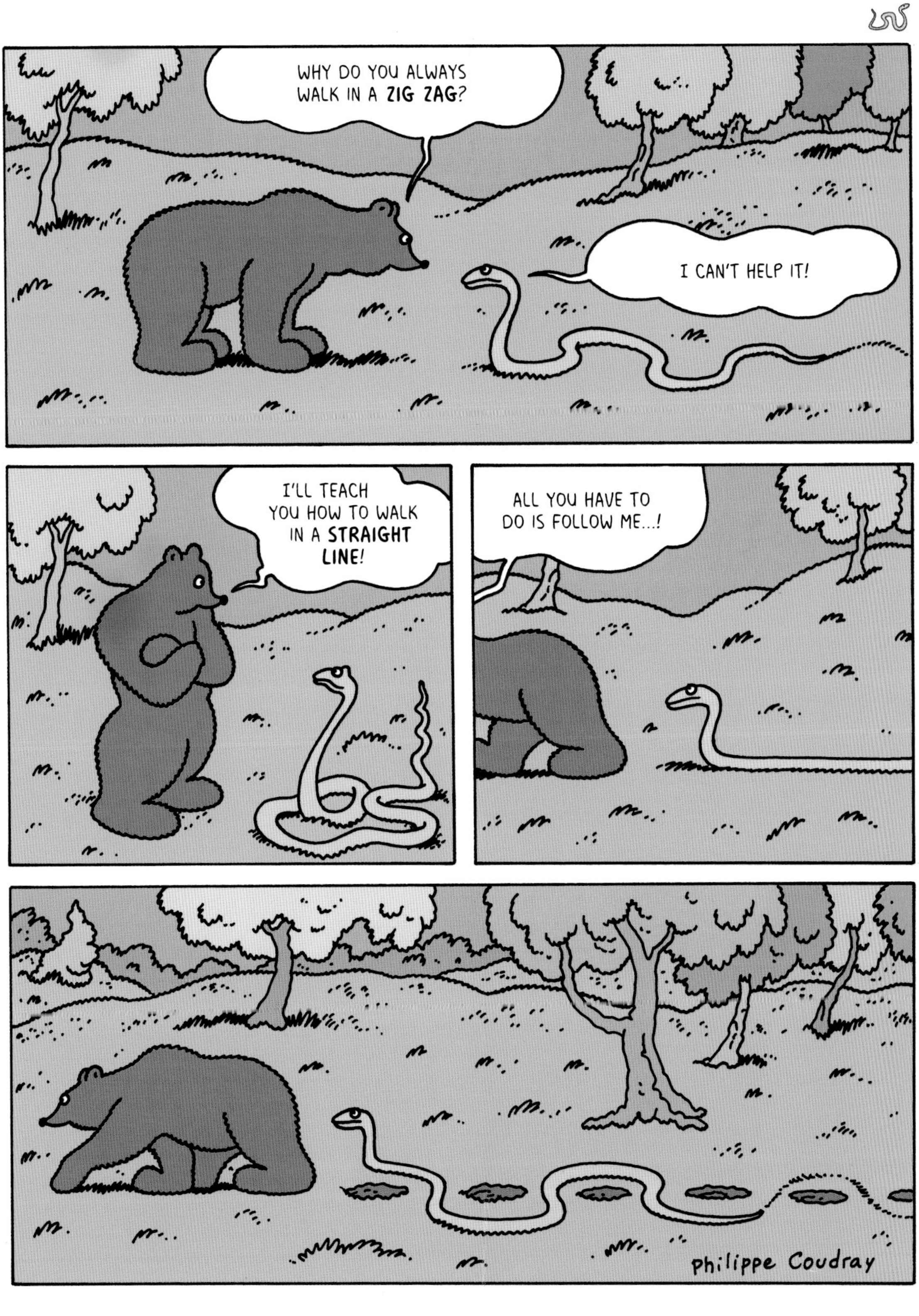
WHY DO YOU ALWAYS WALK IN A **ZIG ZAG**?
I CAN'T HELP IT!
I'LL TEACH YOU HOW TO WALK IN A **STRAIGHT LINE**!
ALL YOU HAVE TO DO IS FOLLOW ME...!
Philippe Coudray

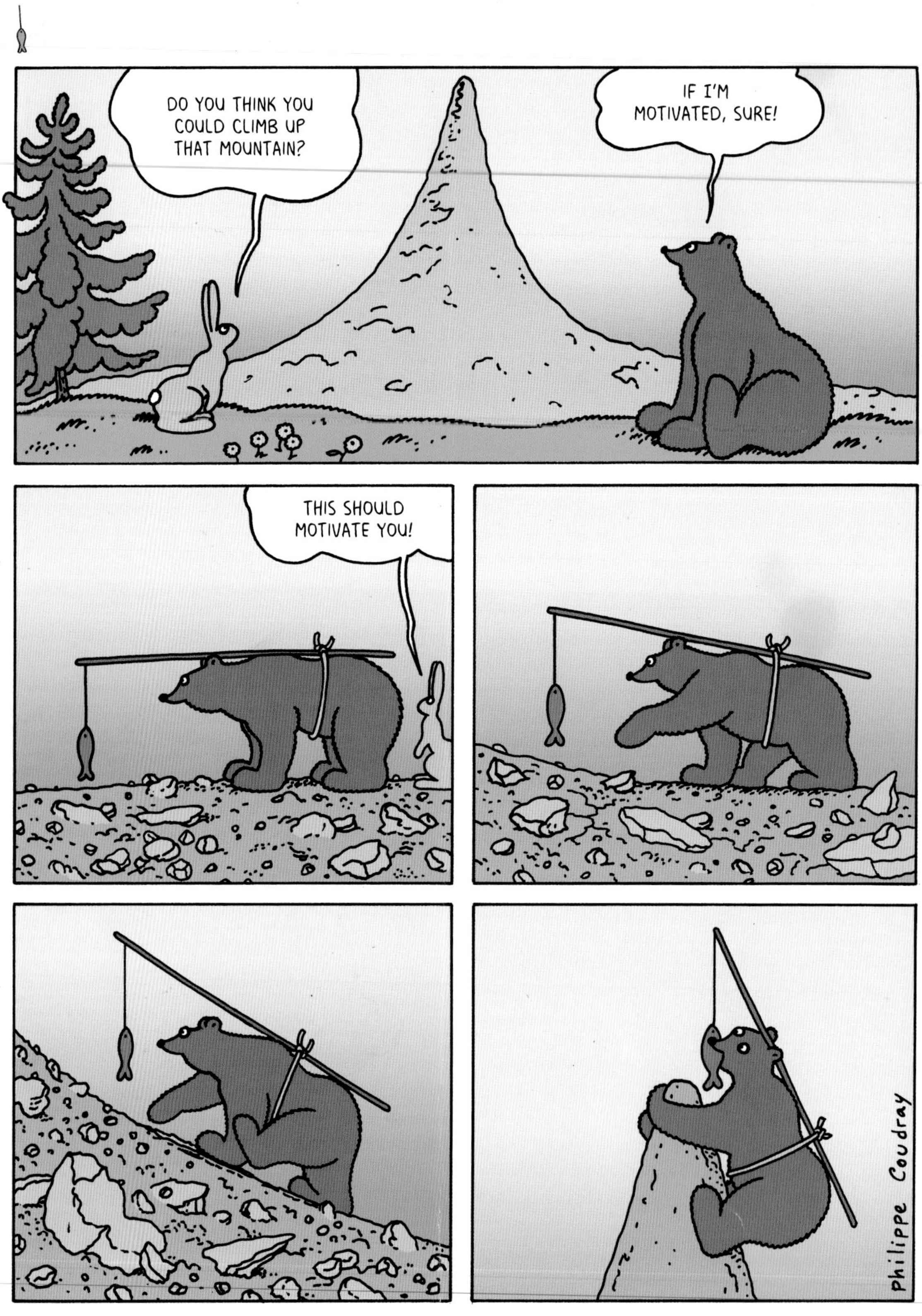
DO YOU THINK YOU COULD CLIMB UP THAT MOUNTAIN?
IF I'M MOTIVATED, SURE!
THIS SHOULD MOTIVATE YOU!
philippe Coudray

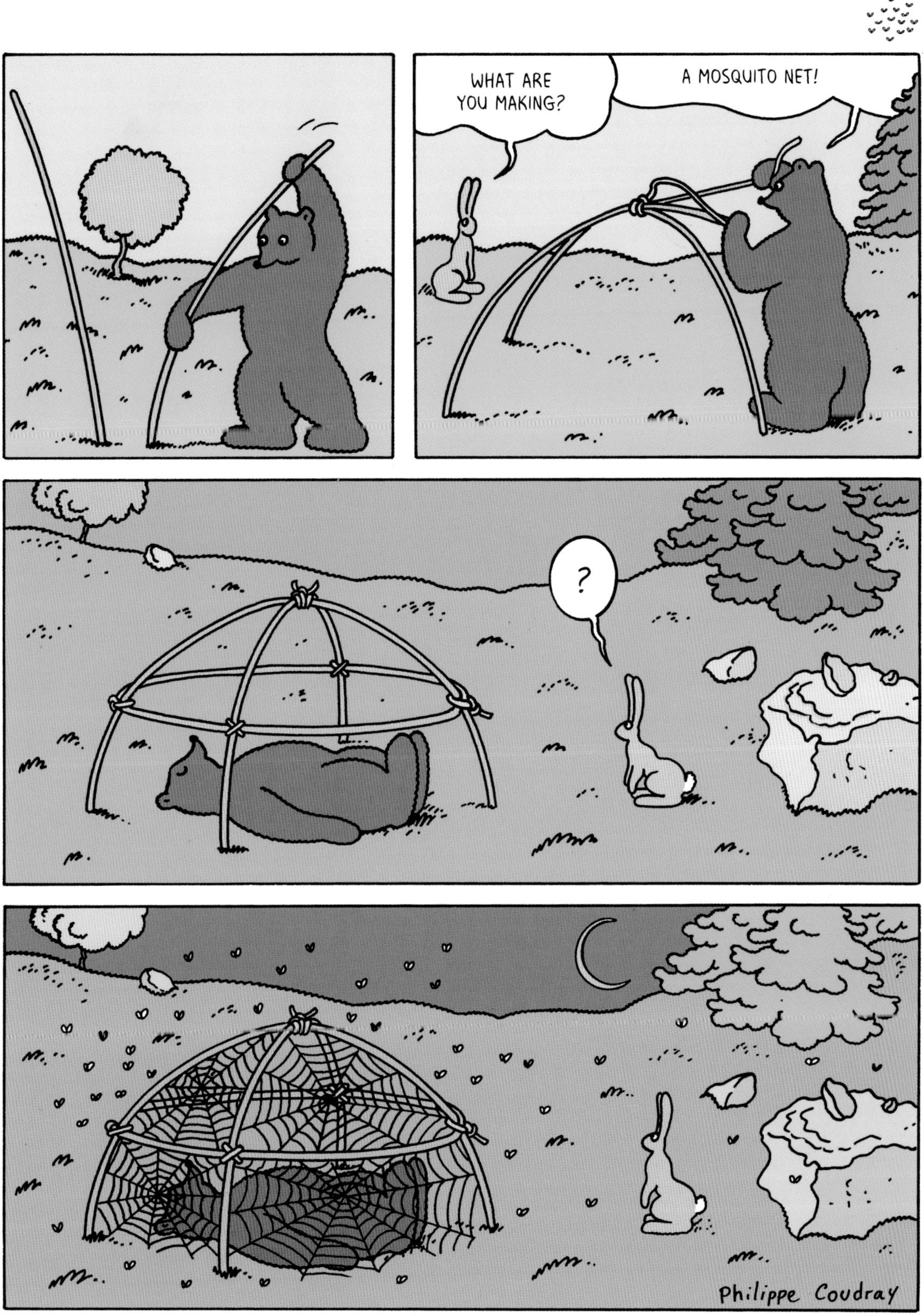
WHAT ARE YOU MAKING?
A MOSQUITO NET!
?
Philippe Coudray

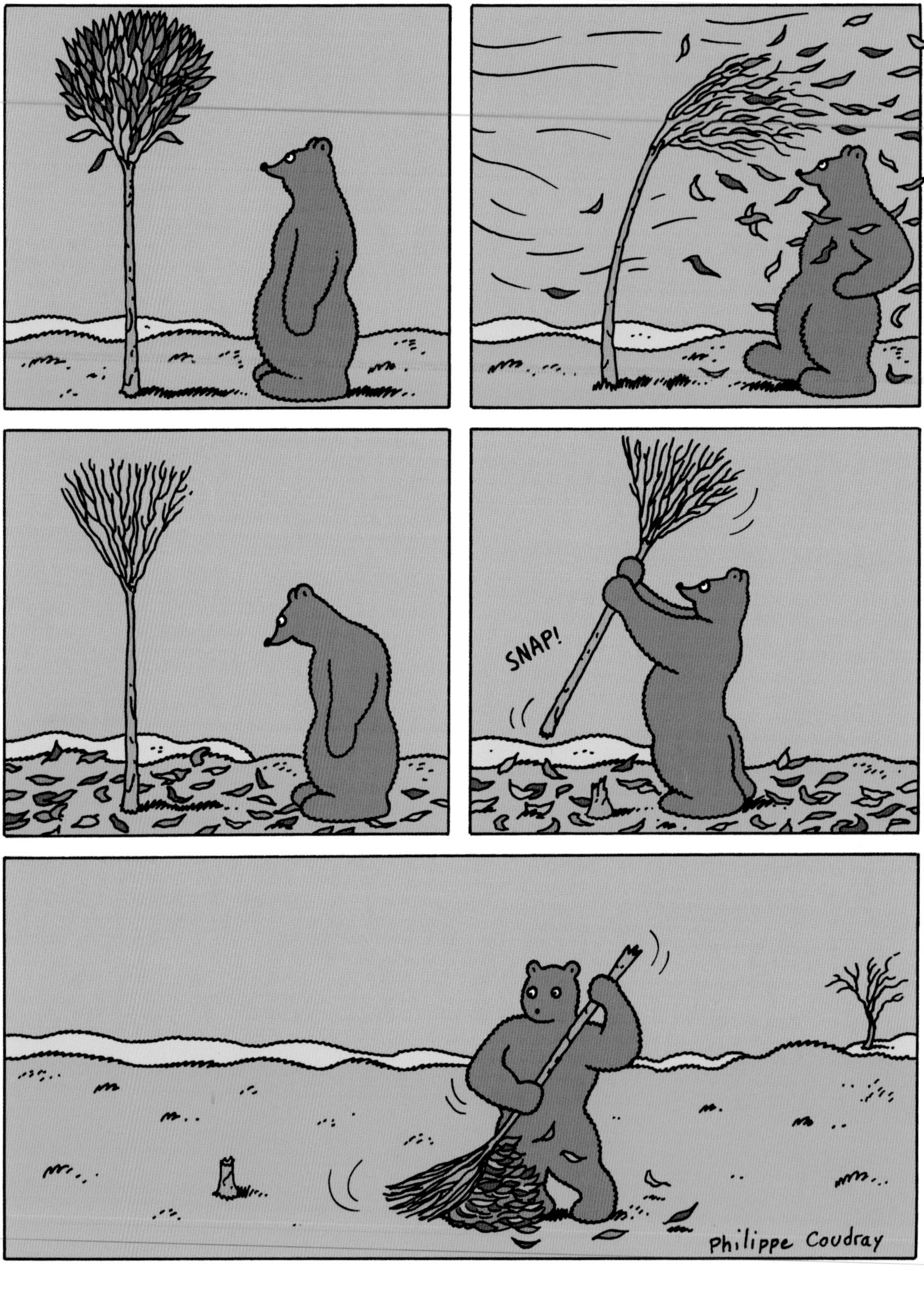
SNAP!
Philippe Coudray

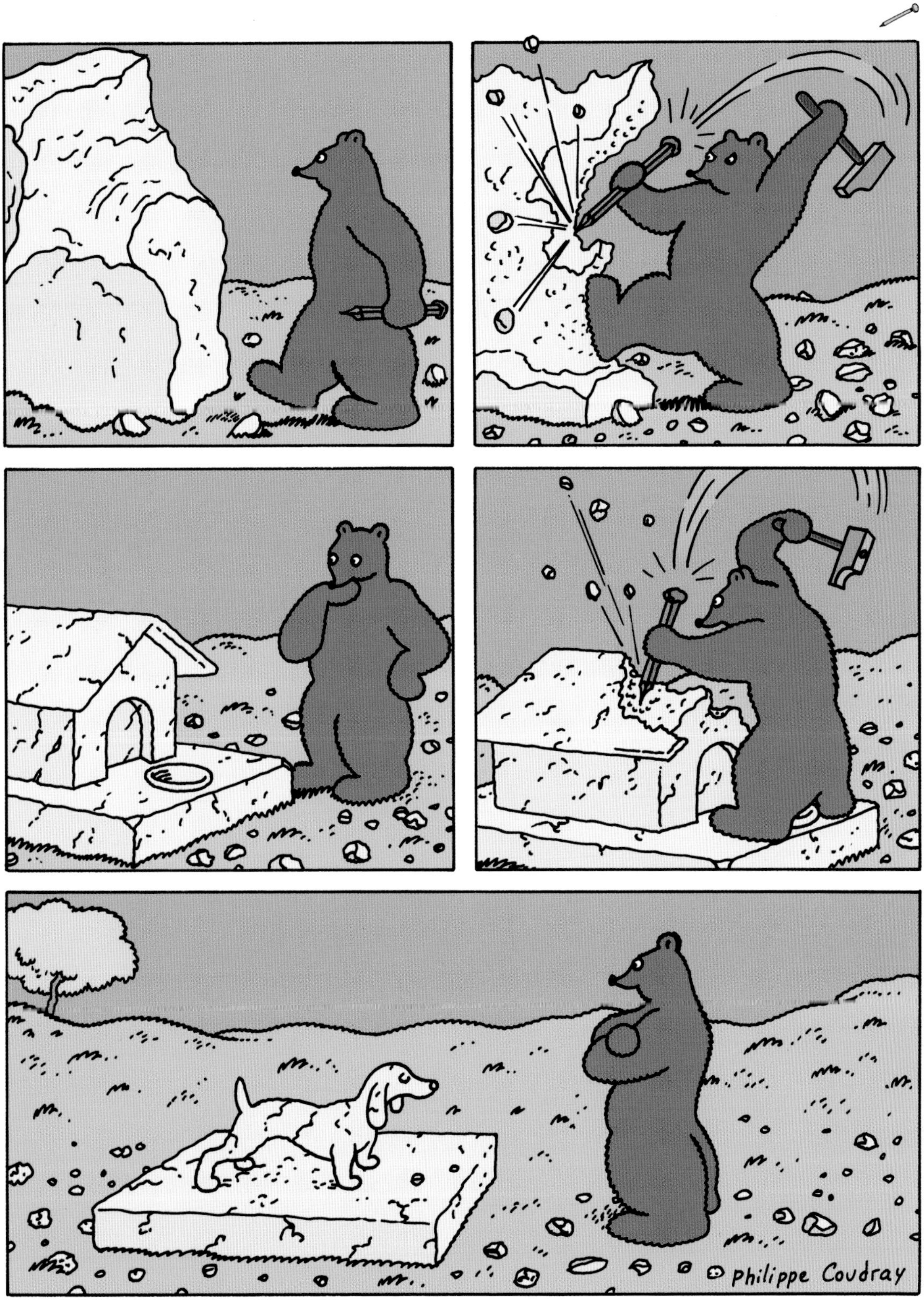
Philippe Coudray

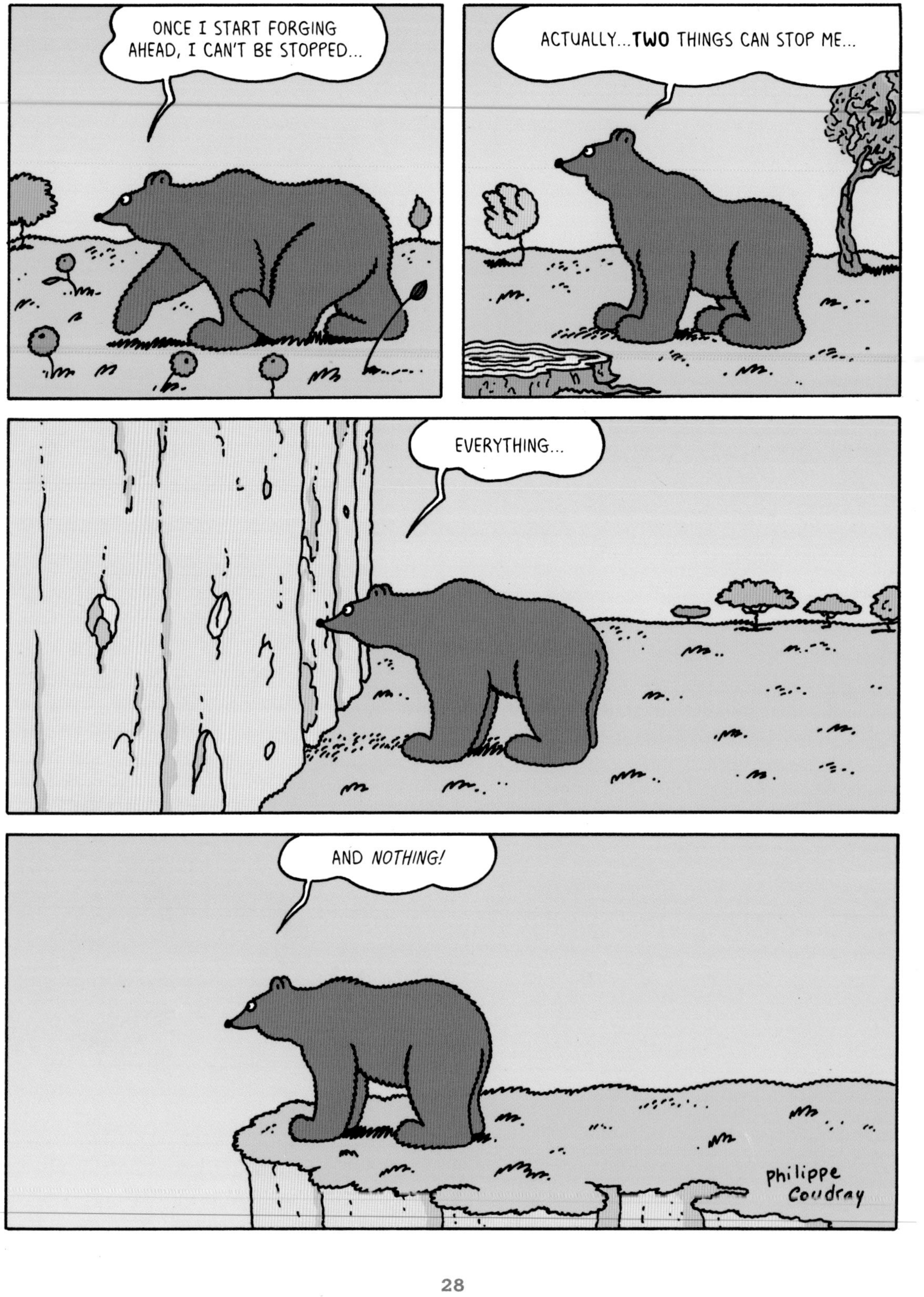
ONCE I START FORGING AHEAD, I CAN'T BE STOPPED...
ACTUALLY...**TWO** THINGS CAN STOP ME...
EVERYTHING...
AND *NOTHING!*
Philippe Coudray

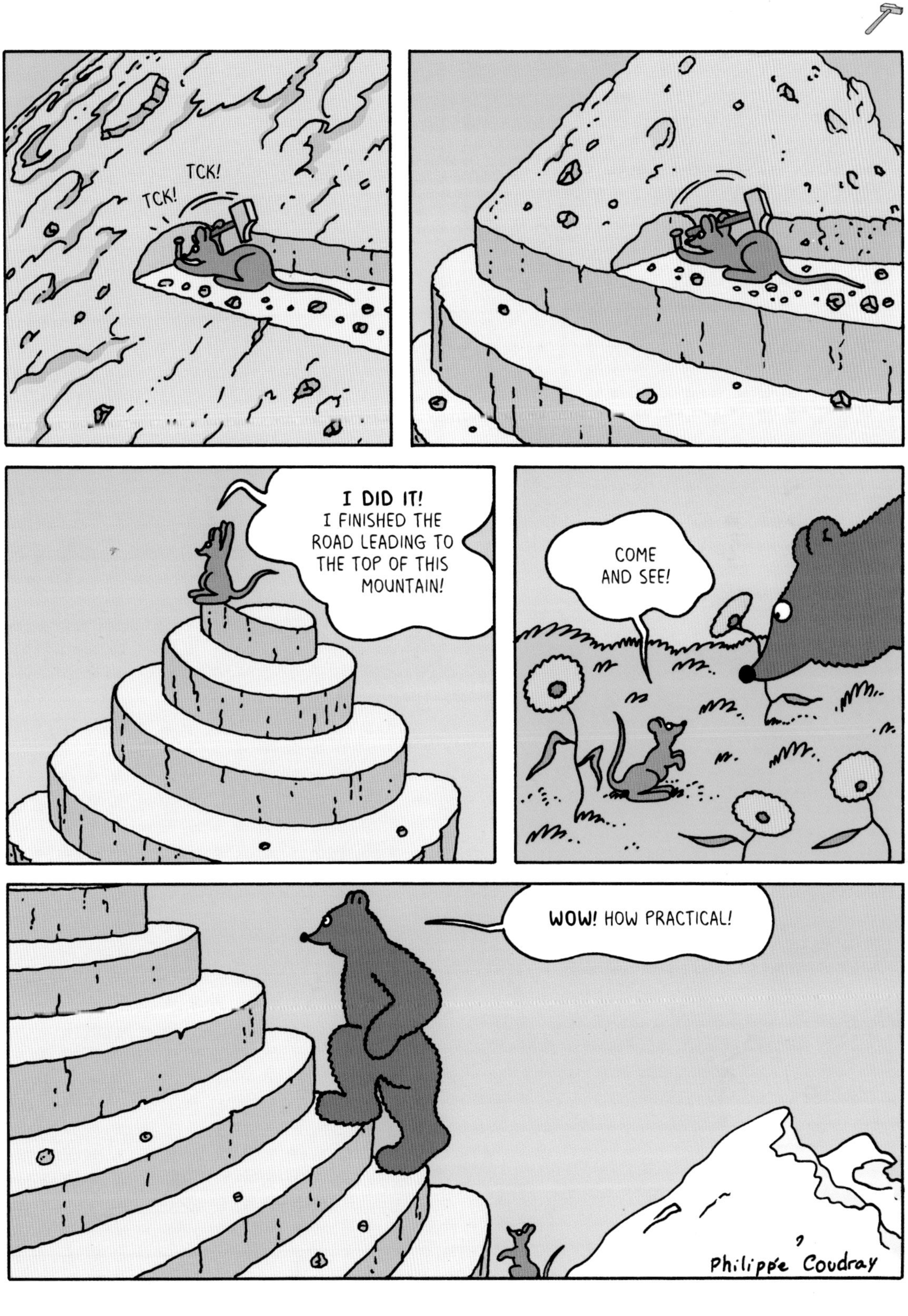
TCK!
TCK!
I DID IT! I FINISHED THE ROAD LEADING TO THE TOP OF THIS MOUNTAIN!
COME AND SEE!
WOW! HOW PRACTICAL!
Philippe Coudray

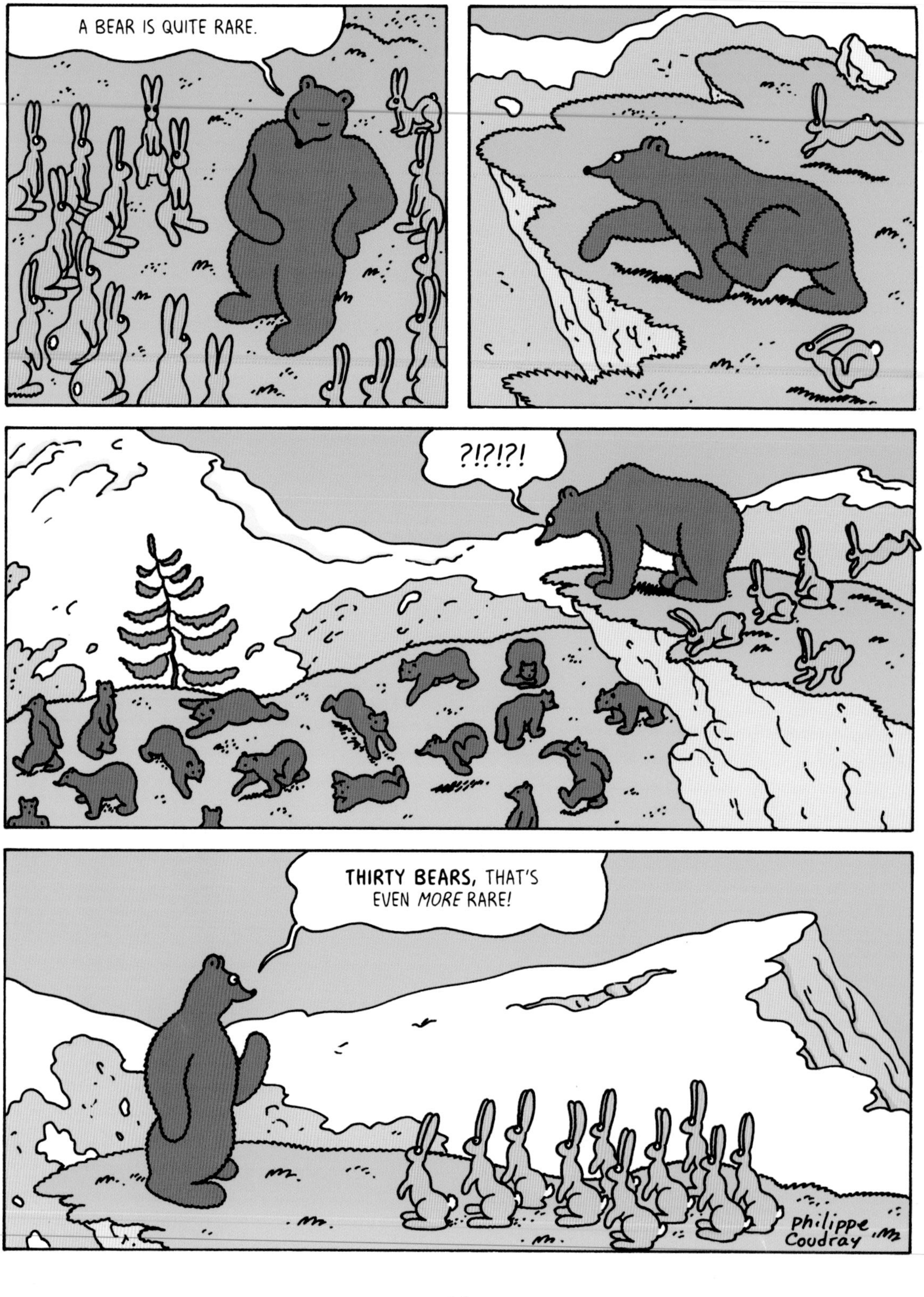
A BEAR IS QUITE RARE.
?!?!?!
THIRTY BEARS, THAT'S EVEN *MORE* RARE!
Philippe Coudray

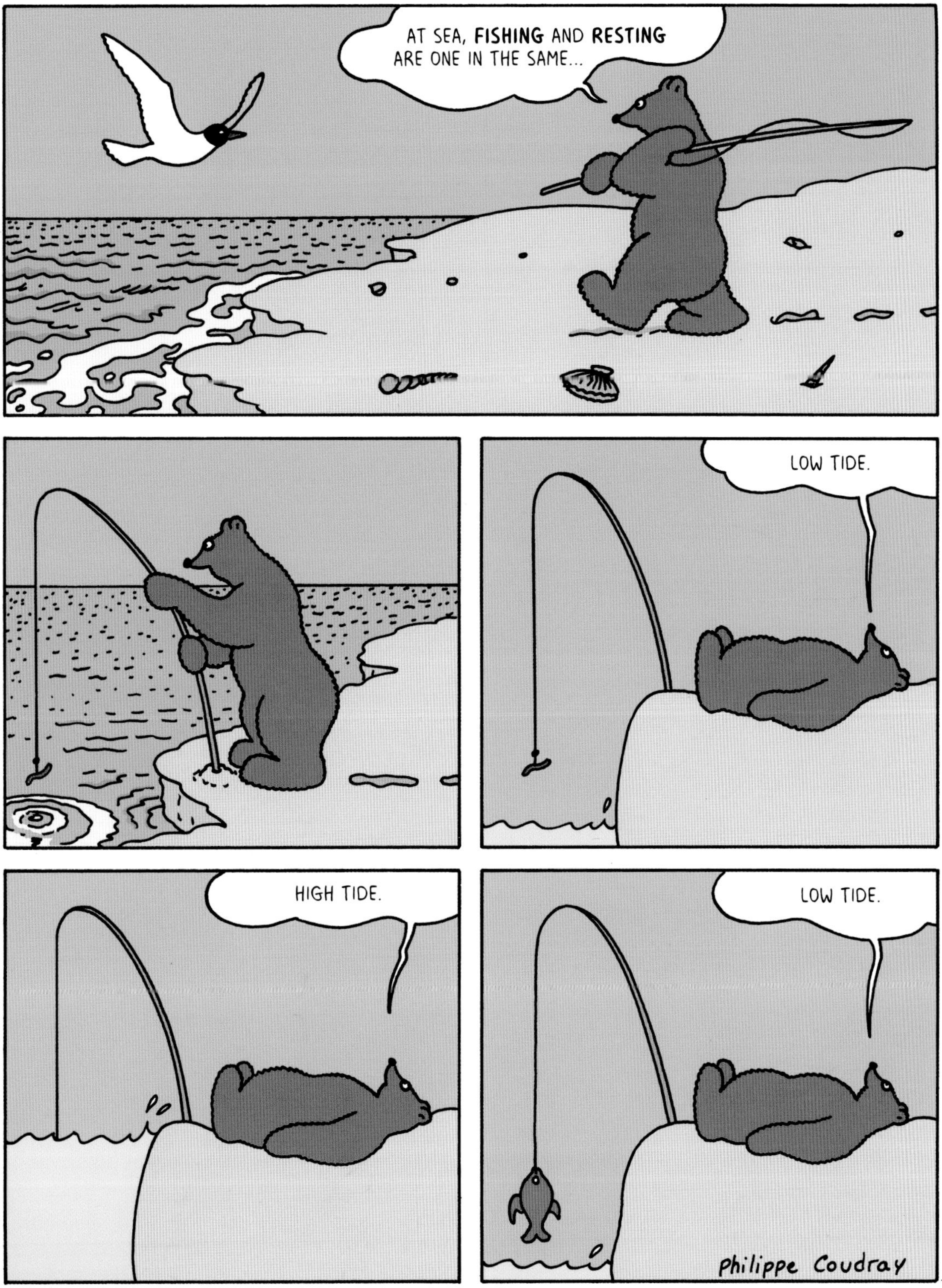
AT SEA, **FISHING** AND **RESTING** ARE ONE IN THE SAME...
LOW TIDE.
HIGH TIDE.
LOW TIDE.
Philippe Coudray

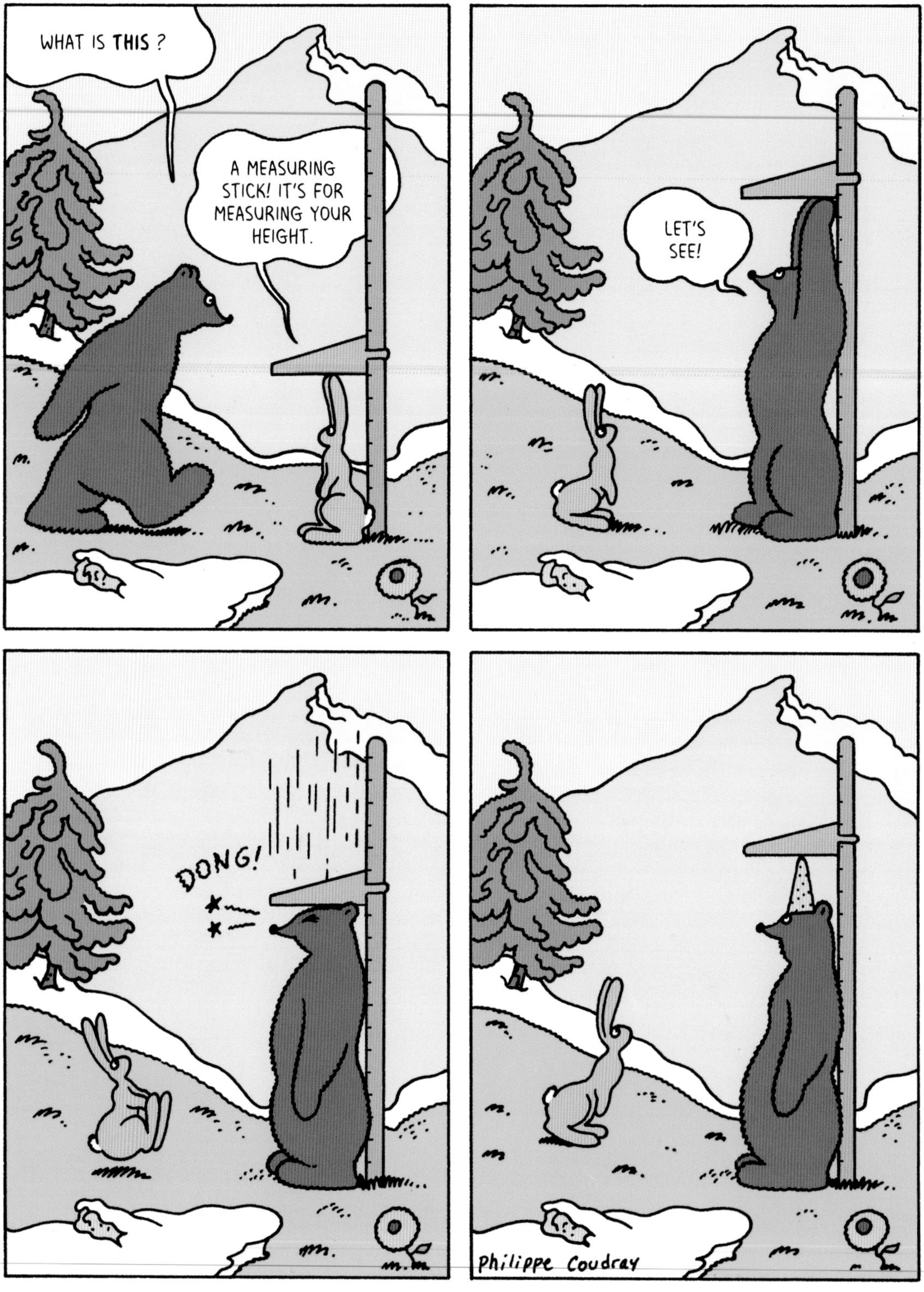
WHAT IS THIS ?
A MEASURING STICK! IT'S FOR MEASURING YOUR HEIGHT.
LET'S SEE!
DONG!
Philippe Coudray

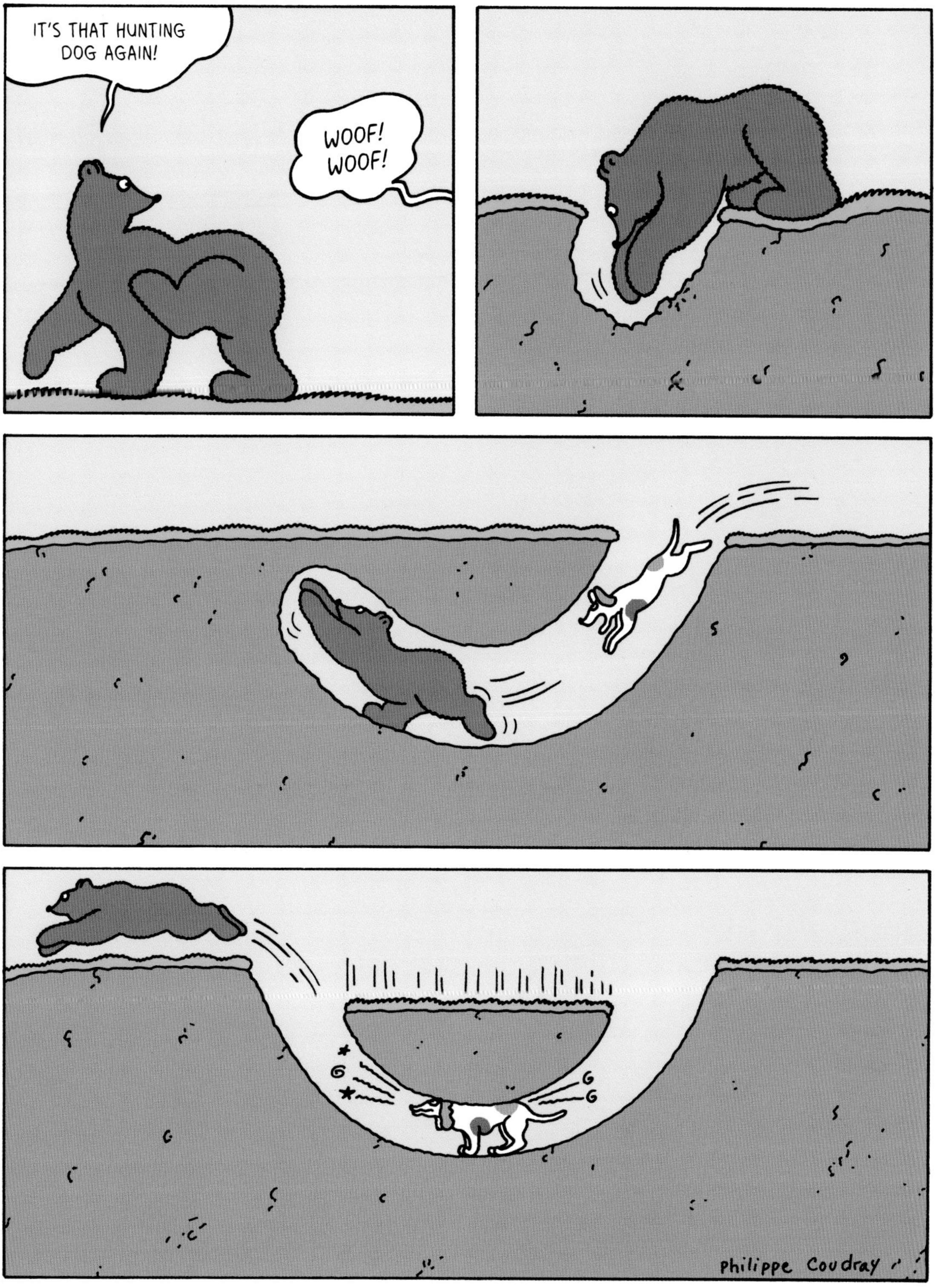
IT'S THAT HUNTING DOG AGAIN!
WOOF! WOOF!
Philippe Coudray

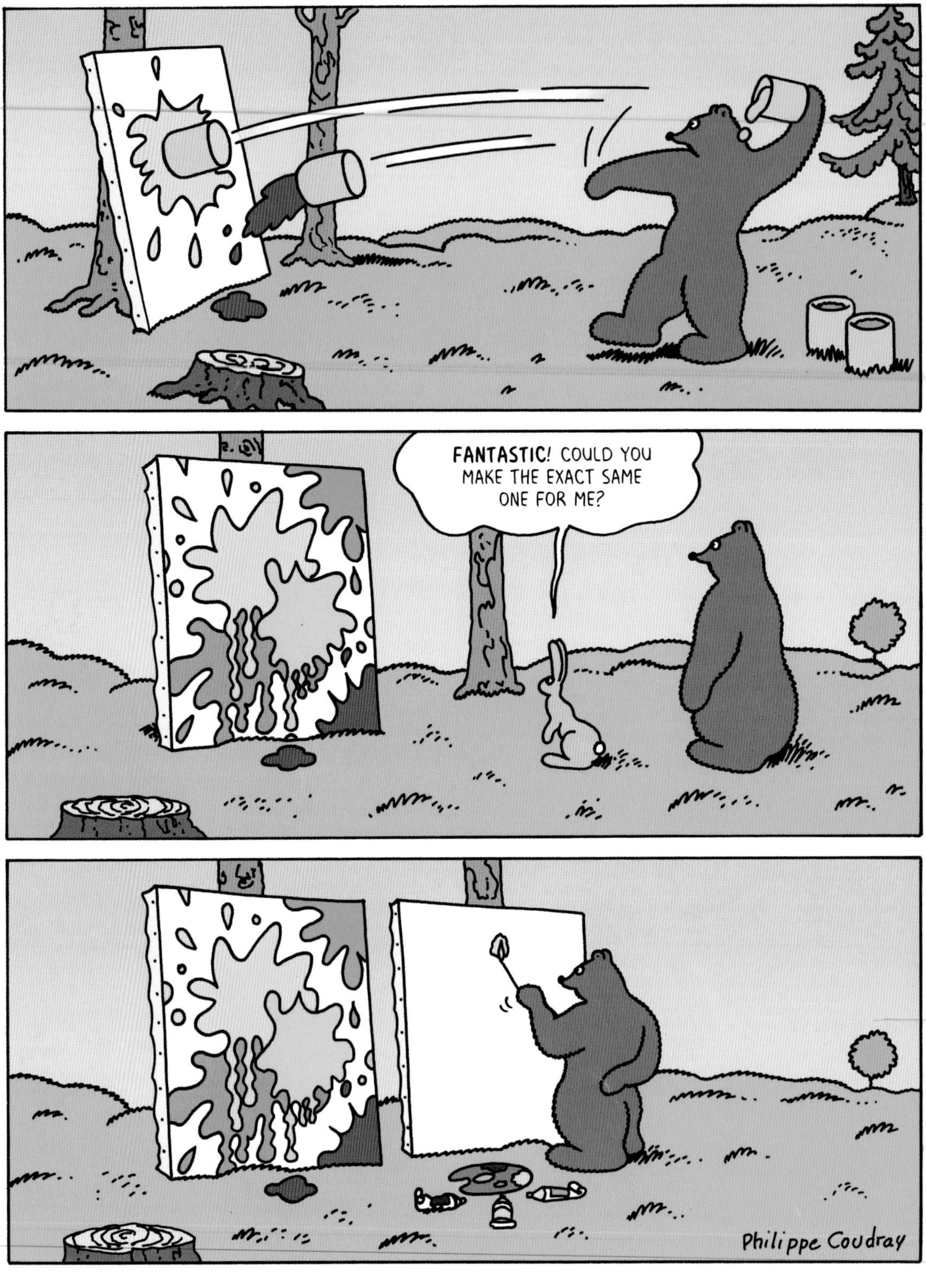
FANTASTIC! COULD YOU MAKE THE EXACT SAME ONE FOR ME?
Philippe Coudray

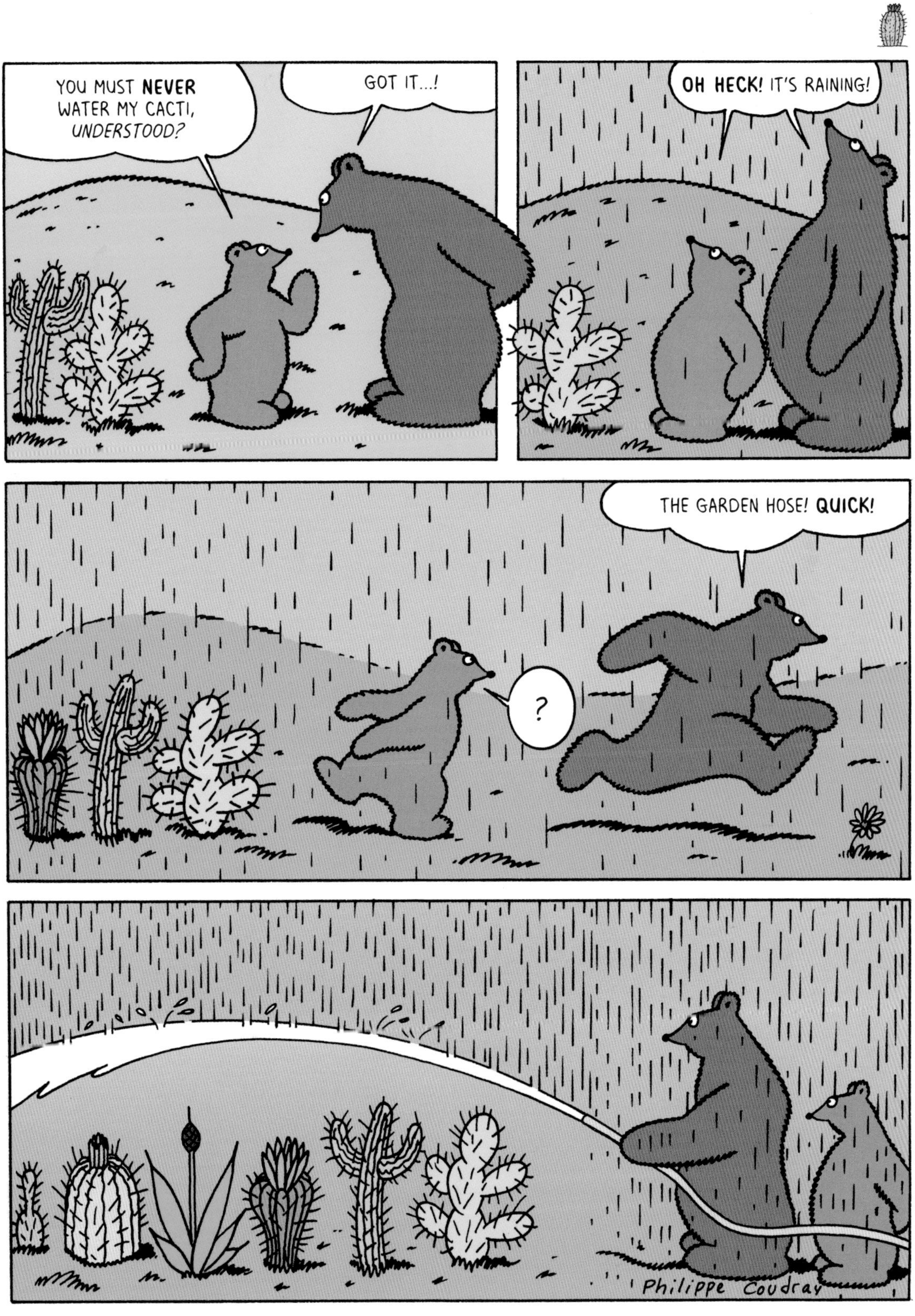
YOU MUST **NEVER** WATER MY CACTI, *UNDERSTOOD?*
GOT IT...!
OH HECK! IT'S RAINING!
THE GARDEN HOSE! **QUICK!**
?
Philippe Coudray

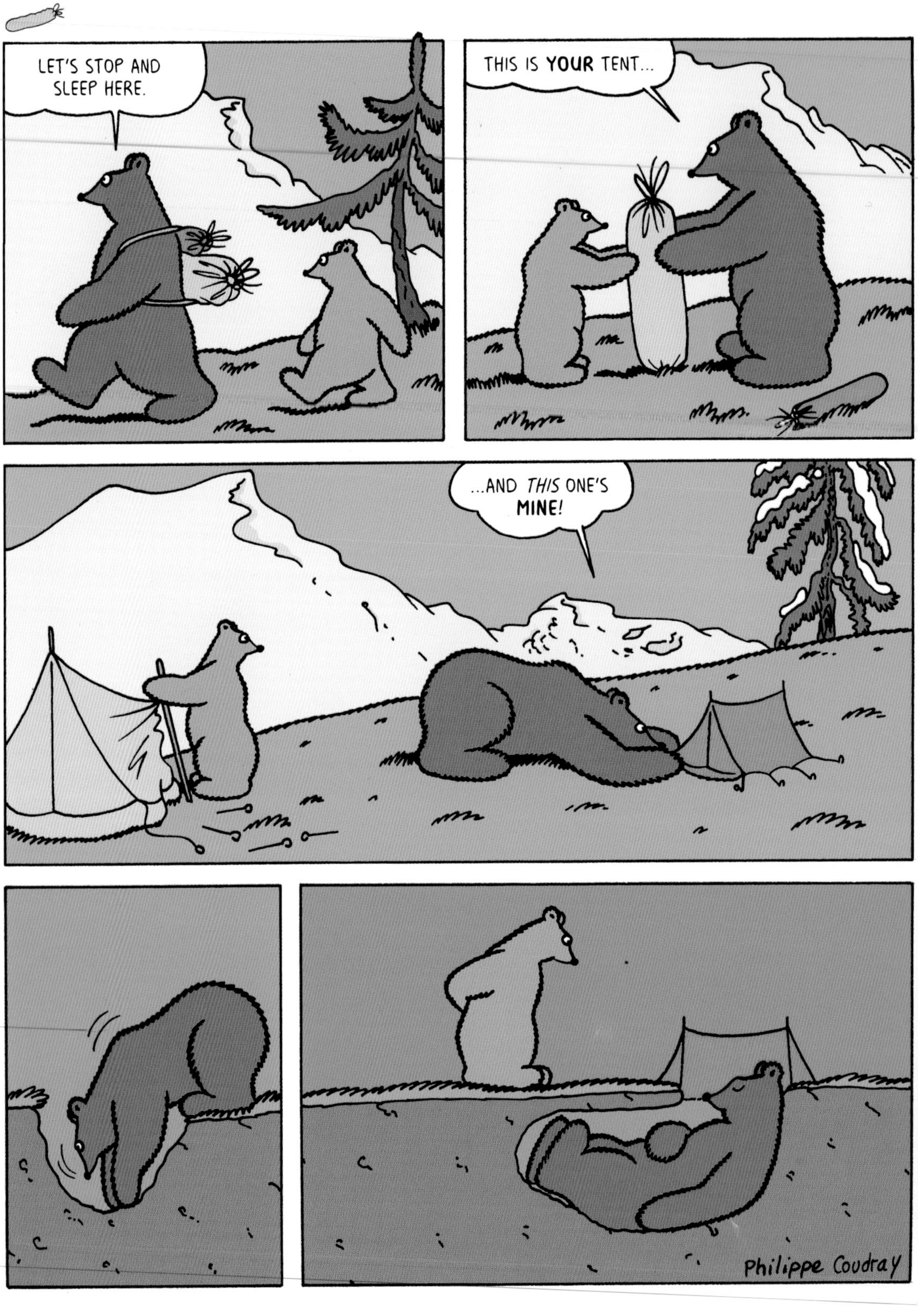
LET'S STOP AND SLEEP HERE.
THIS IS **YOUR** TENT...
...AND *THIS* ONE'S **MINE**!
Philippe Coudray

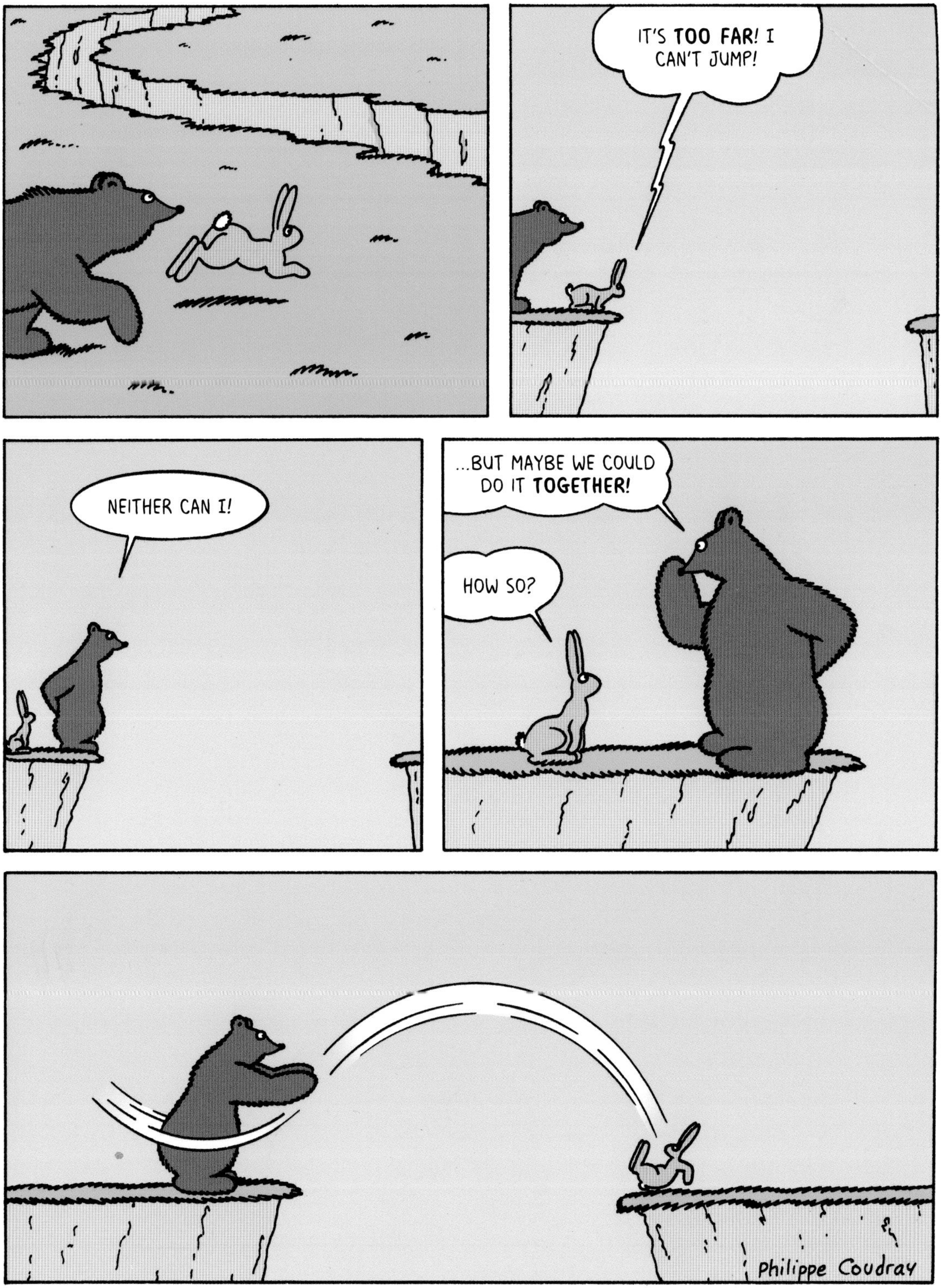
IT'S **TOO FAR**! I CAN'T JUMP!
NEITHER CAN I!
...BUT MAYBE WE COULD DO IT **TOGETHER**!
HOW SO?
Philippe Coudray

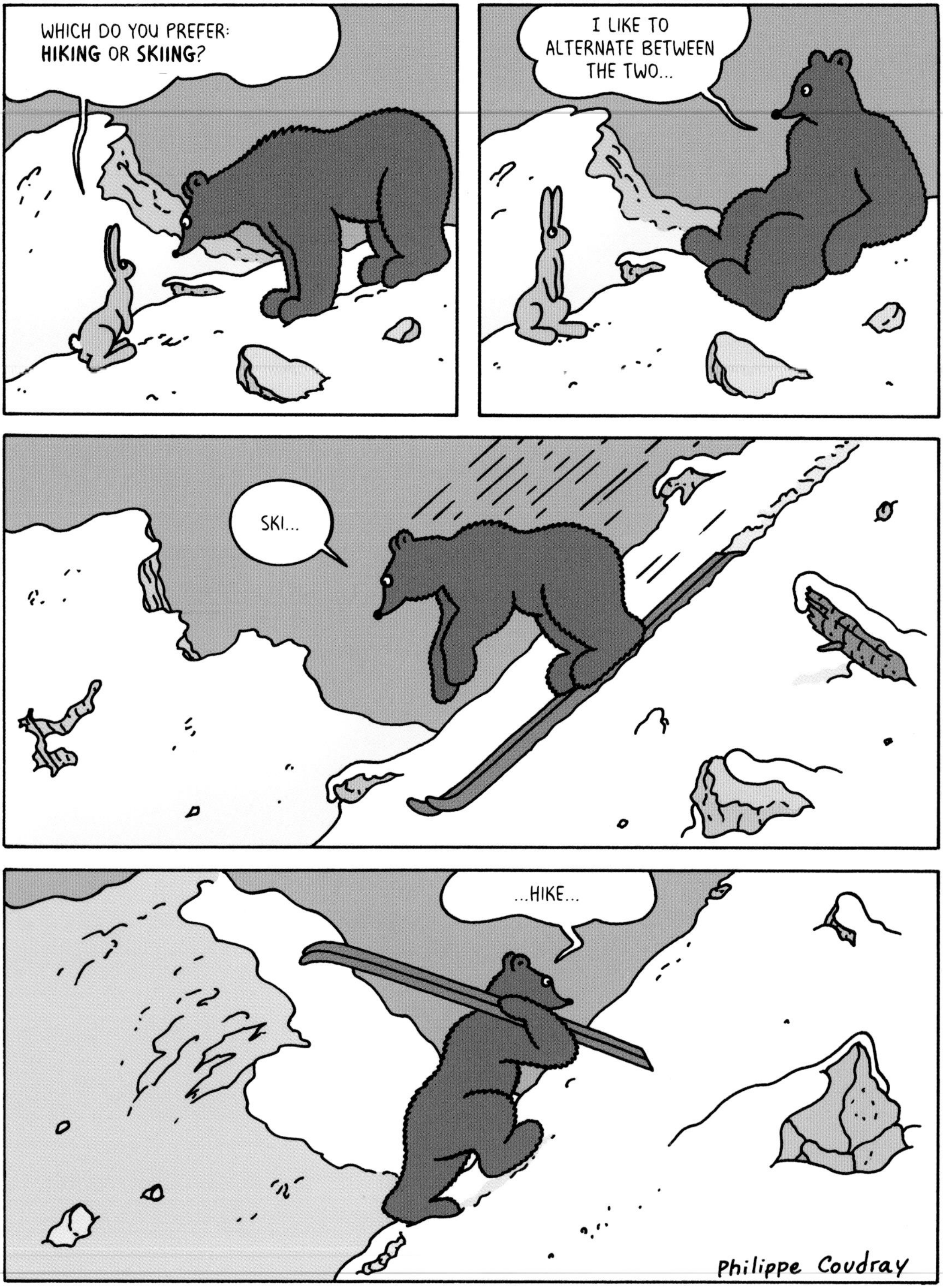
WHICH DO YOU PREFER: **HIKING** OR **SKIING**?
I LIKE TO ALTERNATE BETWEEN THE TWO...
SKI...
...HIKE...
Philippe Coudray

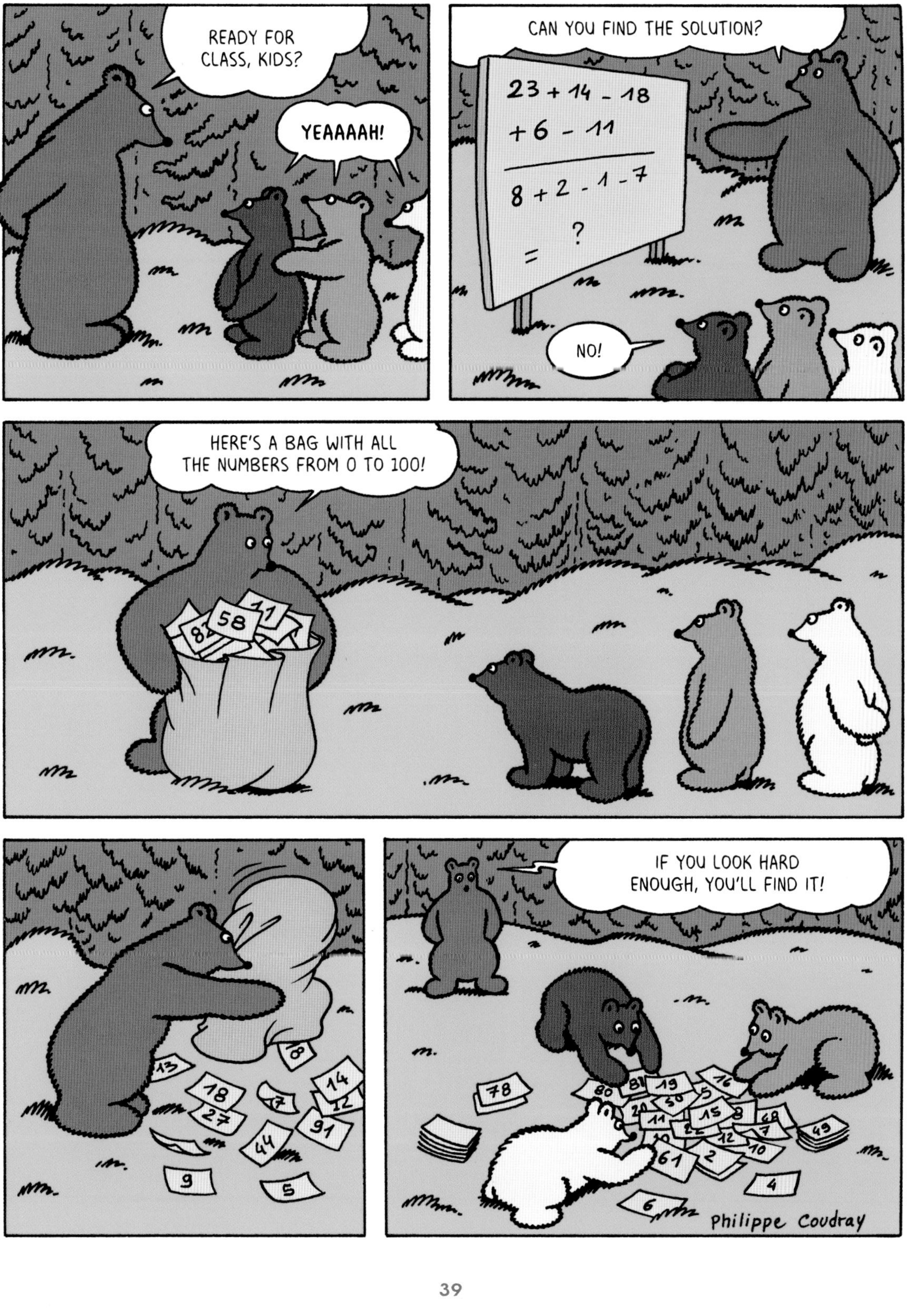
READY FOR CLASS, KIDS?
YEAAAAH!
CAN YOU FIND THE SOLUTION?
23 + 14 - 18
+ 6 - 11
8 + 2 - 1 - 7
= ?
NO!
HERE'S A BAG WITH ALL THE NUMBERS FROM 0 TO 100!
IF YOU LOOK HARD ENOUGH, YOU'LL FIND IT!
Philippe Coudray

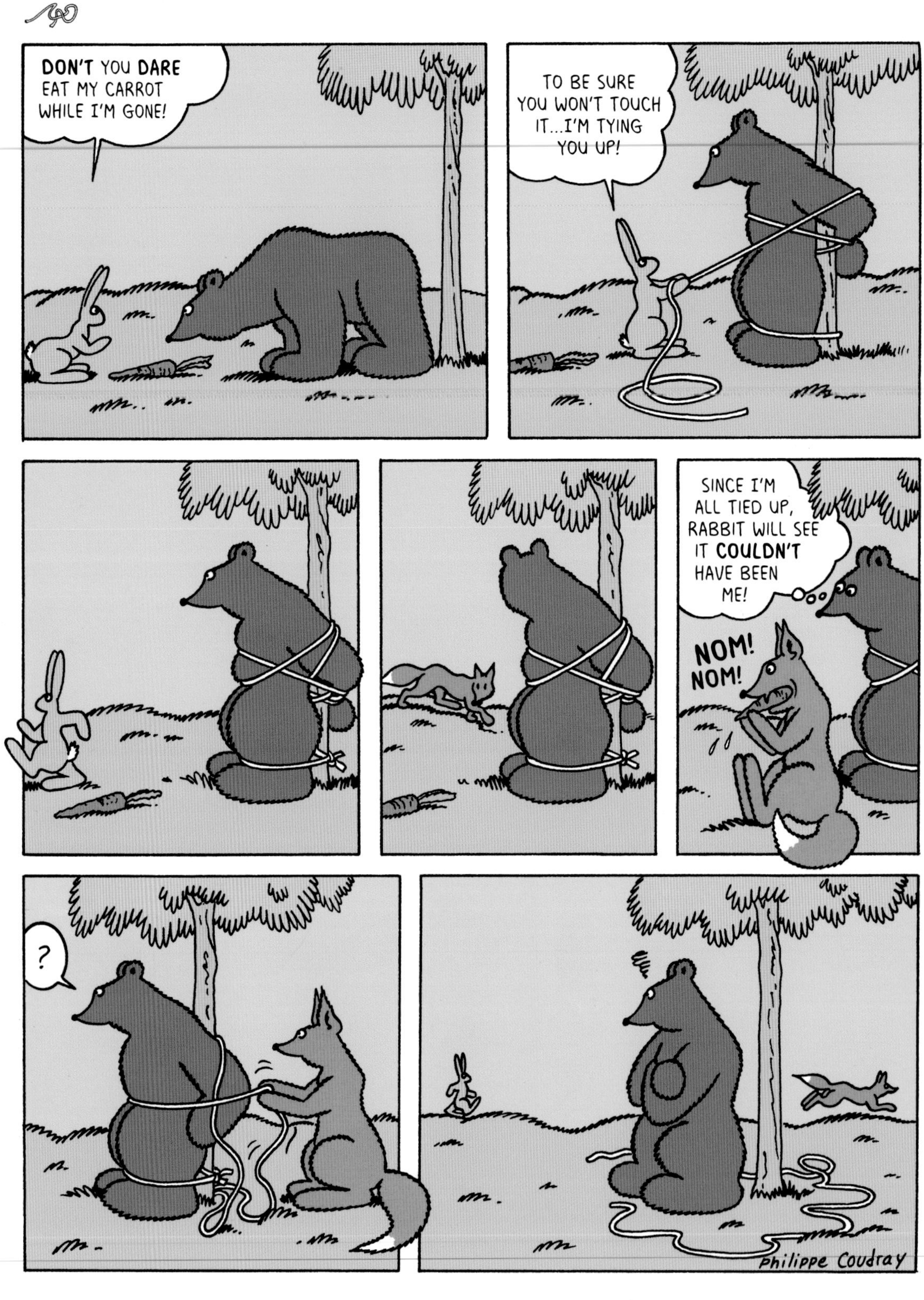

DON'T YOU DARE EAT MY CARROT WHILE I'M GONE!
TO BE SURE YOU WON'T TOUCH IT...I'M TYING YOU UP!
SINCE I'M ALL TIED UP, RABBIT WILL SEE IT COULDN'T HAVE BEEN ME!
NOM! NOM!
?
Philippe Coudray

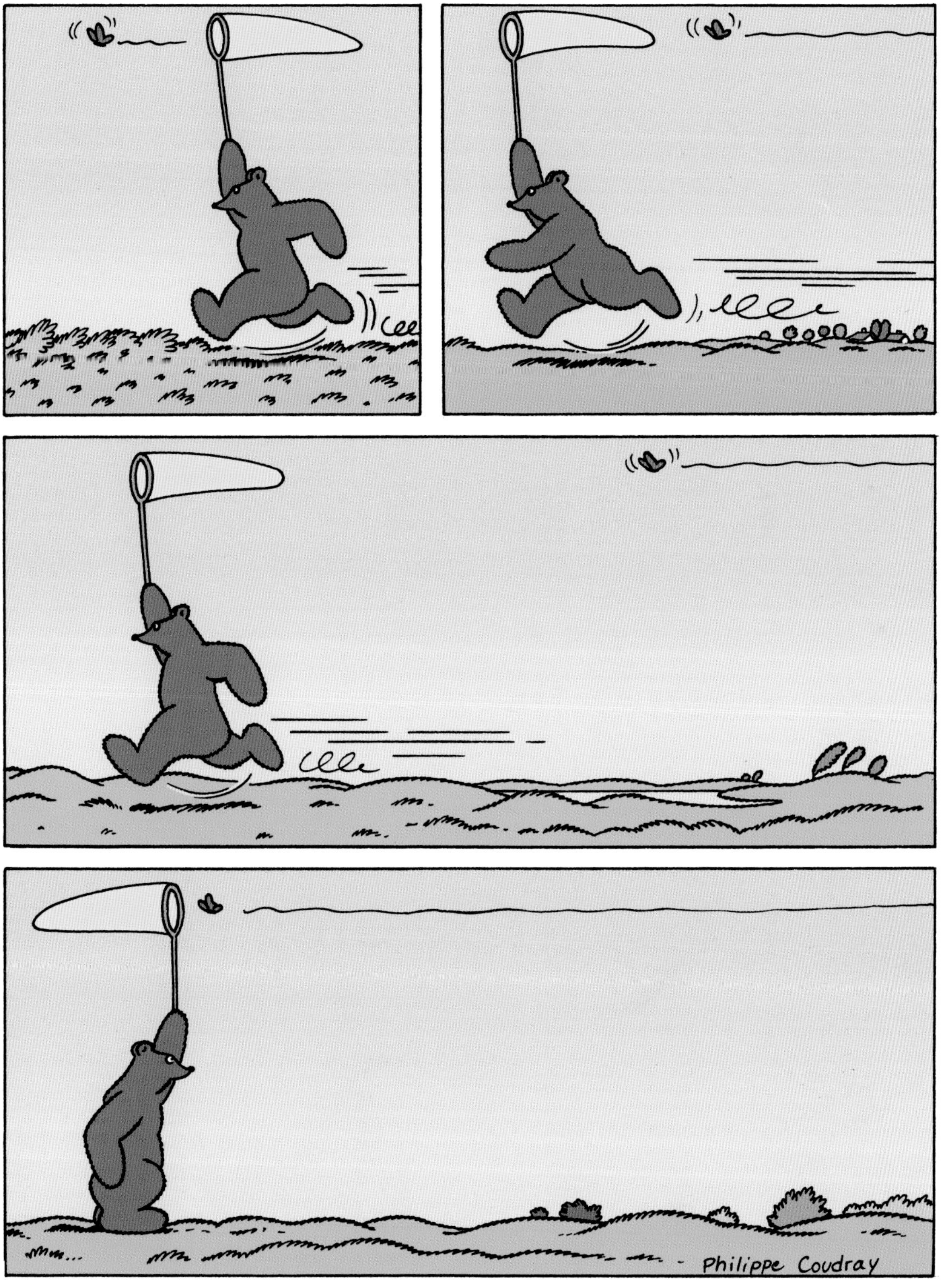
Philippe Coudray

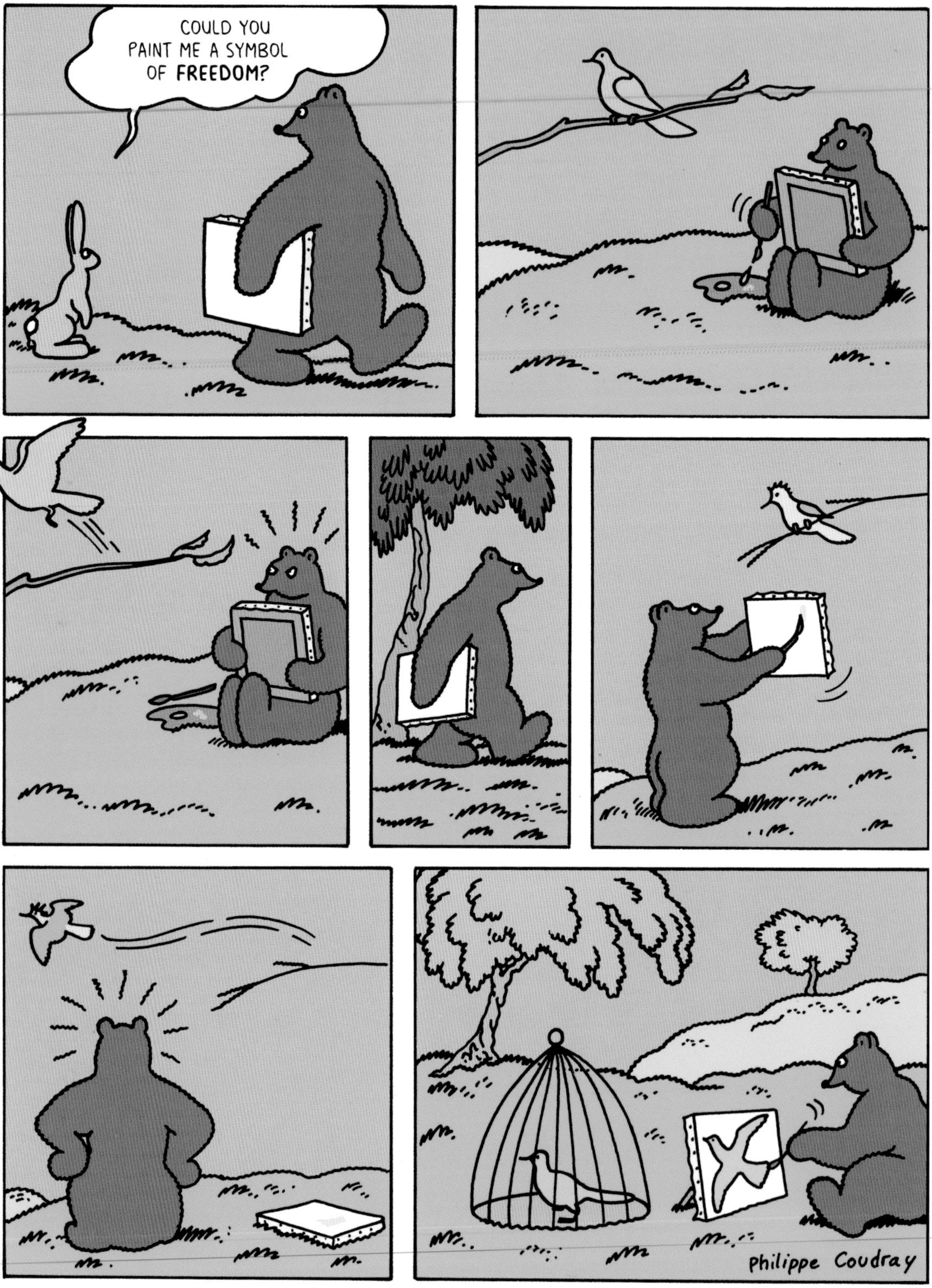
COULD YOU PAINT ME A SYMBOL OF **FREEDOM?**
Philippe Coudray

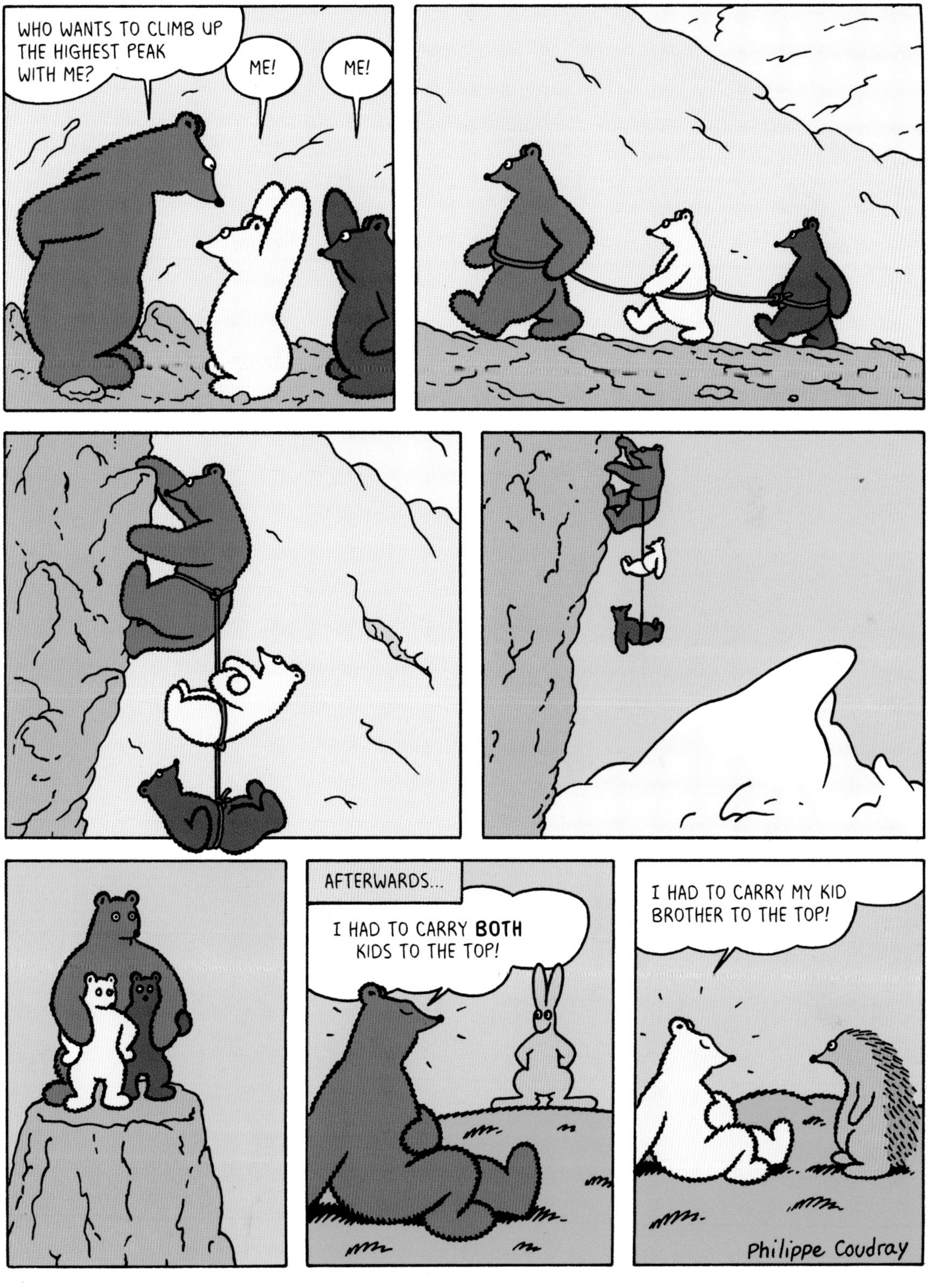
WHO WANTS TO CLIMB UP THE HIGHEST PEAK WITH ME?
ME!
ME!
AFTERWARDS...
I HAD TO CARRY **BOTH** KIDS TO THE TOP!
I HAD TO CARRY MY KID BROTHER TO THE TOP!
Philippe Coudray

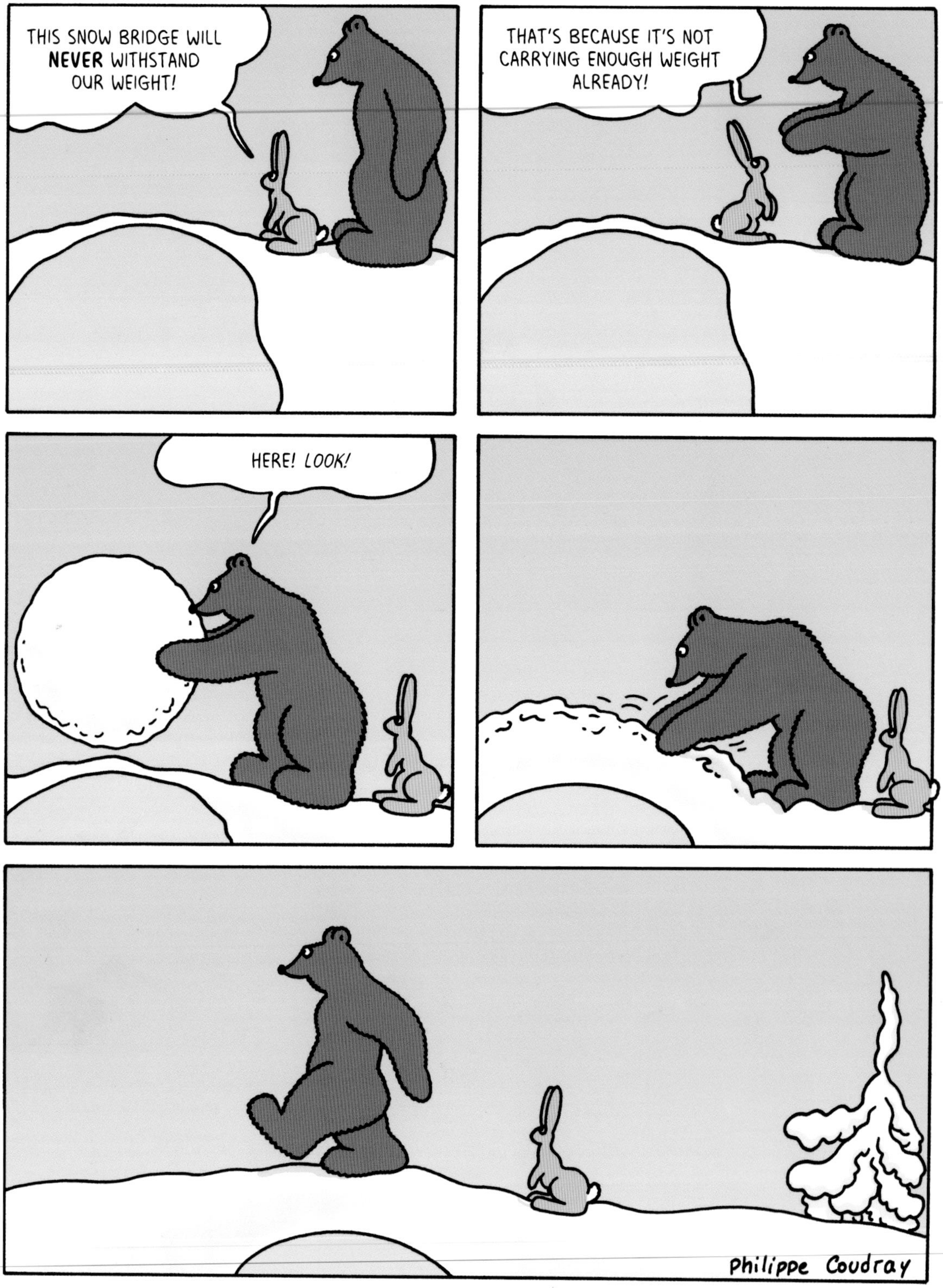
THIS SNOW BRIDGE WILL **NEVER** WITHSTAND OUR WEIGHT!
THAT'S BECAUSE IT'S NOT CARRYING ENOUGH WEIGHT ALREADY!
HERE! *LOOK!*
Philippe Coudray

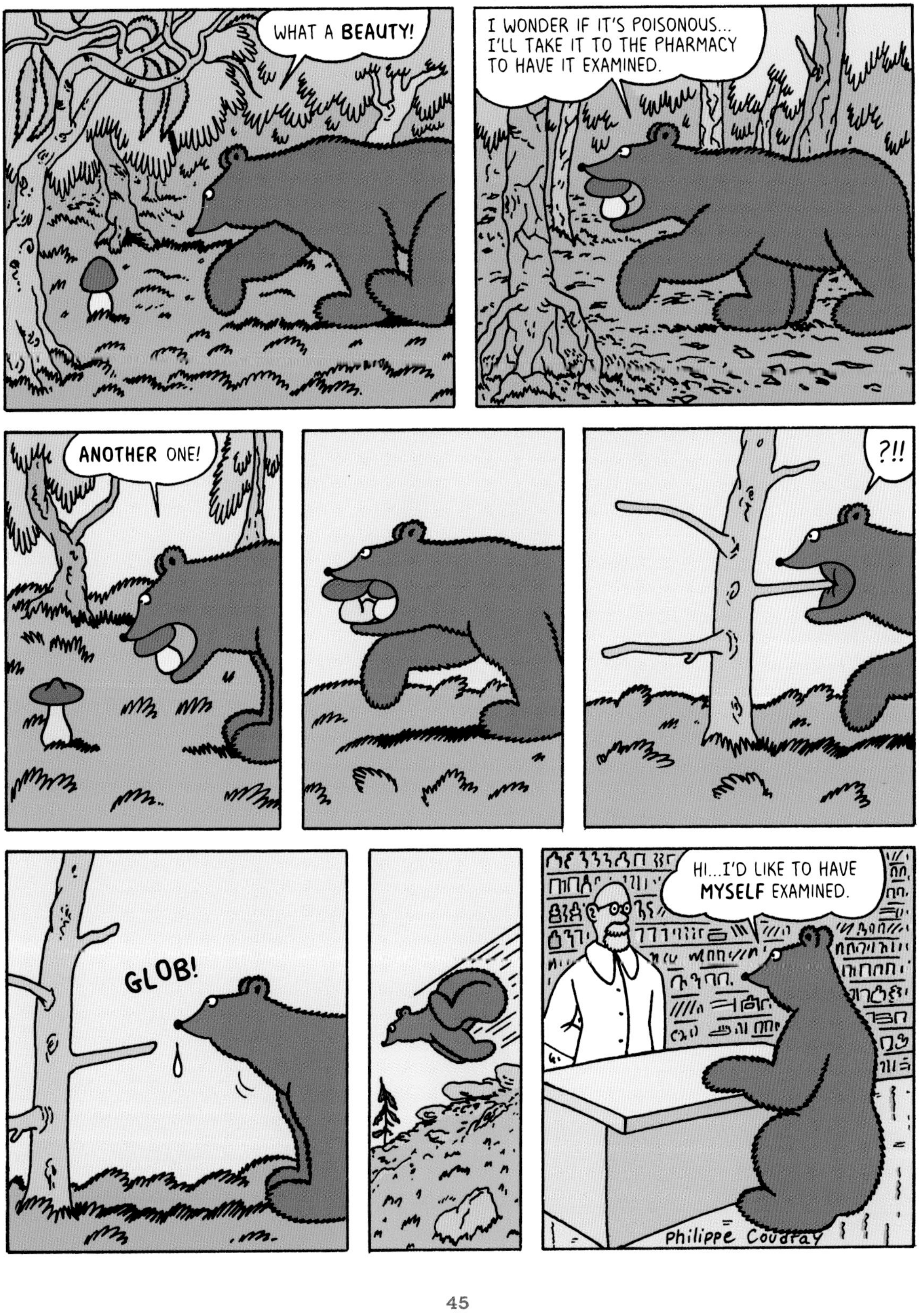
WHAT A BEAUTY!
I WONDER IF IT'S POISONOUS... I'LL TAKE IT TO THE PHARMACY TO HAVE IT EXAMINED.
ANOTHER ONE!
?!!
GLOB!
HI...I'D LIKE TO HAVE MYSELF EXAMINED.
Philippe Coudray

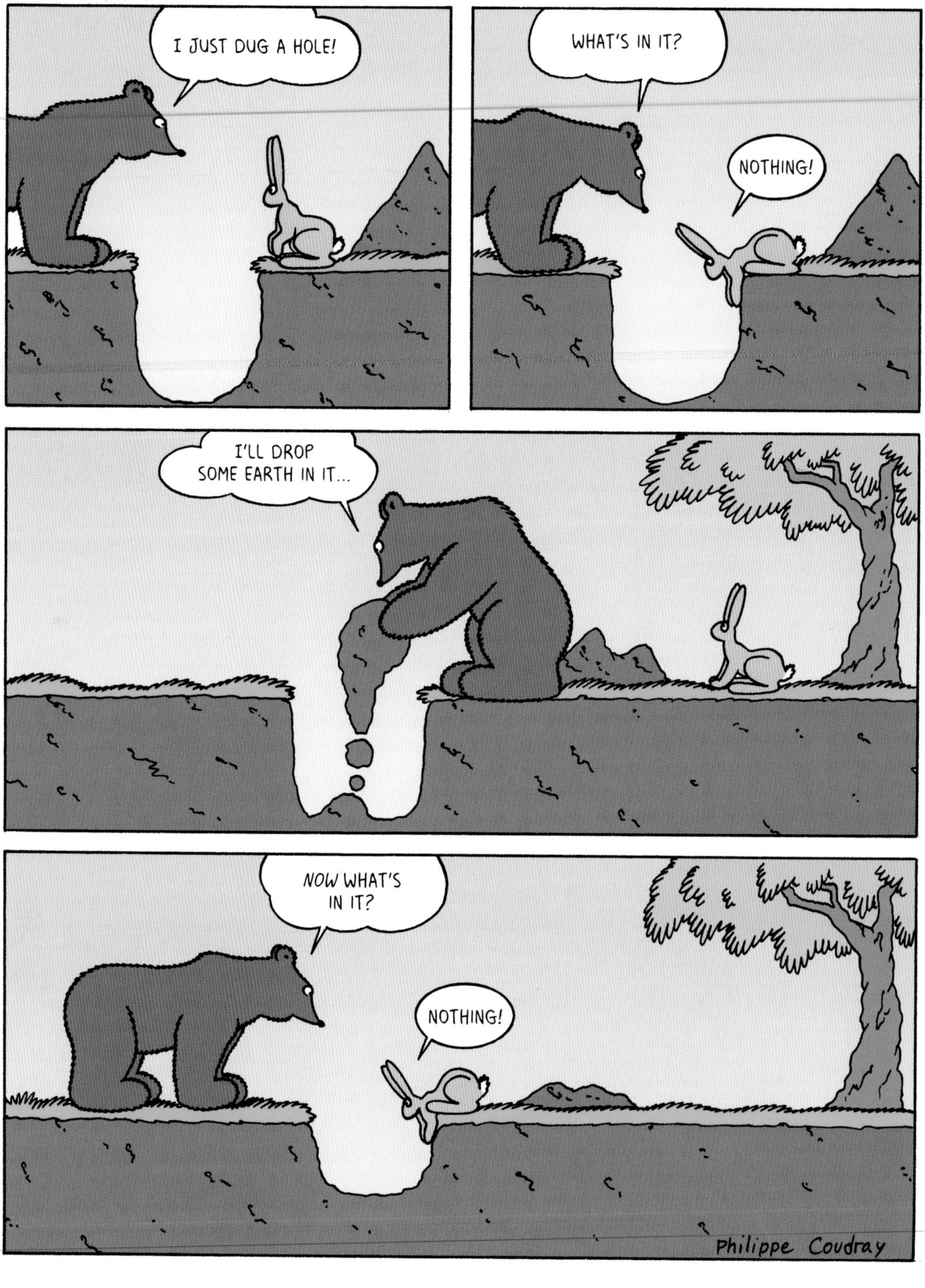

I JUST DUG A HOLE!
WHAT'S IN IT?
NOTHING!
I'LL DROP SOME EARTH IN IT...
NOW WHAT'S IN IT?
NOTHING!
Philippe Coudray

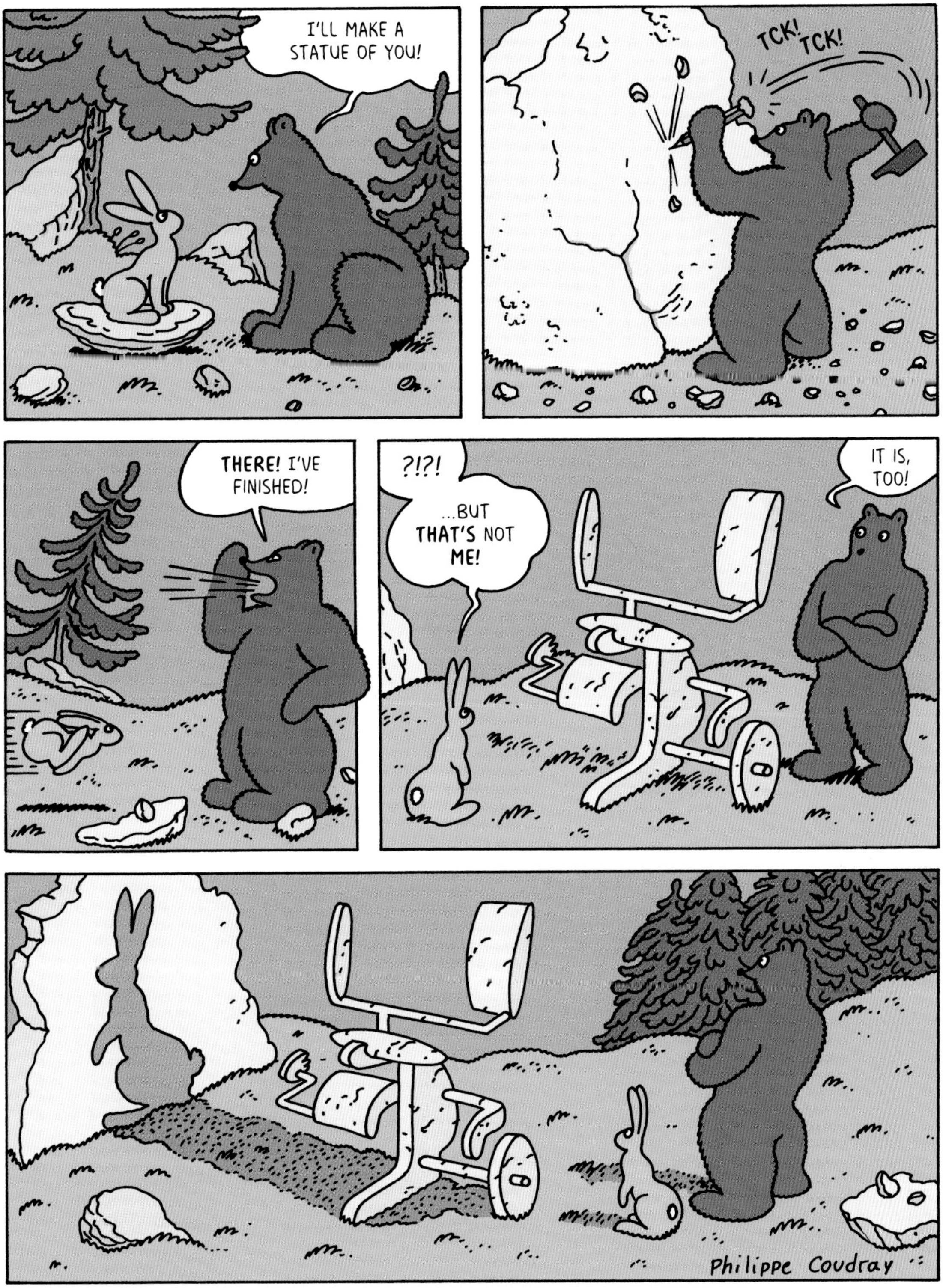

I'LL MAKE A STATUE OF YOU!
TCK! TCK!
THERE! I'VE FINISHED!
?!?!
...BUT THAT'S NOT ME!
IT IS, TOO!
Philippe Coudray

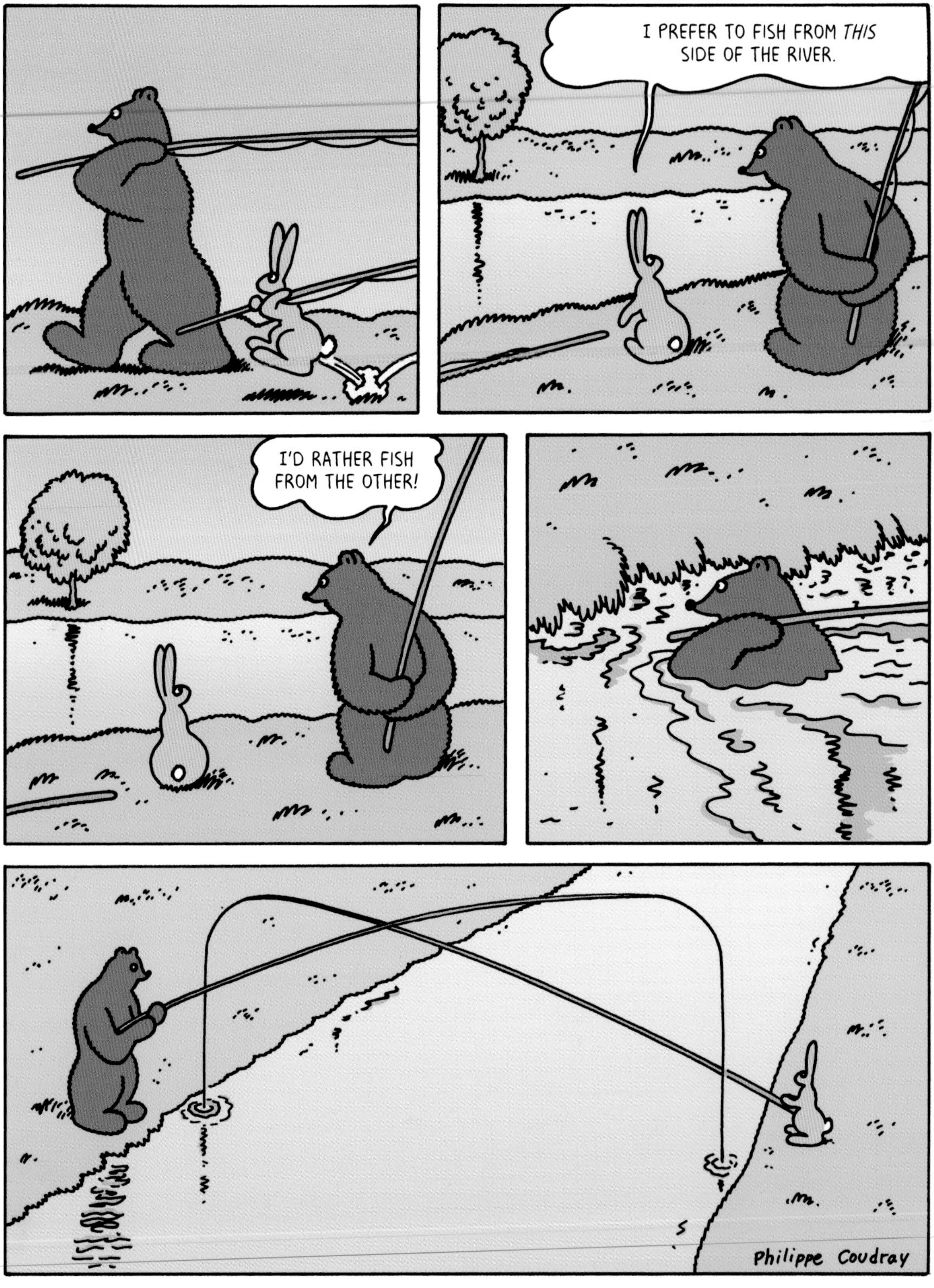
I PREFER TO FISH FROM *THIS* SIDE OF THE RIVER.
I'D RATHER FISH FROM THE OTHER!
Philippe Coudray

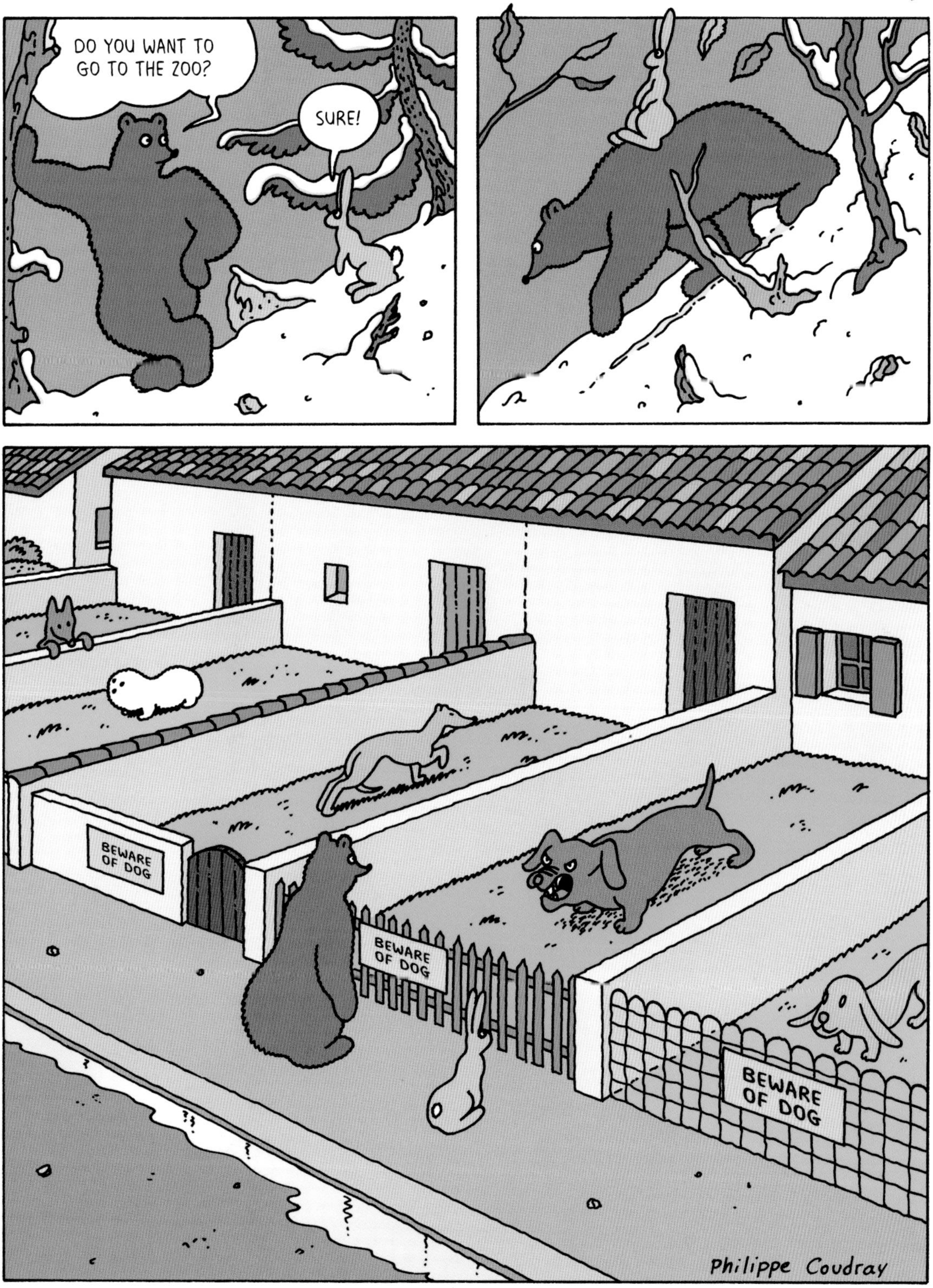
DO YOU WANT TO GO TO THE ZOO?
SURE!
BEWARE OF DOG
BEWARE OF DOG
BEWARE OF DOG
Philippe Coudray

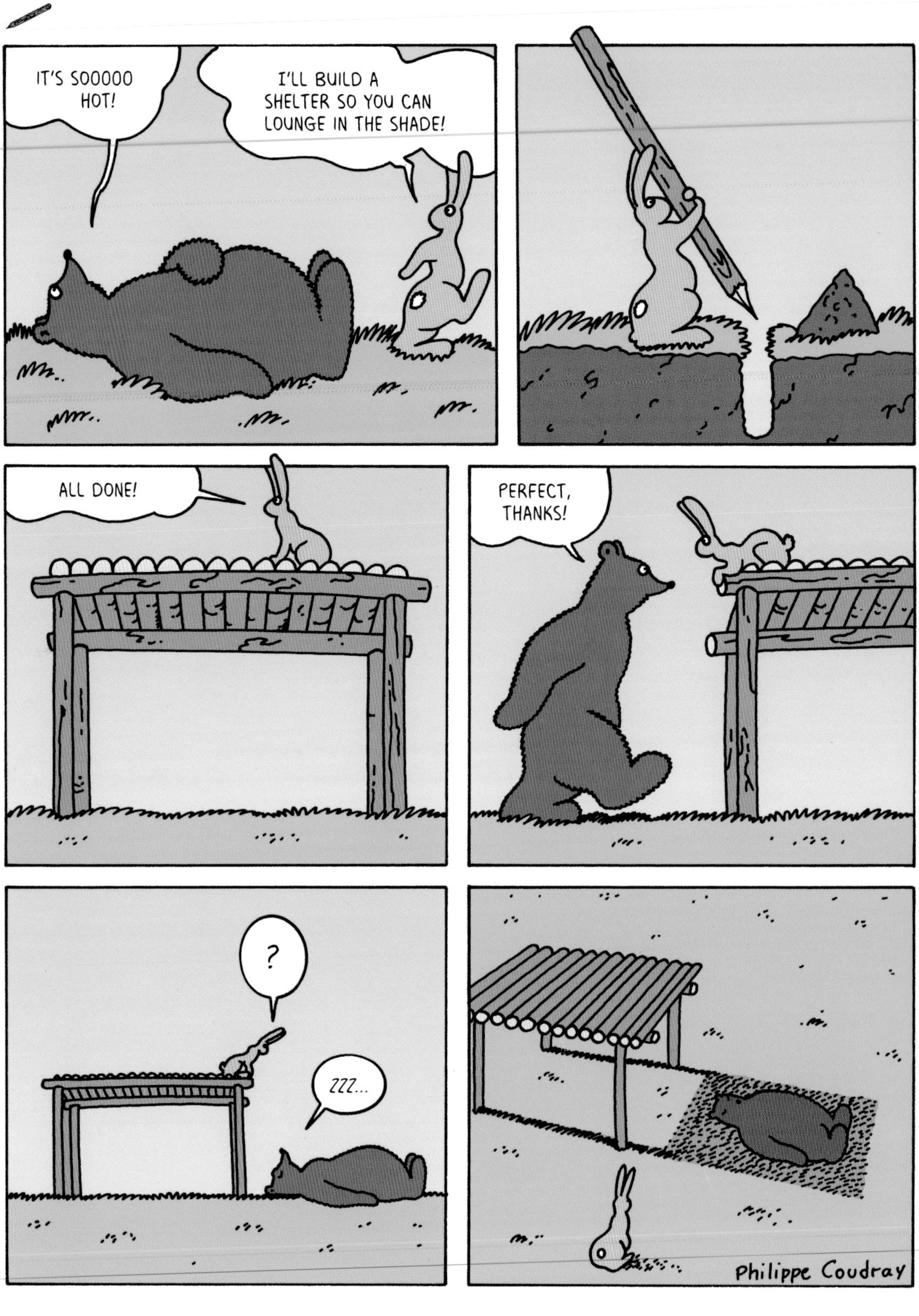
IT'S SOOOOO HOT!
I'LL BUILD A SHELTER SO YOU CAN LOUNGE IN THE SHADE!
ALL DONE!
PERFECT, THANKS!
?
ZZZ...
Philippe Coudray

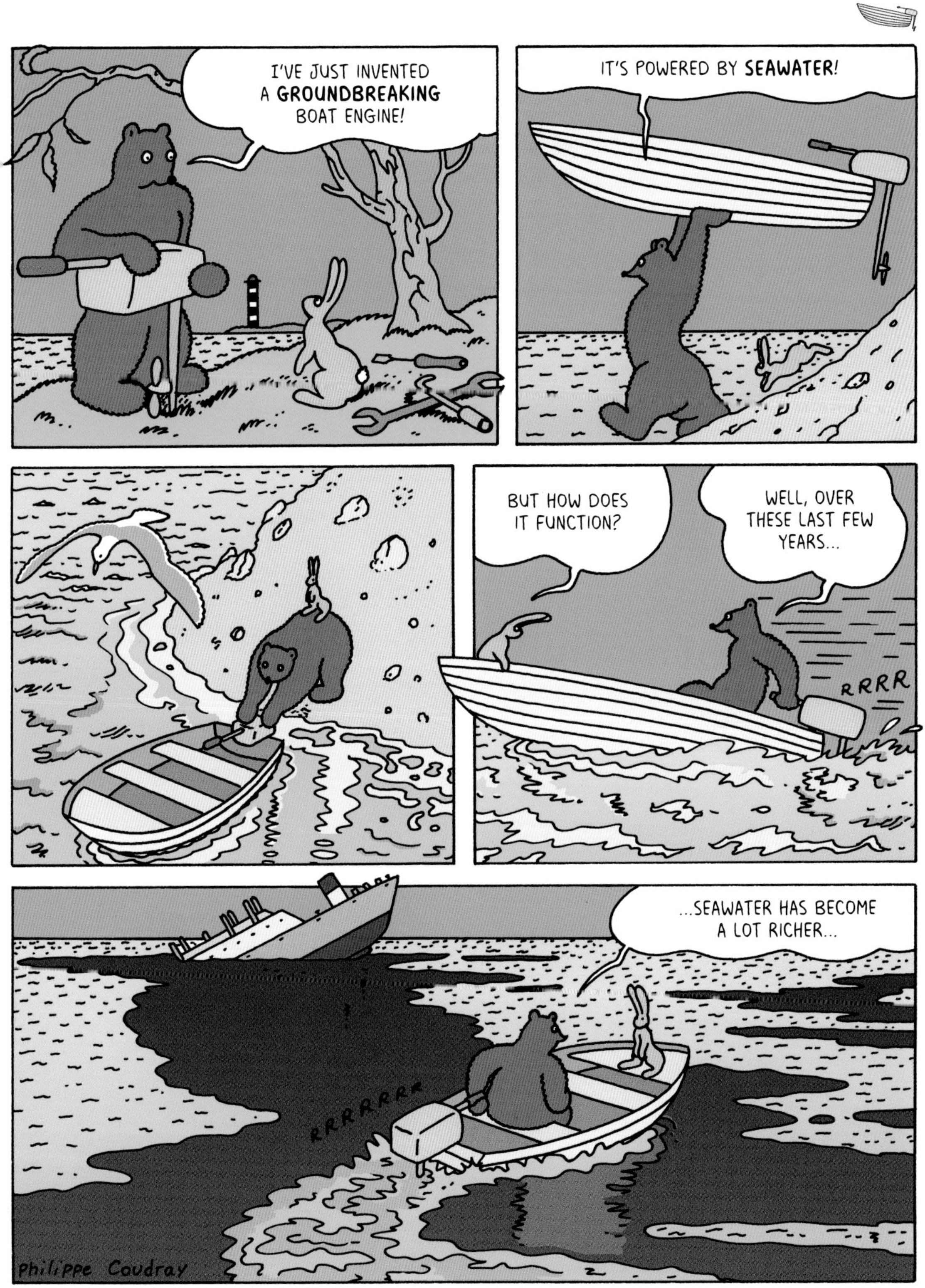
I'VE JUST INVENTED A **GROUNDBREAKING** BOAT ENGINE!
IT'S POWERED BY **SEAWATER**!
BUT HOW DOES IT FUNCTION?
WELL, OVER THESE LAST FEW YEARS...
RRRR
...SEAWATER HAS BECOME A LOT RICHER...
RRRRRRR
Philippe Coudray

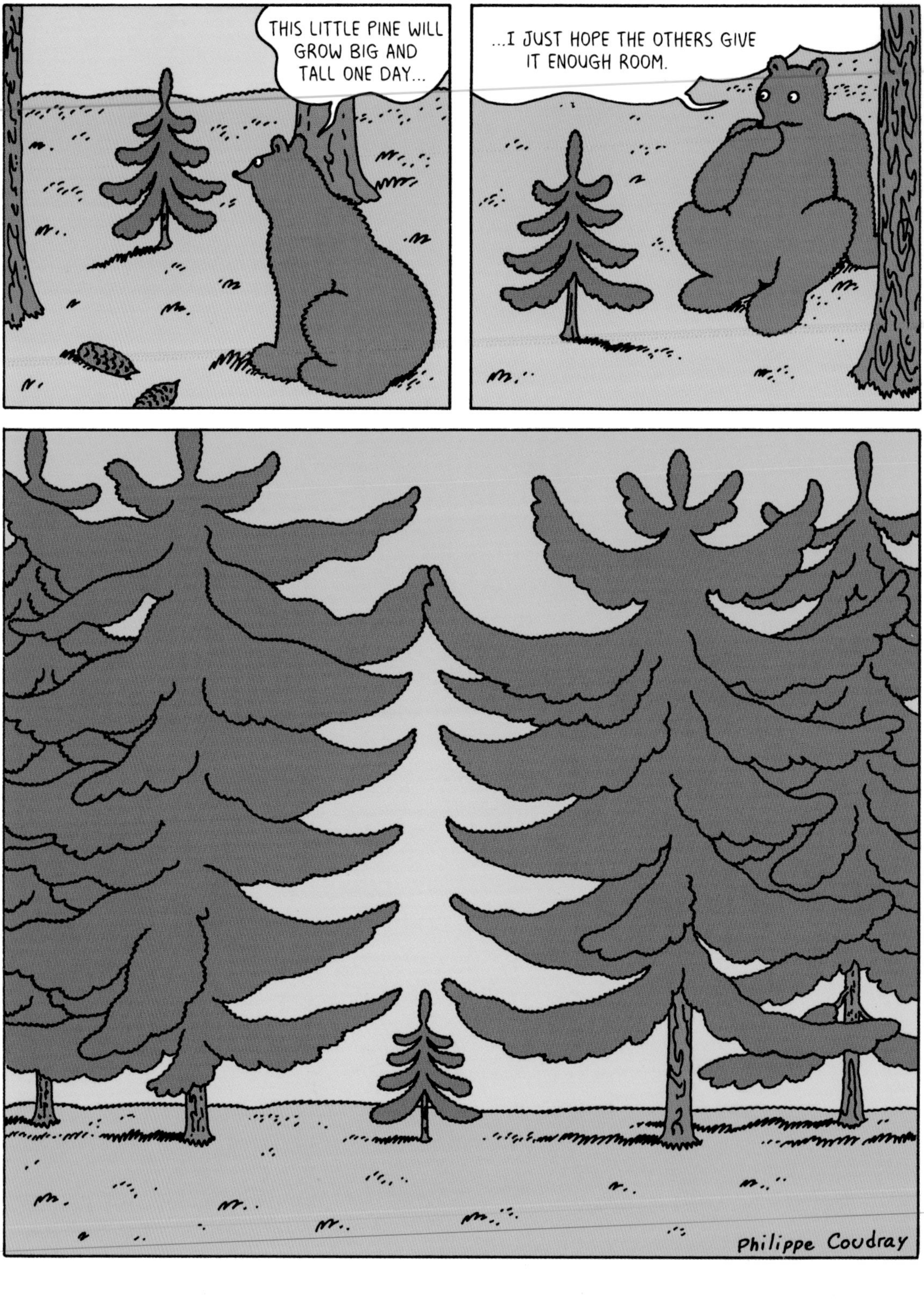
THIS LITTLE PINE WILL GROW BIG AND TALL ONE DAY...
...I JUST HOPE THE OTHERS GIVE IT ENOUGH ROOM.
Philippe Coudray

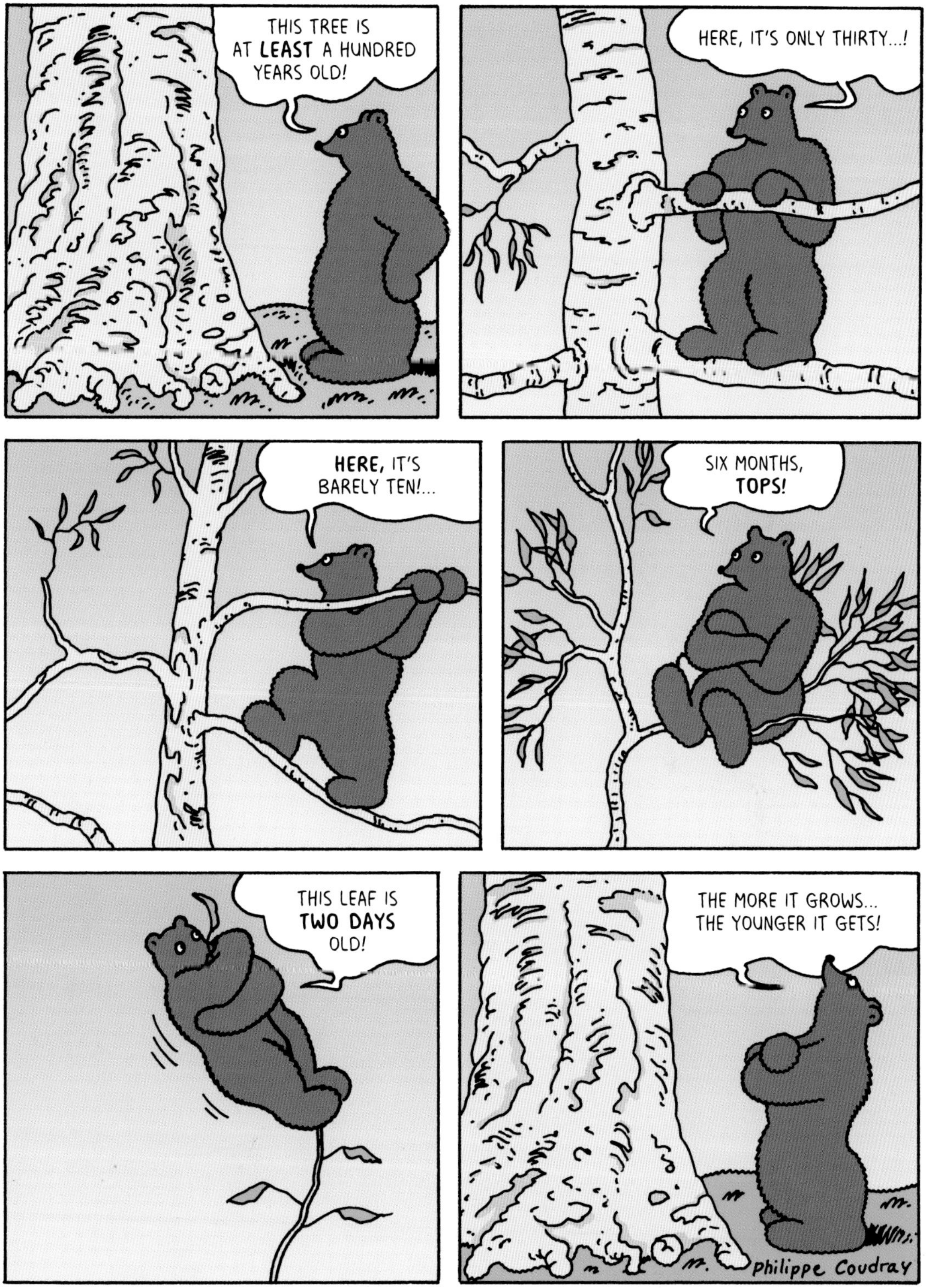
THIS TREE IS AT **LEAST** A HUNDRED YEARS OLD!
HERE, IT'S ONLY THIRTY...!
HERE, IT'S BARELY TEN!...
SIX MONTHS, **TOPS!**
THIS LEAF IS **TWO DAYS** OLD!
THE MORE IT GROWS... THE YOUNGER IT GETS!
Philippe Coudray

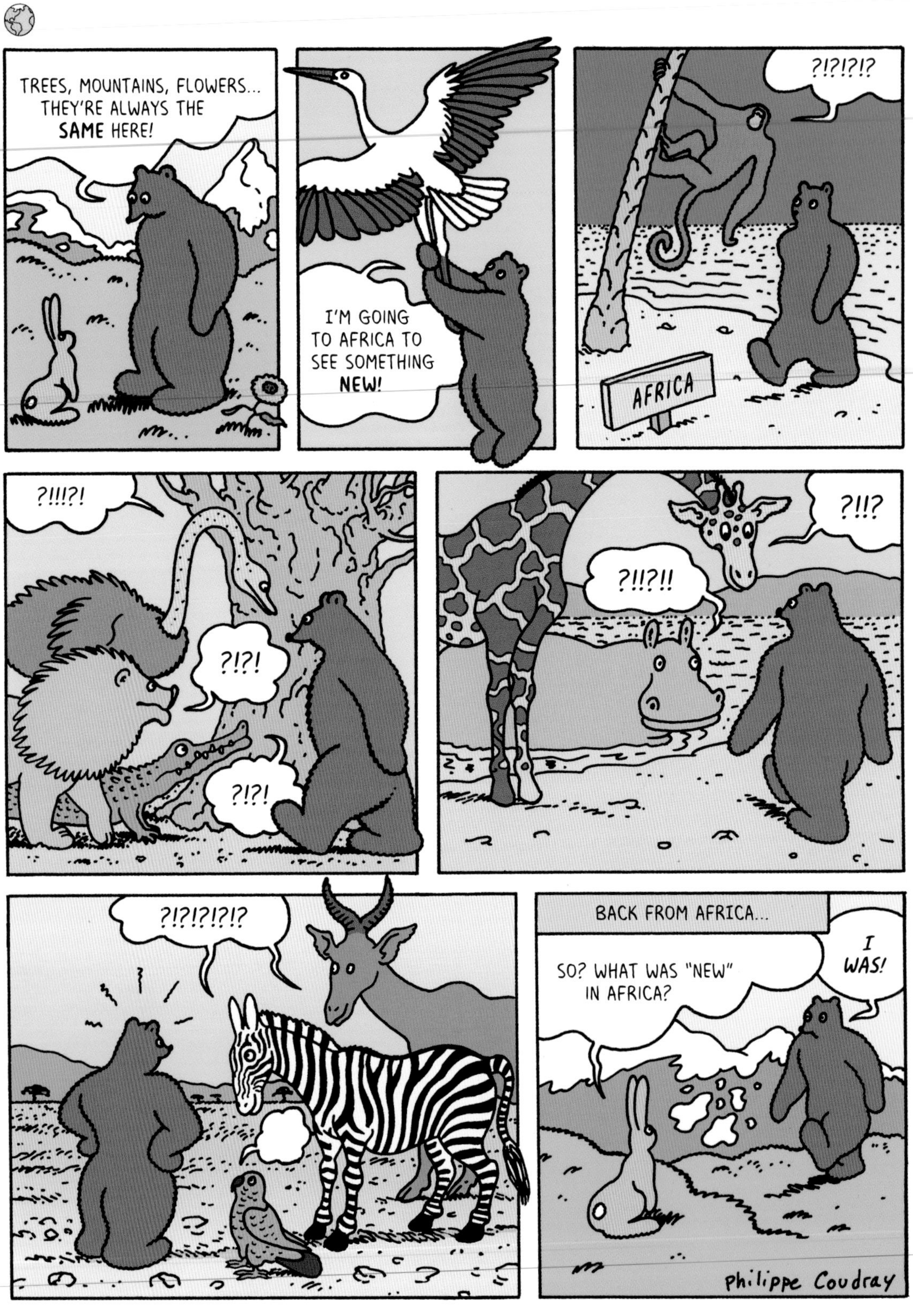
TREES, MOUNTAINS, FLOWERS... THEY'RE ALWAYS THE SAME HERE!
I'M GOING TO AFRICA TO SEE SOMETHING NEW!
?!?!?!?
AFRICA
?!!!?!
?!?!
?!?!
?!!?!!
?!!?
?!?!?!?!?
BACK FROM AFRICA...
SO? WHAT WAS "NEW" IN AFRICA?
I WAS!
Philippe Coudray

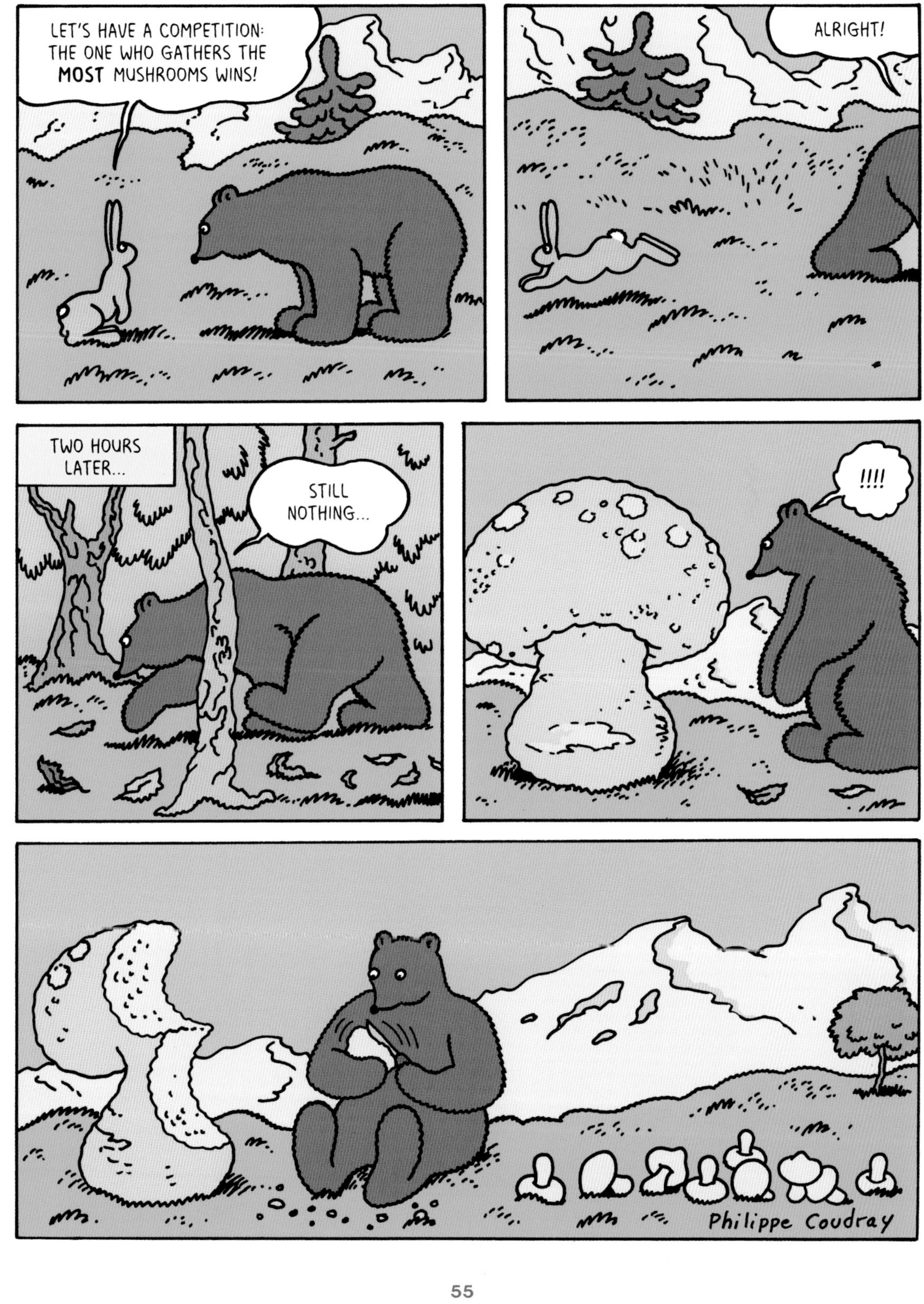
LET'S HAVE A COMPETITION: THE ONE WHO GATHERS THE **MOST** MUSHROOMS WINS!
ALRIGHT!
TWO HOURS LATER...
STILL NOTHING...
!!!!
Philippe Coudray

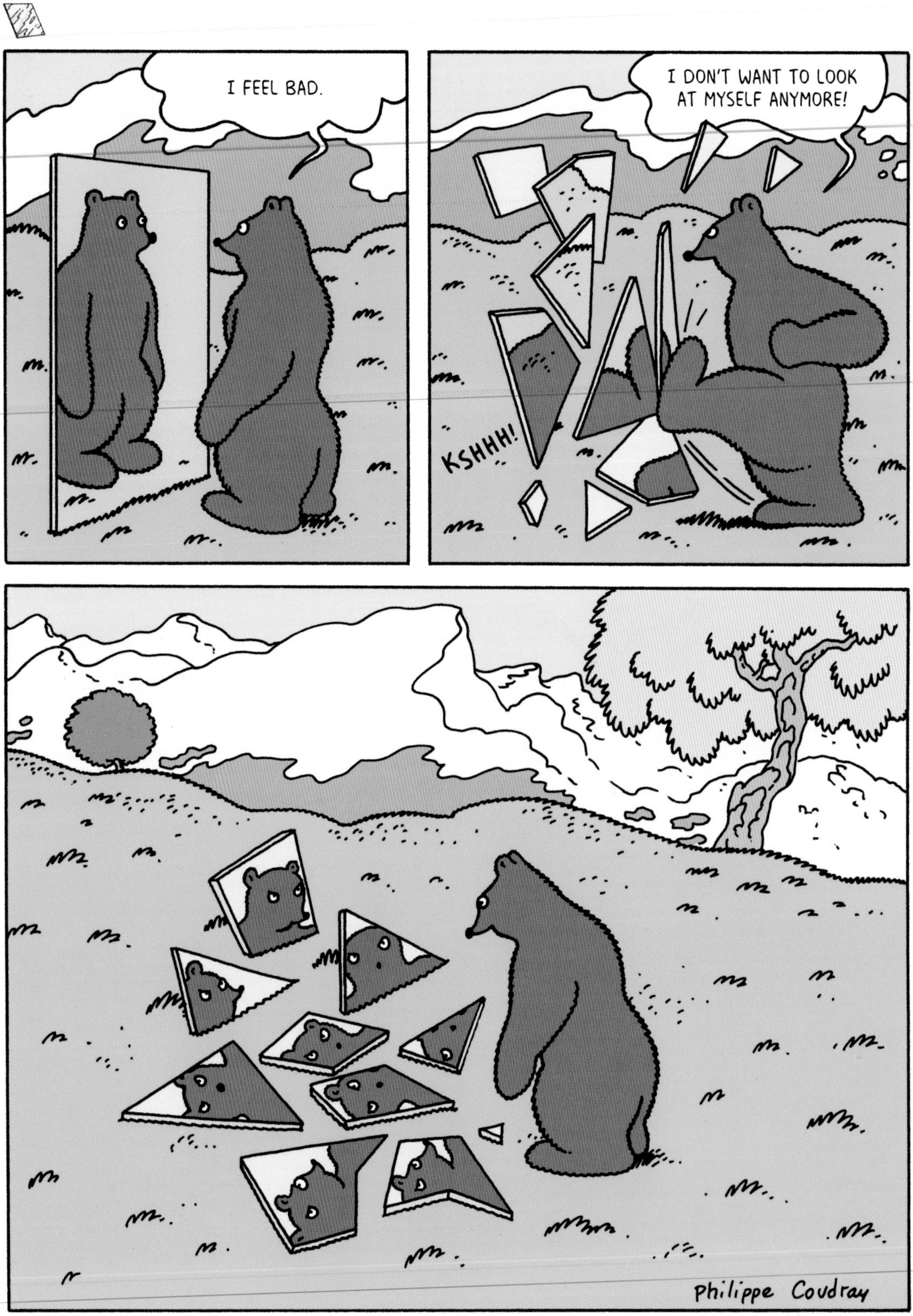
I FEEL BAD.
I DON'T WANT TO LOOK AT MYSELF ANYMORE!
KSHHH!
Philippe Coudray

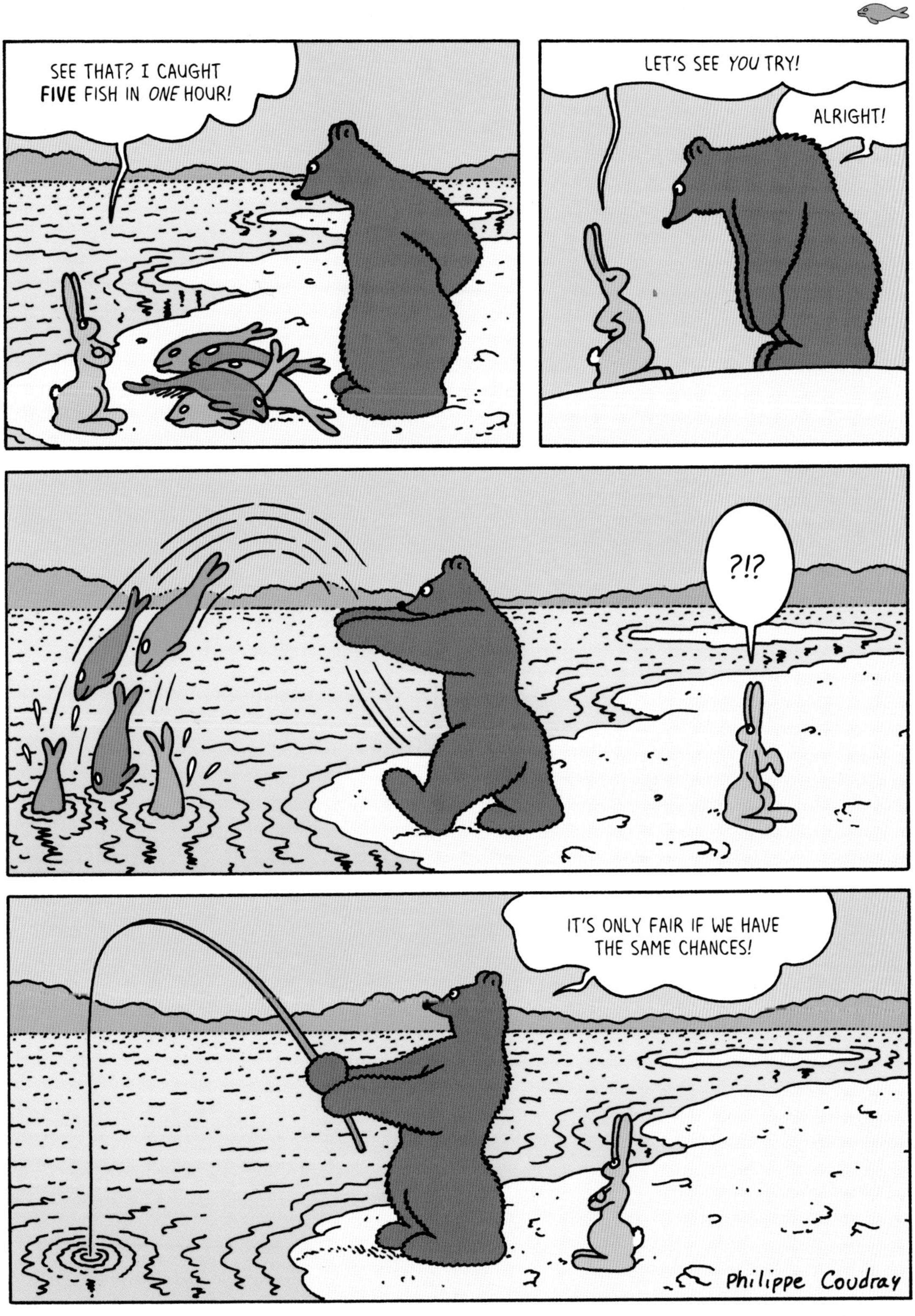
SEE THAT? I CAUGHT **FIVE** FISH IN *ONE* HOUR!
LET'S SEE *YOU* TRY!
ALRIGHT!
?!?
IT'S ONLY FAIR IF WE HAVE THE SAME CHANCES!
Philippe Coudray

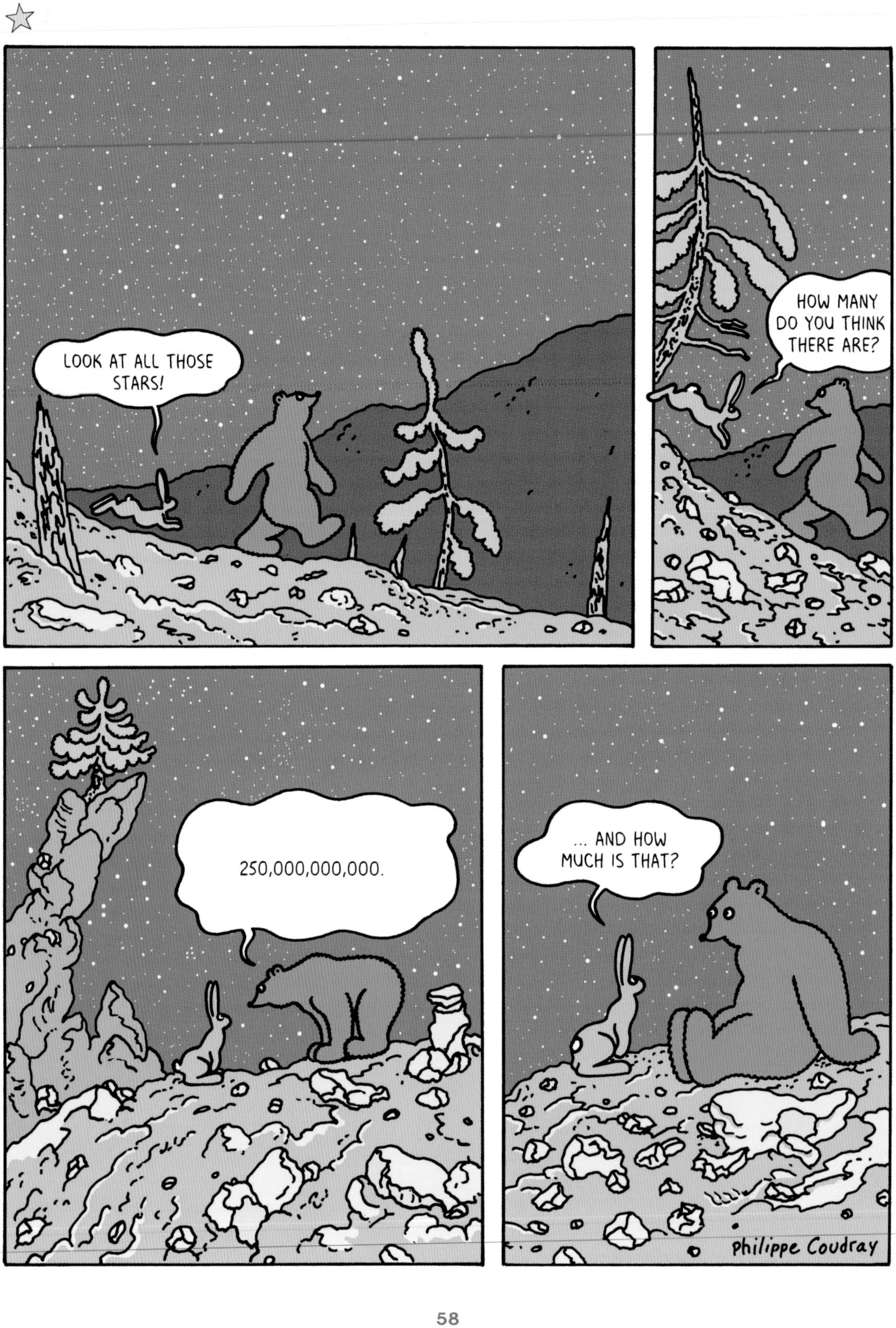
LOOK AT ALL THOSE STARS!
HOW MANY DO YOU THINK THERE ARE?
250,000,000,000.
... AND HOW MUCH IS THAT?
Philippe Coudray

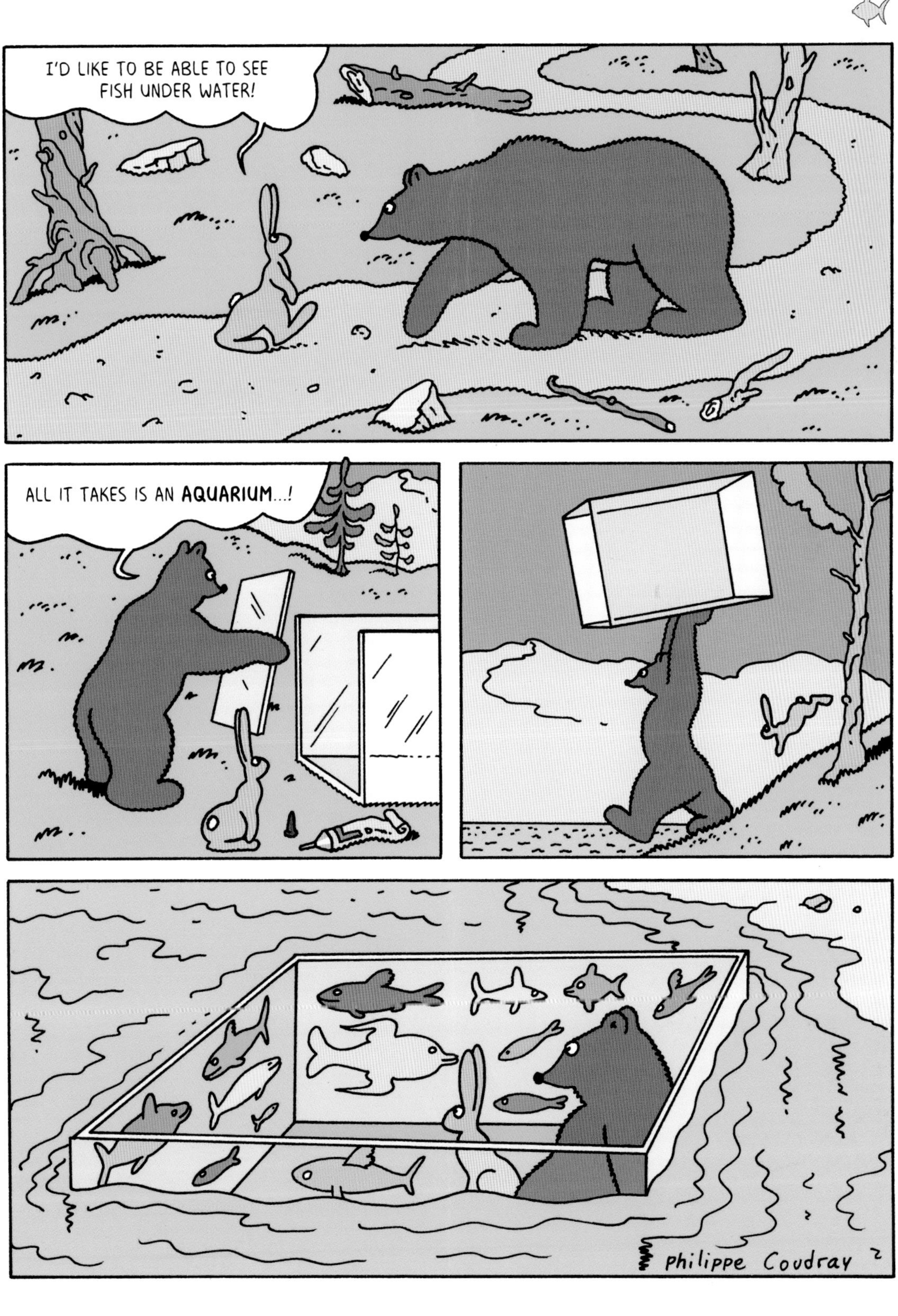
I'D LIKE TO BE ABLE TO SEE FISH UNDER WATER!
ALL IT TAKES IS AN **AQUARIUM**...!
philippe Coudray

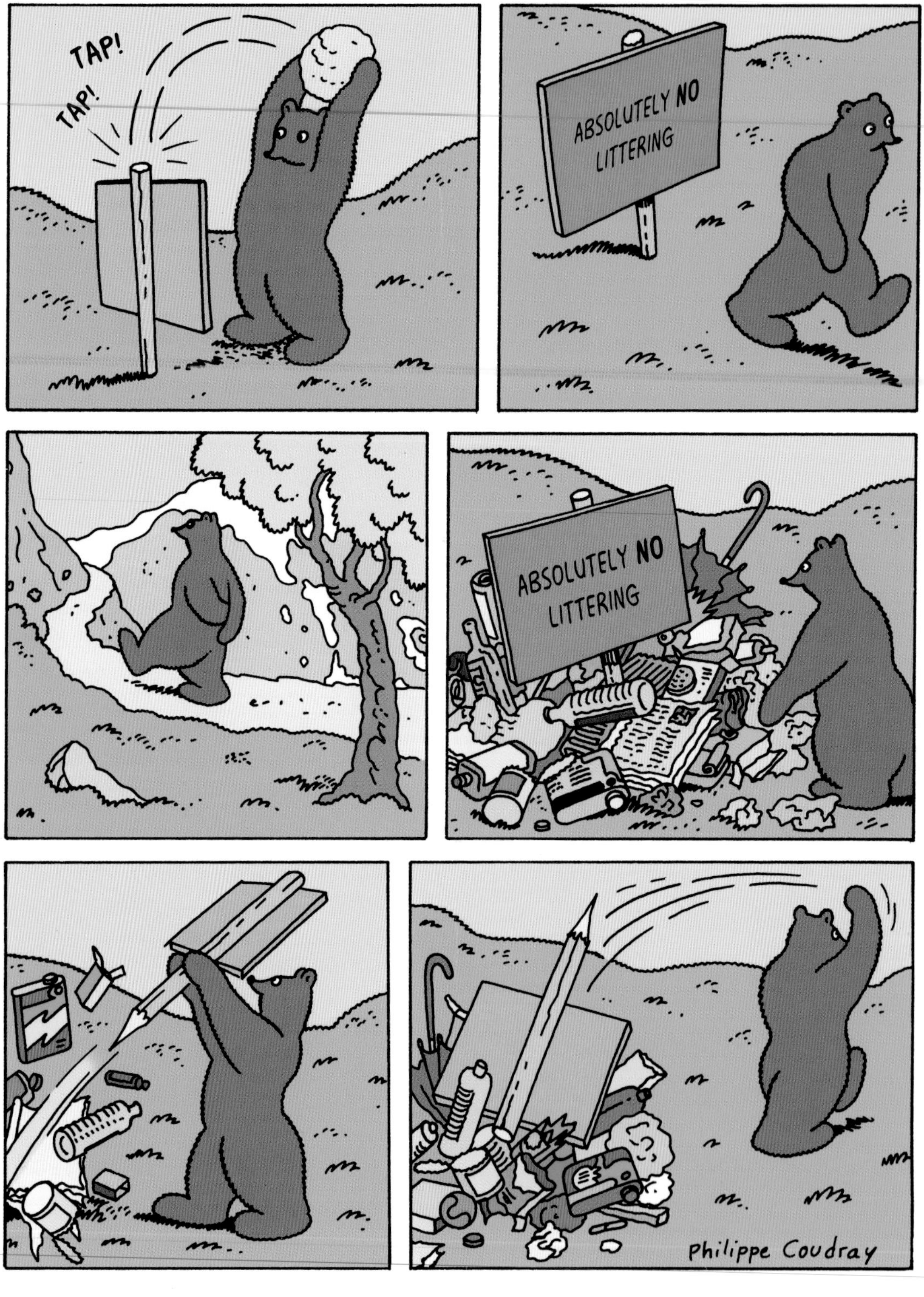
TAP!
TAP!
ABSOLUTELY NO LITTERING
ABSOLUTELY NO LITTERING
Philippe Coudray

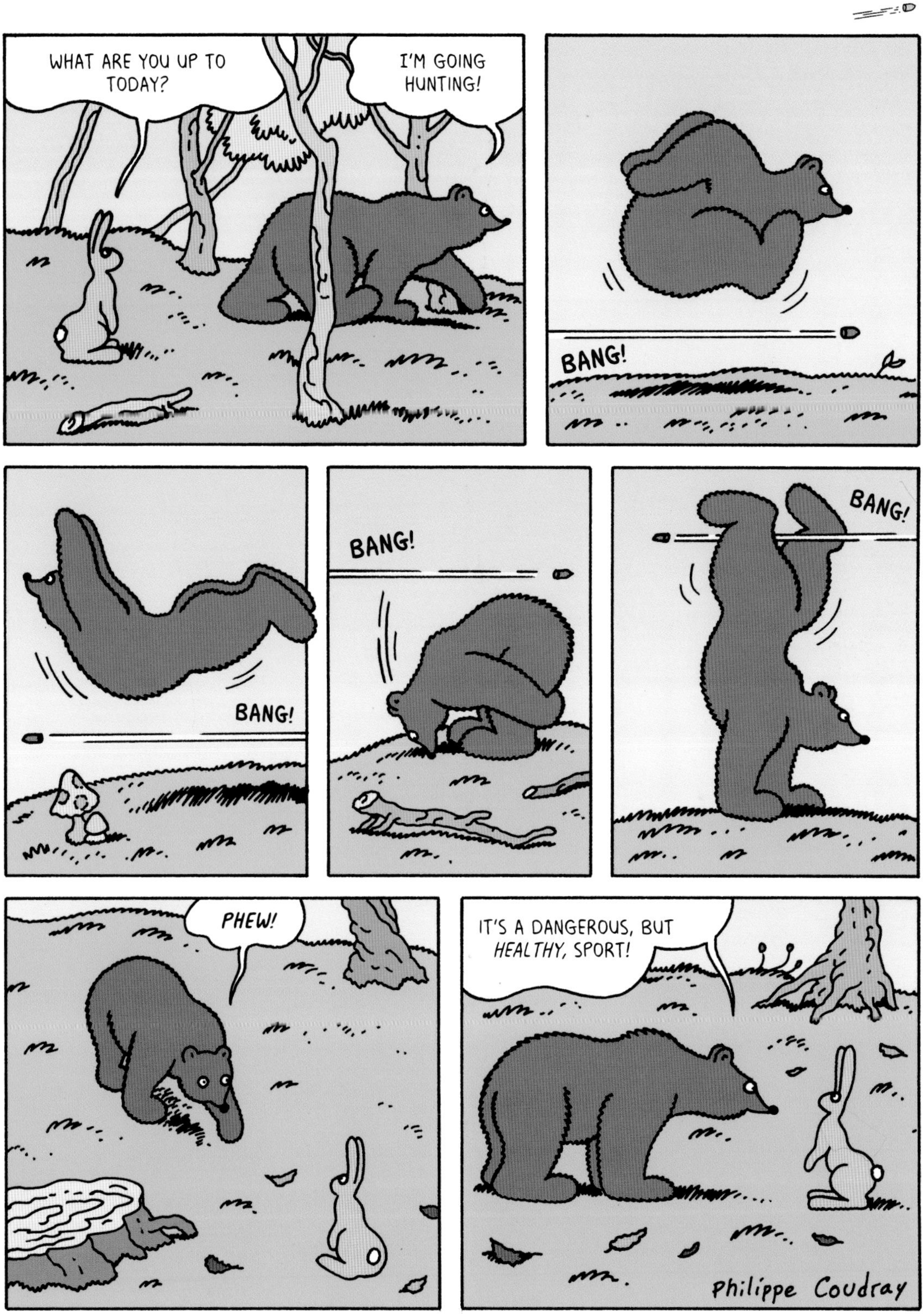
WHAT ARE YOU UP TO TODAY?
I'M GOING HUNTING!
BANG!
BANG!
BANG!
BANG!
PHEW!
IT'S A DANGEROUS, BUT *HEALTHY*, SPORT!
Philippe Coudray

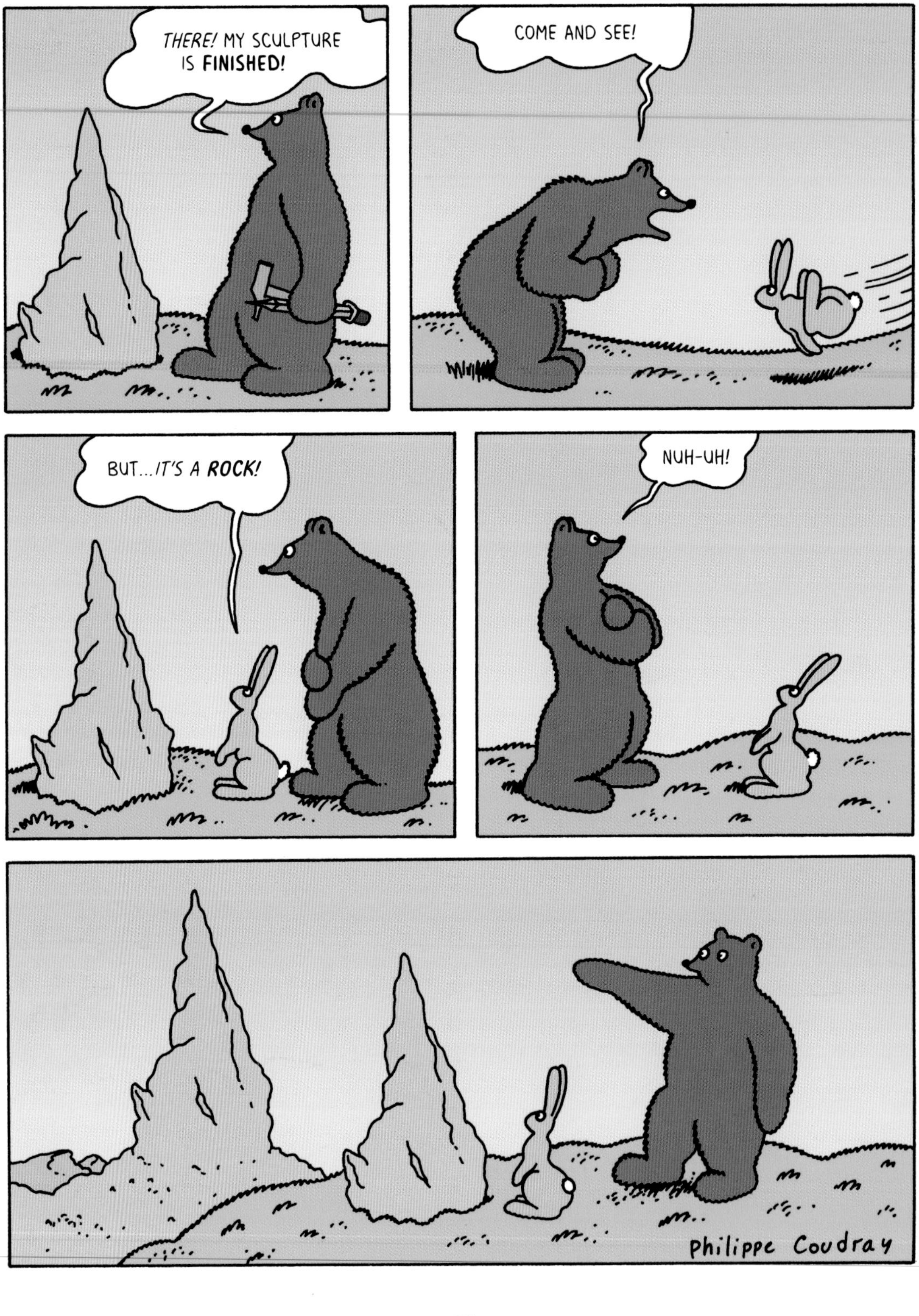
THERE! MY SCULPTURE IS FINISHED!
COME AND SEE!
BUT...IT'S A ROCK!
NUH-UH!
Philippe Coudray

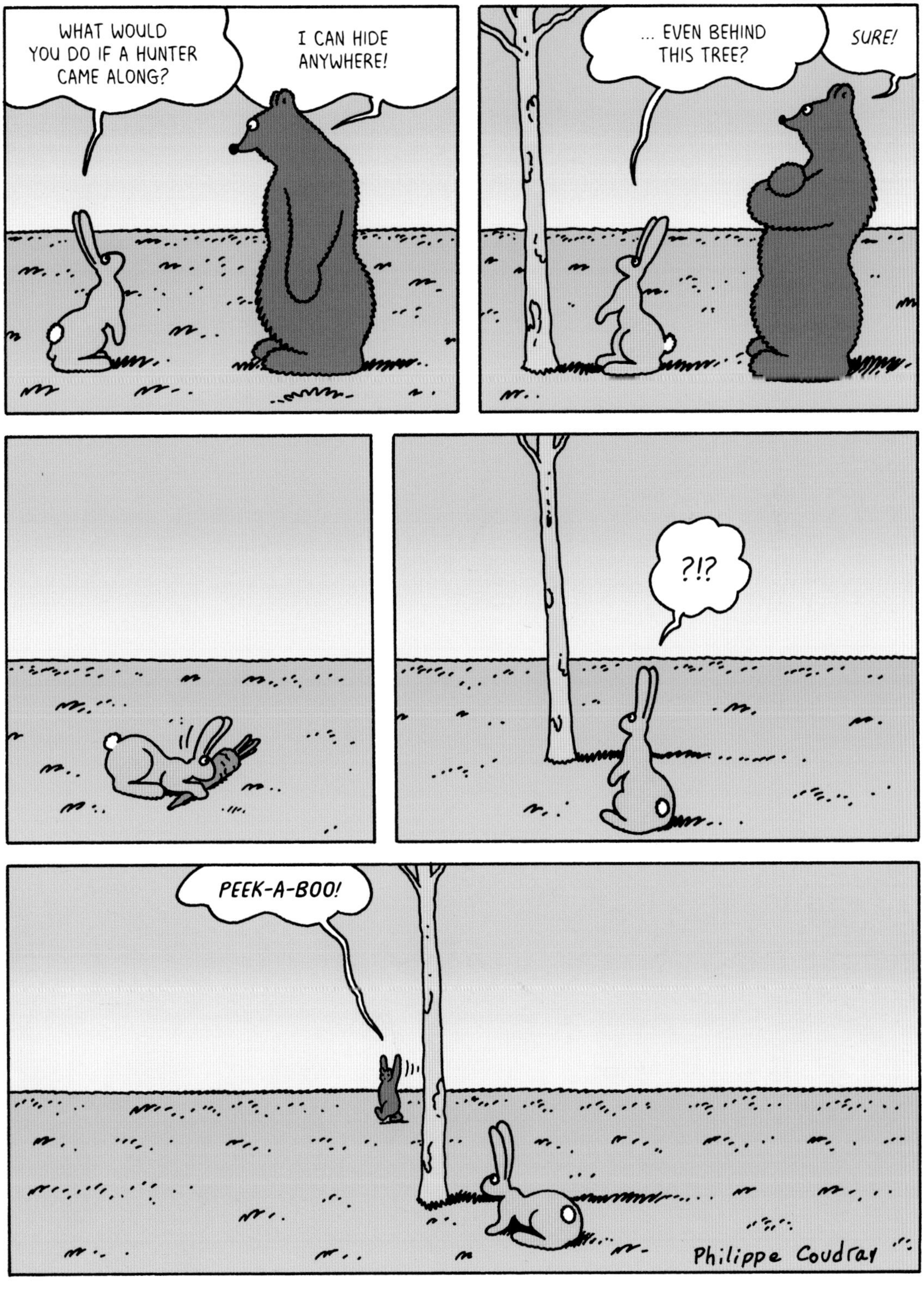
WHAT WOULD YOU DO IF A HUNTER CAME ALONG?
I CAN HIDE ANYWHERE!
... EVEN BEHIND THIS TREE?
SURE!
?!?
PEEK-A-BOO!
Philippe Coudray

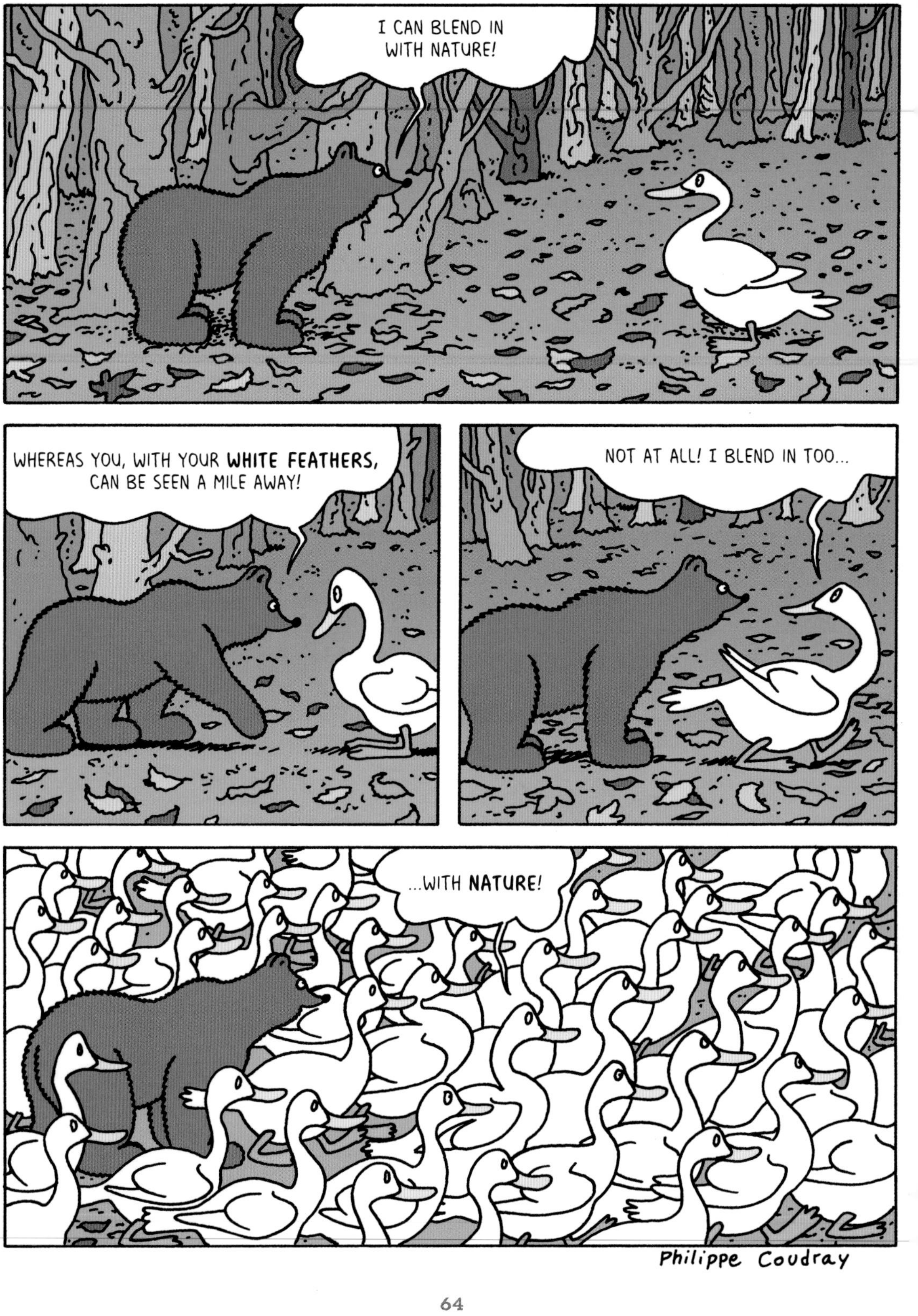
I CAN BLEND IN WITH NATURE!
WHEREAS YOU, WITH YOUR **WHITE FEATHERS,** CAN BE SEEN A MILE AWAY!
NOT AT ALL! I BLEND IN TOO...
...WITH **NATURE!**

Philippe Coudray

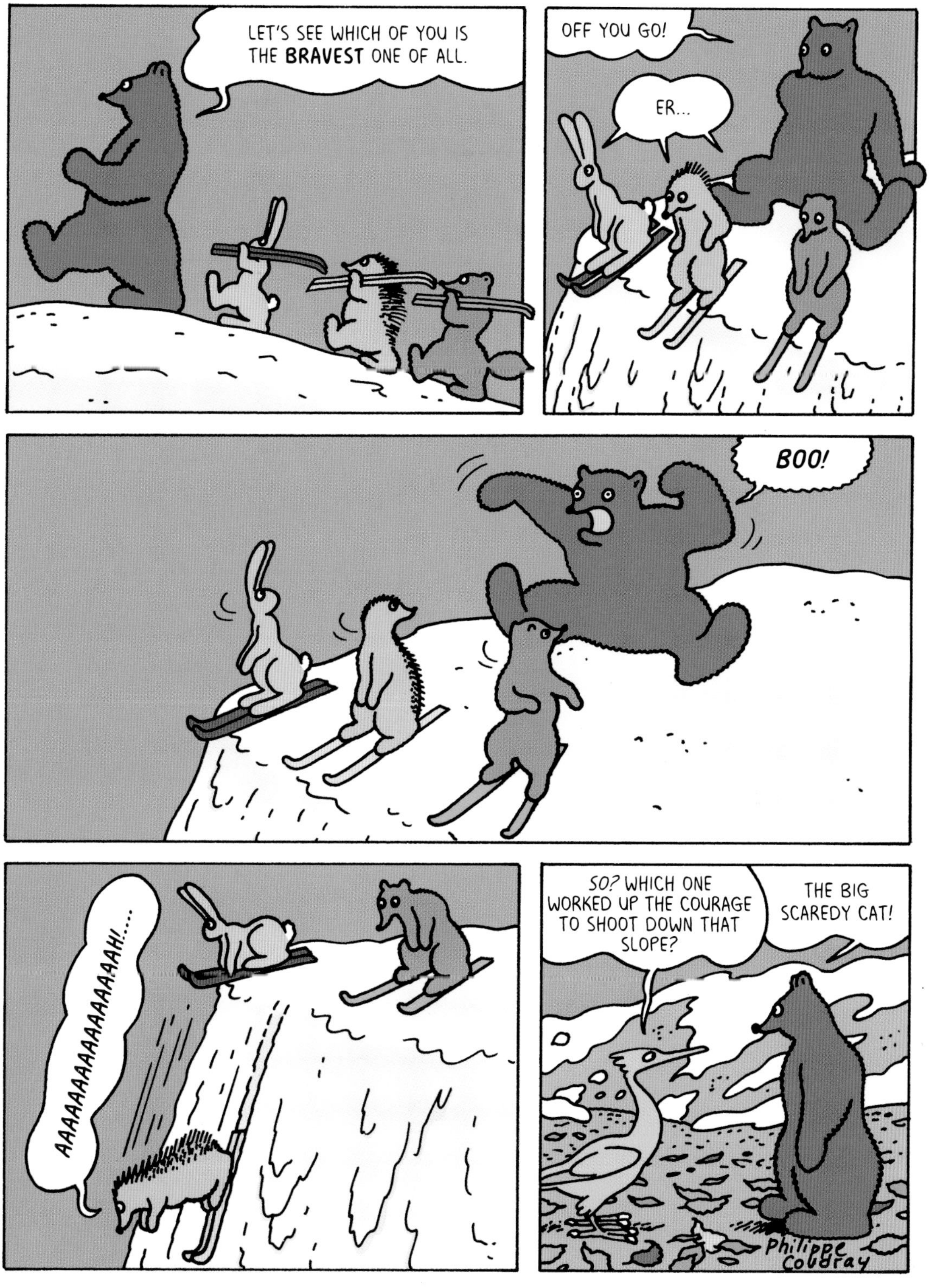
LET'S SEE WHICH OF YOU IS THE **BRAVEST** ONE OF ALL.
OFF YOU GO!
ER...
BOO!
AAAAAAAAAAAAH!....
SO? WHICH ONE WORKED UP THE COURAGE TO SHOOT DOWN THAT SLOPE?
THE BIG SCAREDY CAT!
Philippe Coudray

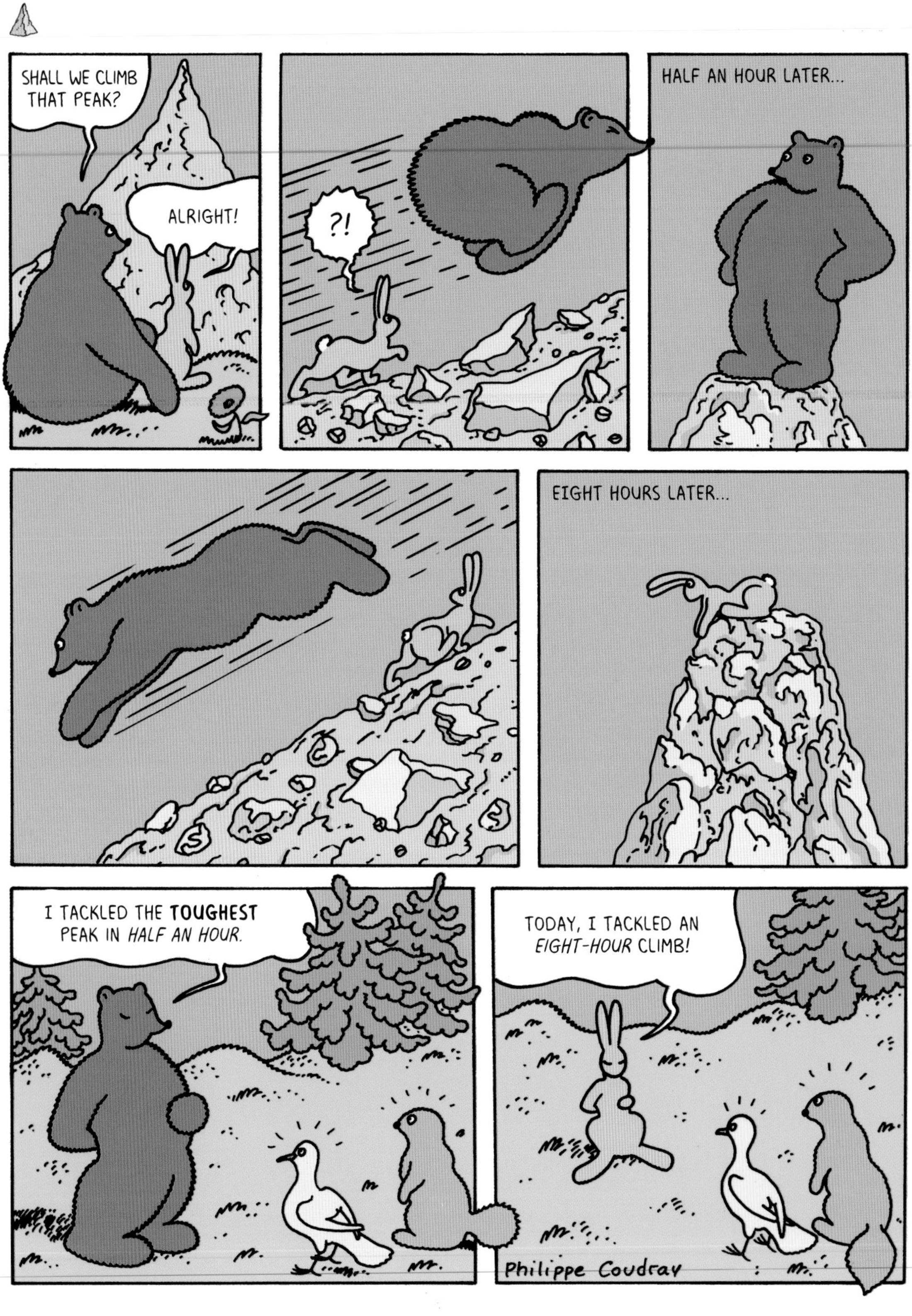
SHALL WE CLIMB THAT PEAK?
ALRIGHT!
?!
HALF AN HOUR LATER...
EIGHT HOURS LATER...
I TACKLED THE **TOUGHEST** PEAK IN *HALF AN HOUR*.
TODAY, I TACKLED AN *EIGHT-HOUR* CLIMB!
Philippe Coudray

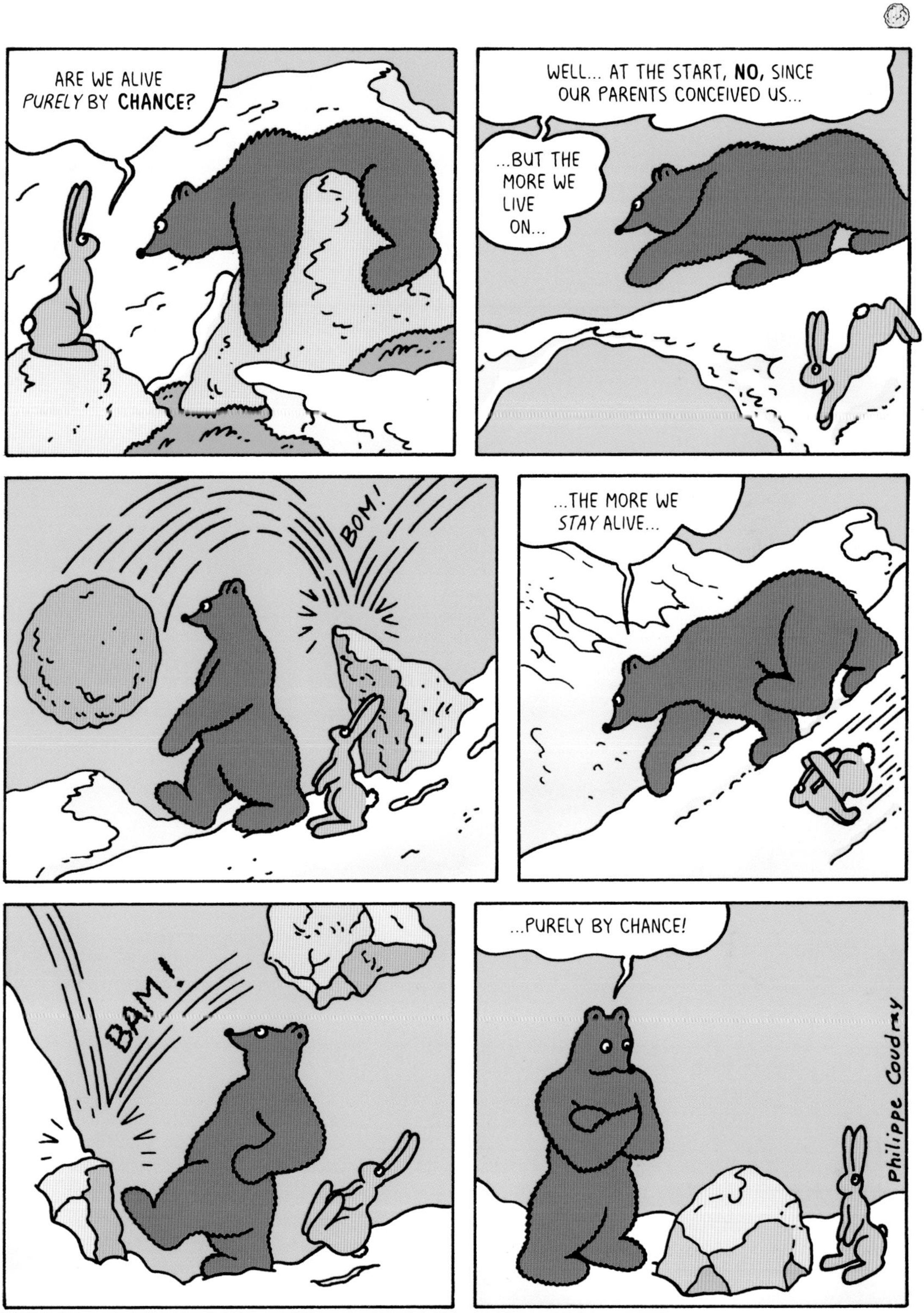
ARE WE ALIVE *PURELY* BY **CHANCE**?
WELL... AT THE START, **NO,** SINCE OUR PARENTS CONCEIVED US...
...BUT THE MORE WE LIVE ON...
BOM!
...THE MORE WE *STAY* ALIVE...
BAM!
...PURELY BY CHANCE!
Philippe Coudray

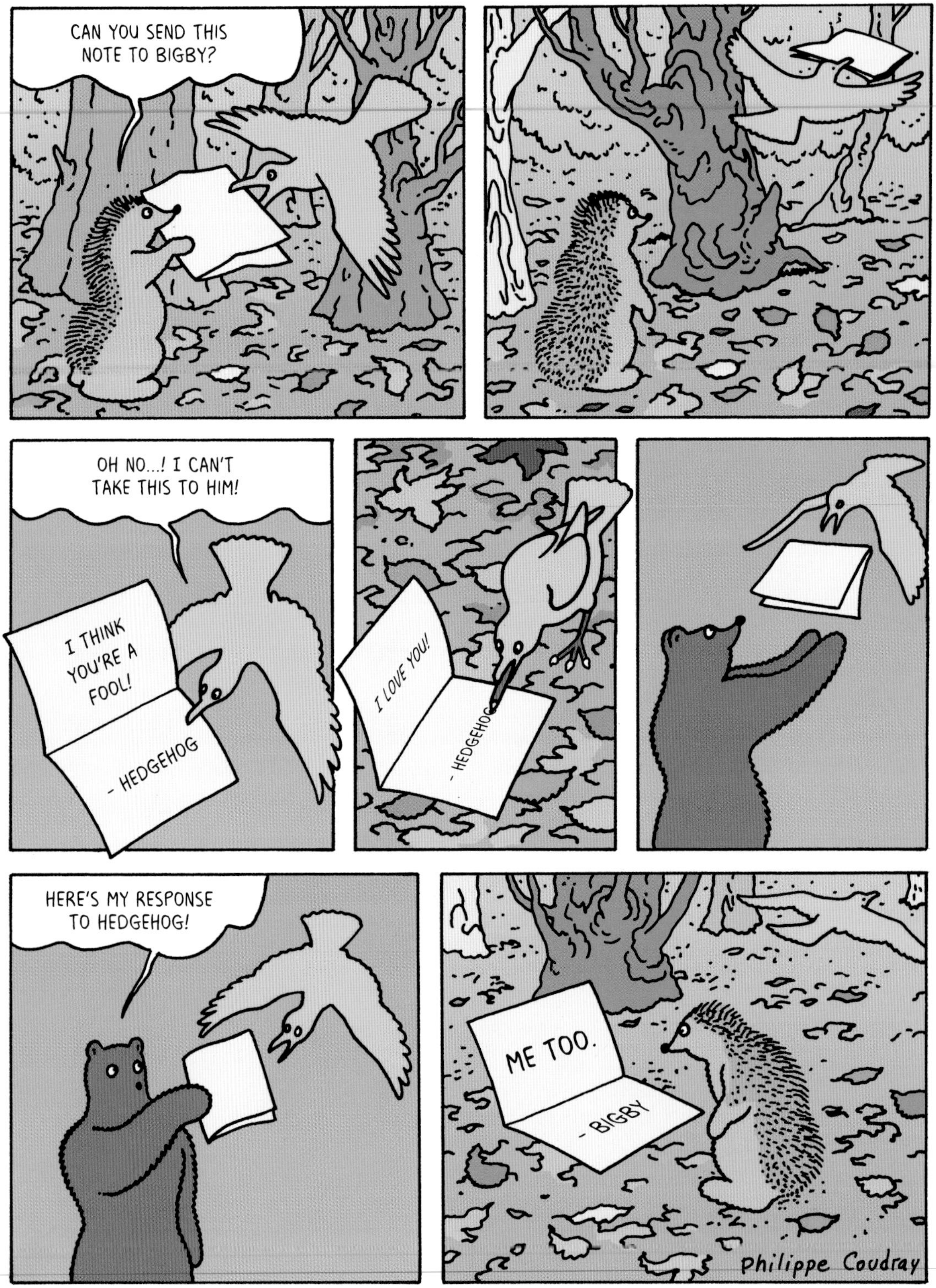

CAN YOU SEND THIS NOTE TO BIGBY?
OH NO...! I CAN'T TAKE THIS TO HIM!
I THINK YOU'RE A FOOL!
- HEDGEHOG
I LOVE YOU!
- HEDGEHOG
HERE'S MY RESPONSE TO HEDGEHOG!
ME TOO.
- BIGBY
Philippe Coudray

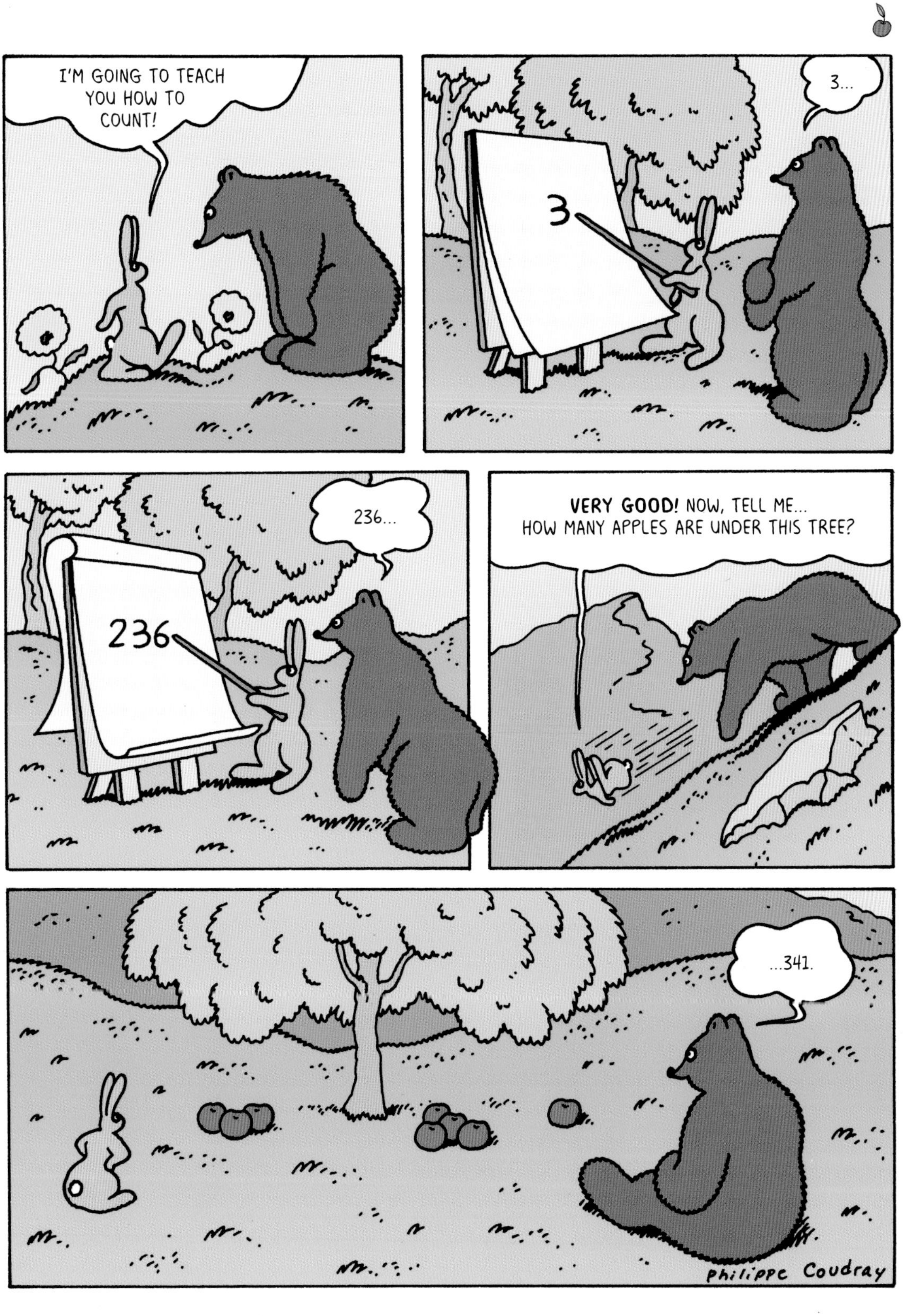
I'M GOING TO TEACH YOU HOW TO COUNT!
3...
3
236
236...
VERY GOOD! NOW, TELL ME... HOW MANY APPLES ARE UNDER THIS TREE?
...341.
Philippe Coudray

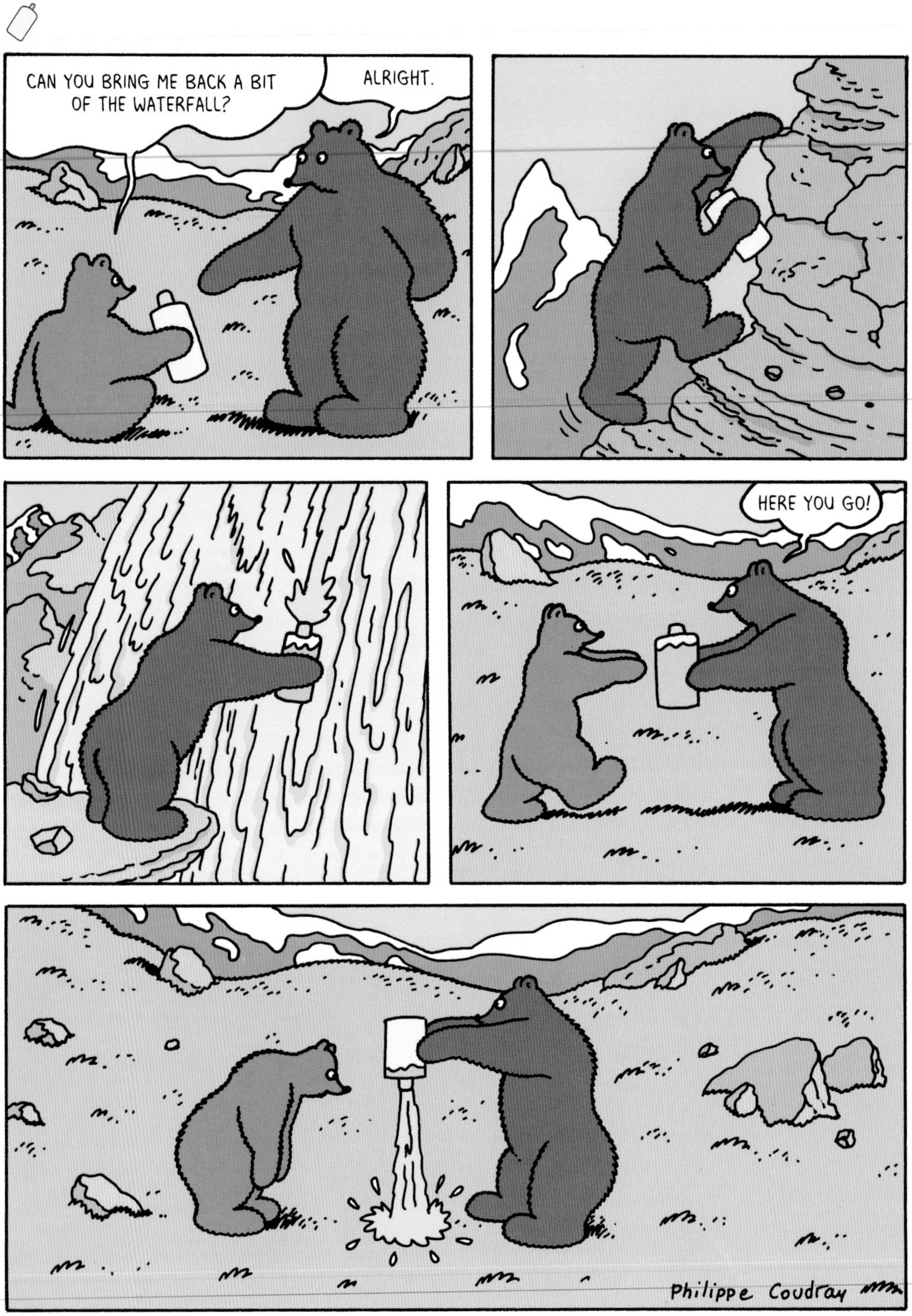
CAN YOU BRING ME BACK A BIT OF THE WATERFALL?
ALRIGHT.
HERE YOU GO!
Philippe Coudray

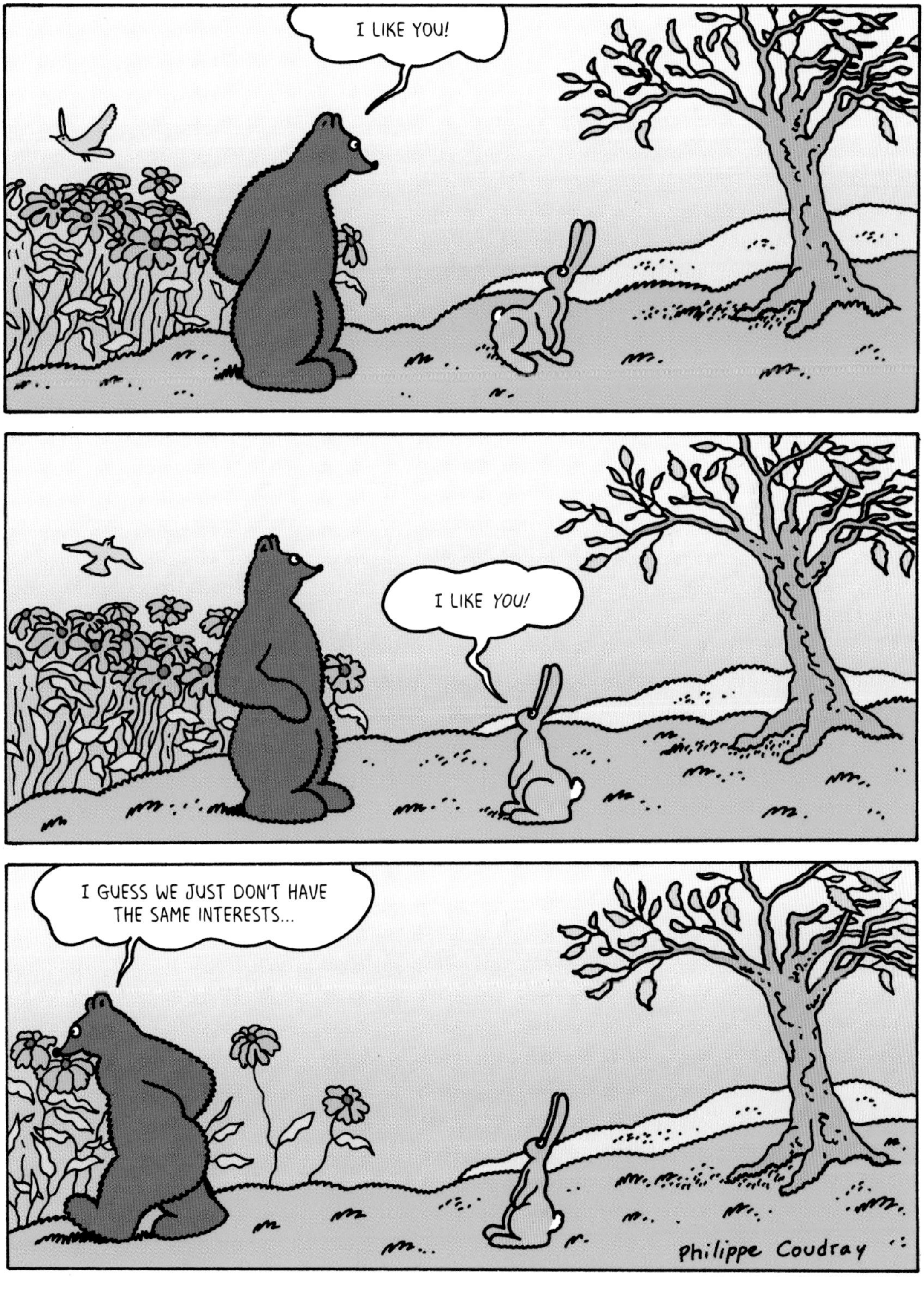
I LIKE YOU!
I LIKE *YOU!*
I GUESS WE JUST DON'T HAVE THE SAME INTERESTS...
Philippe Coudray

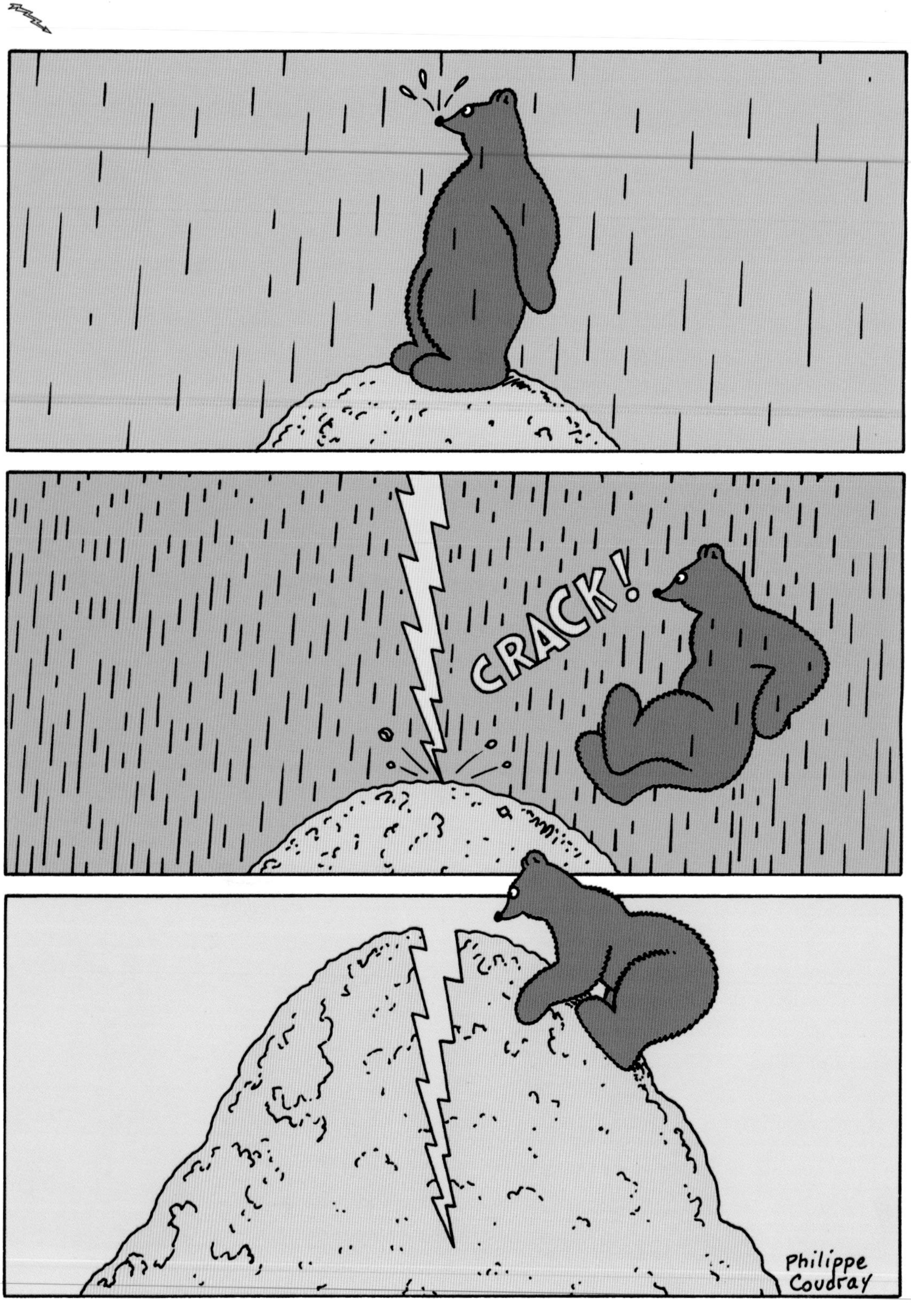
CRACK!
Philippe Coudray

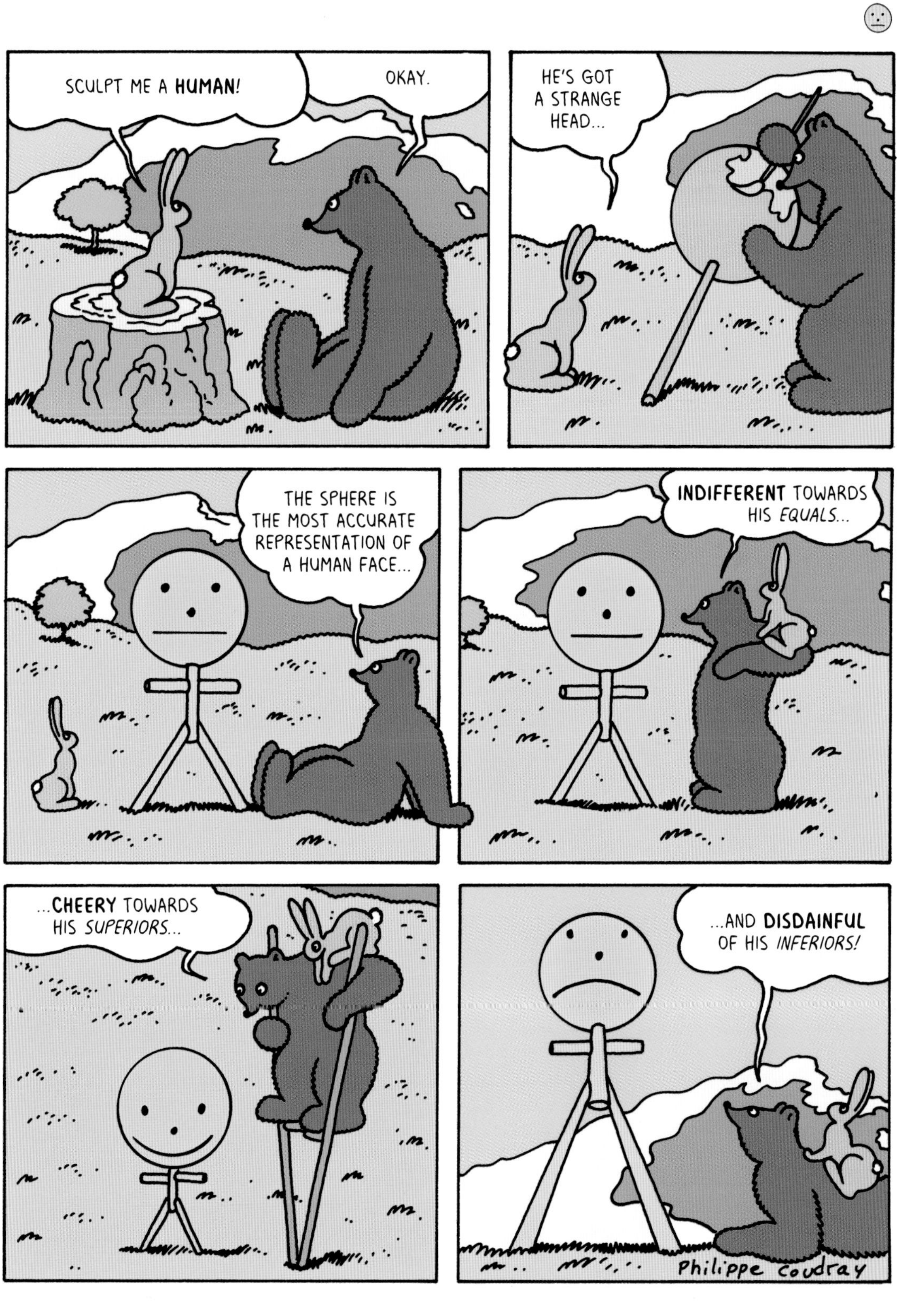
SCULPT ME A **HUMAN**!
OKAY.
HE'S GOT A STRANGE HEAD...
THE SPHERE IS THE MOST ACCURATE REPRESENTATION OF A HUMAN FACE...
INDIFFERENT TOWARDS HIS *EQUALS*...
...**CHEERY** TOWARDS HIS *SUPERIORS*...
...AND **DISDAINFUL** OF HIS *INFERIORS*!
Philippe Coudray

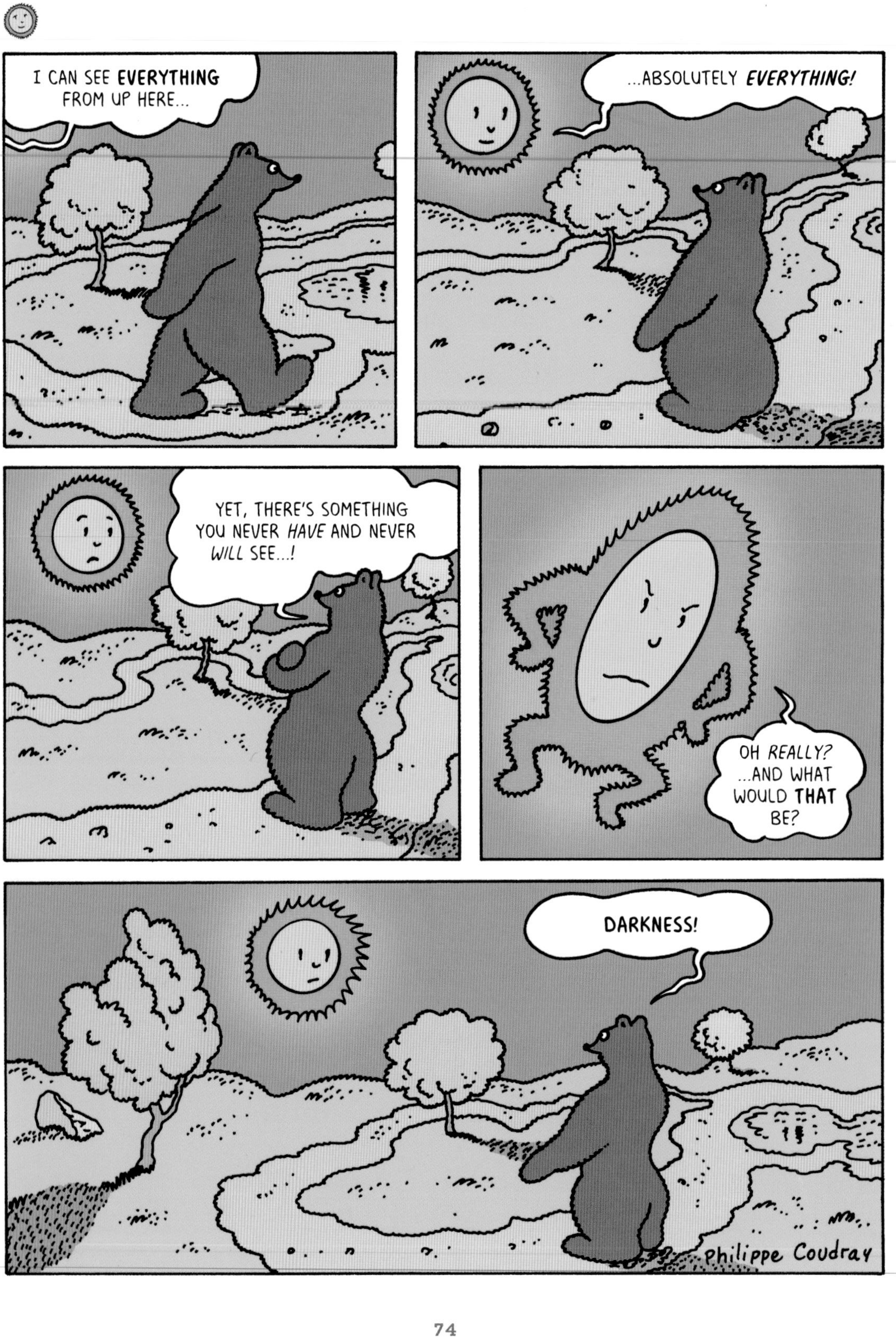
I CAN SEE EVERYTHING FROM UP HERE...
...ABSOLUTELY EVERYTHING!
YET, THERE'S SOMETHING YOU NEVER HAVE AND NEVER WILL SEE...!
OH REALLY? ...AND WHAT WOULD THAT BE?
DARKNESS!
Philippe Coudray

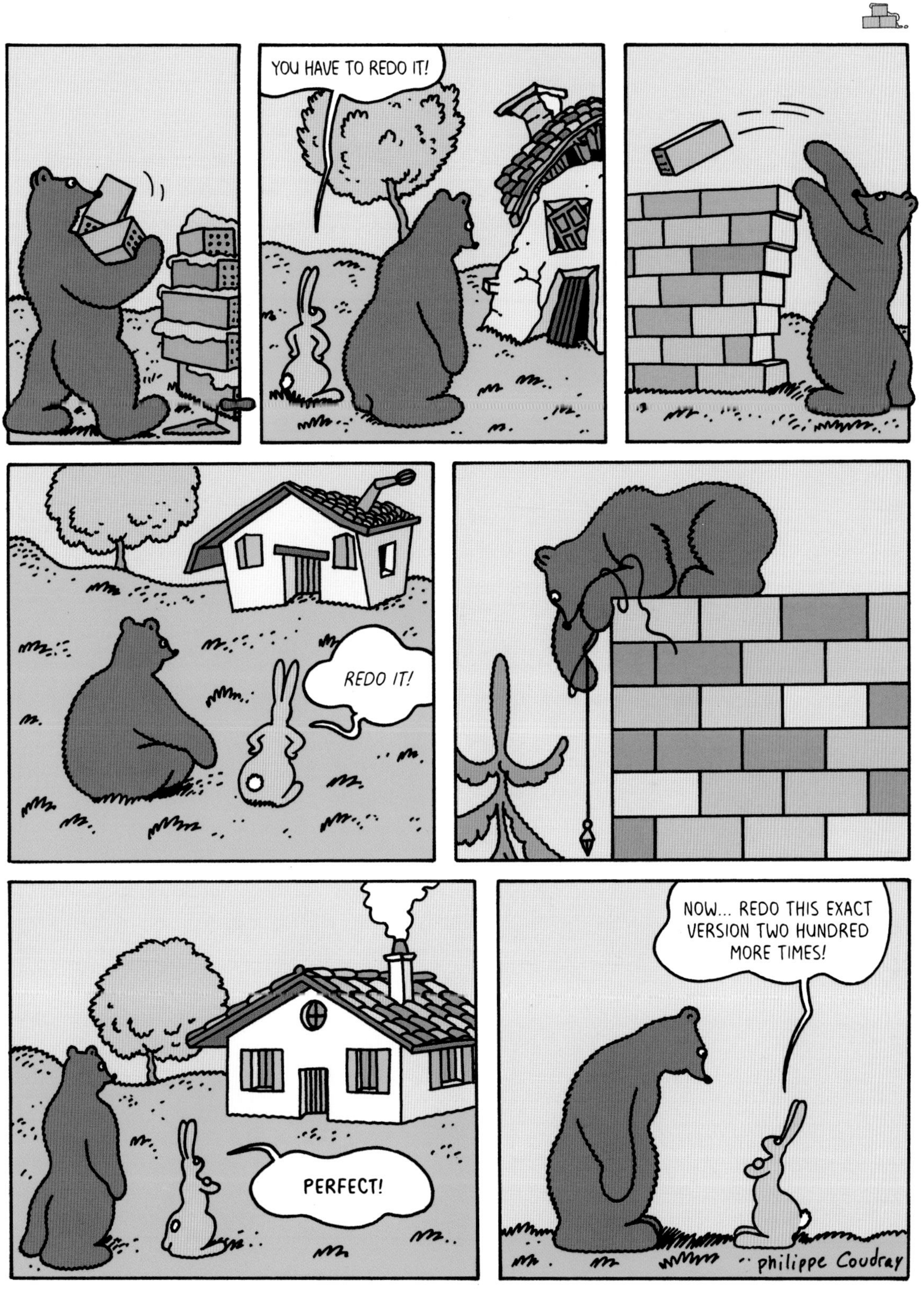
YOU HAVE TO REDO IT!
REDO IT!
PERFECT!
NOW... REDO THIS EXACT VERSION TWO HUNDRED MORE TIMES!
philippe Coudray

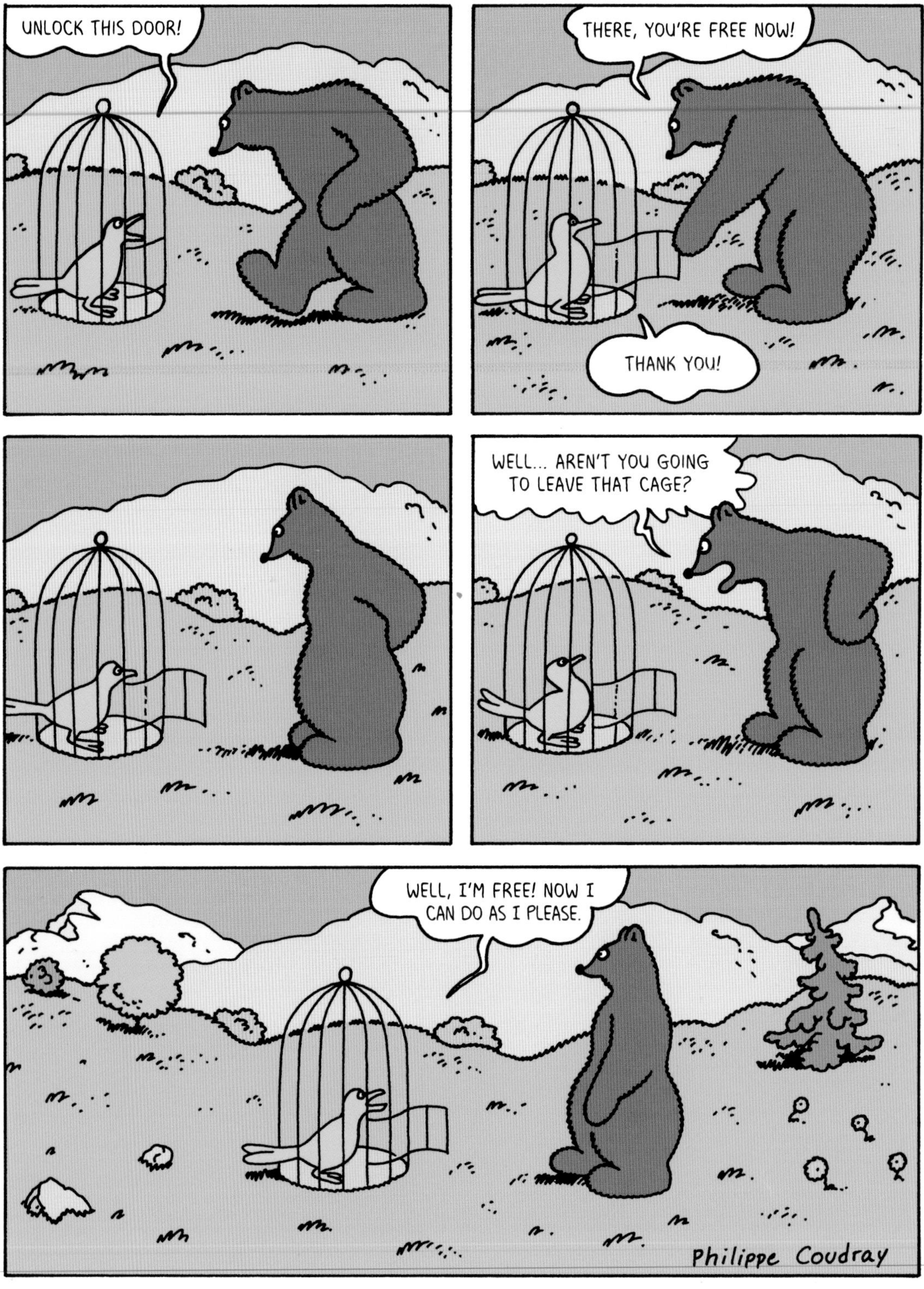
UNLOCK THIS DOOR!
THERE, YOU'RE FREE NOW!
THANK YOU!
WELL... AREN'T YOU GOING TO LEAVE THAT CAGE?
WELL, I'M FREE! NOW I CAN DO AS I PLEASE.
Philippe Coudray

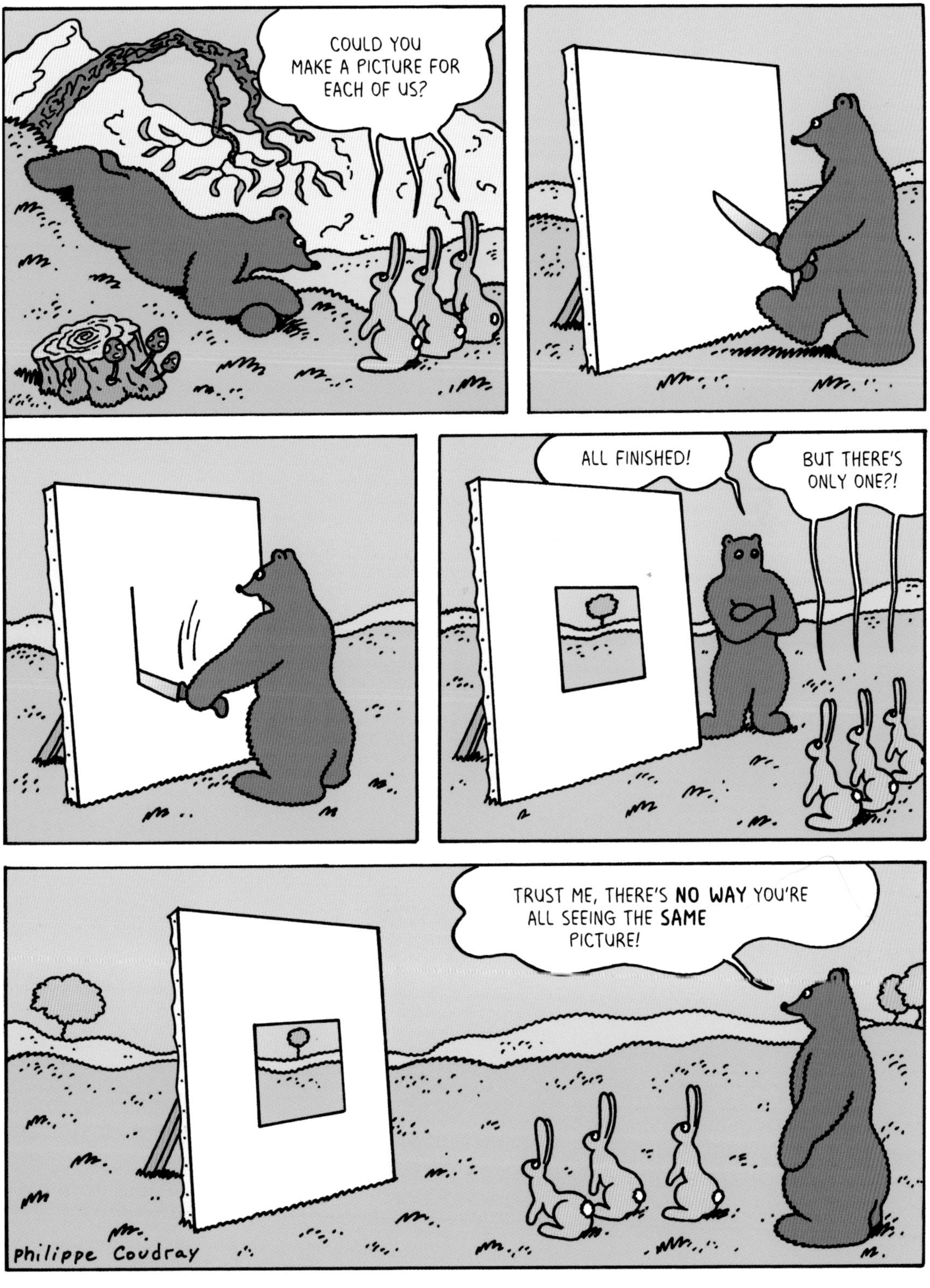
COULD YOU MAKE A PICTURE FOR EACH OF US?
ALL FINISHED!
BUT THERE'S ONLY ONE?!
TRUST ME, THERE'S **NO WAY** YOU'RE ALL SEEING THE **SAME** PICTURE!
Philippe Coudray

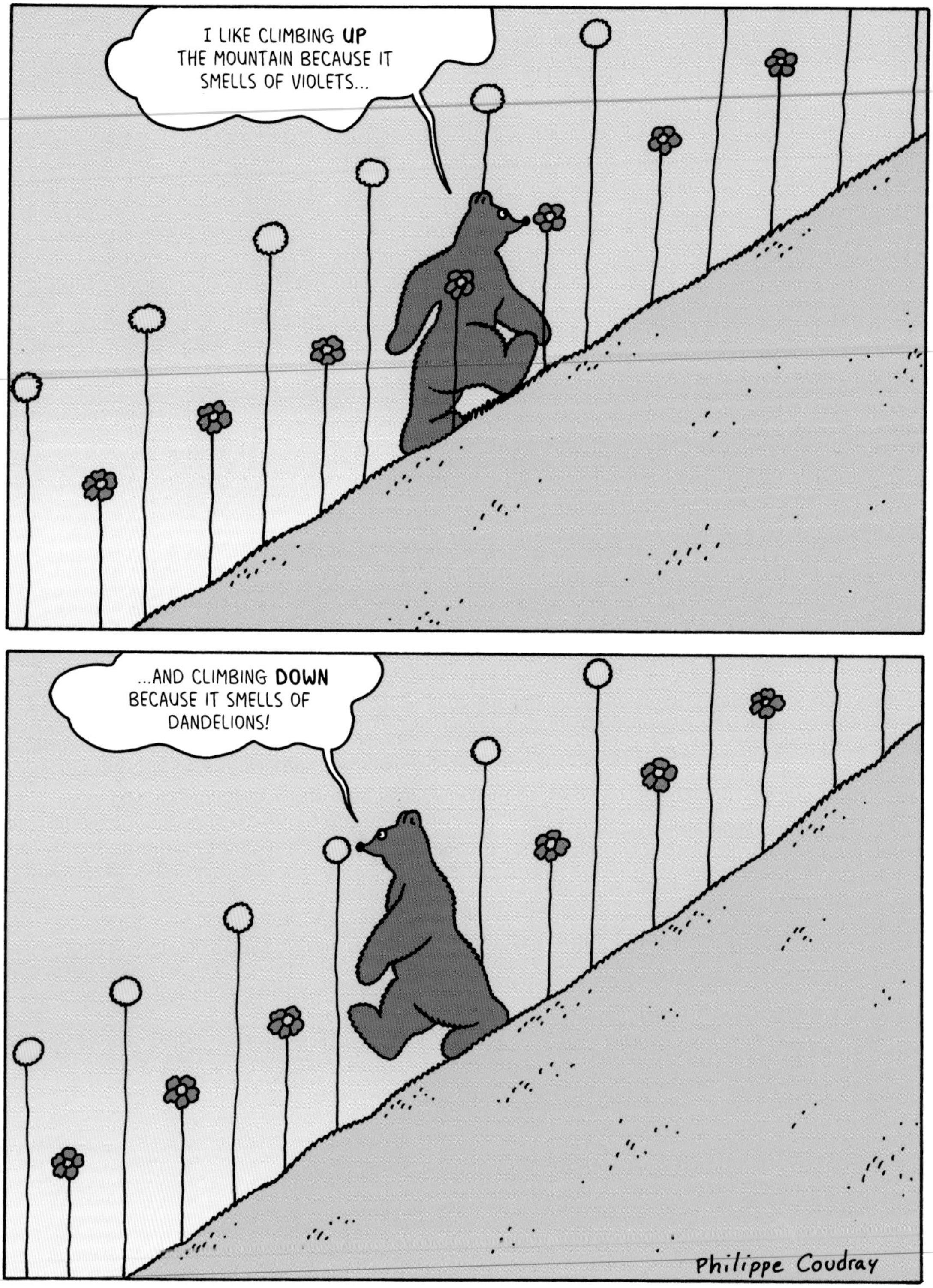
I LIKE CLIMBING **UP** THE MOUNTAIN BECAUSE IT SMELLS OF VIOLETS...
...AND CLIMBING **DOWN** BECAUSE IT SMELLS OF DANDELIONS!
Philippe Coudray

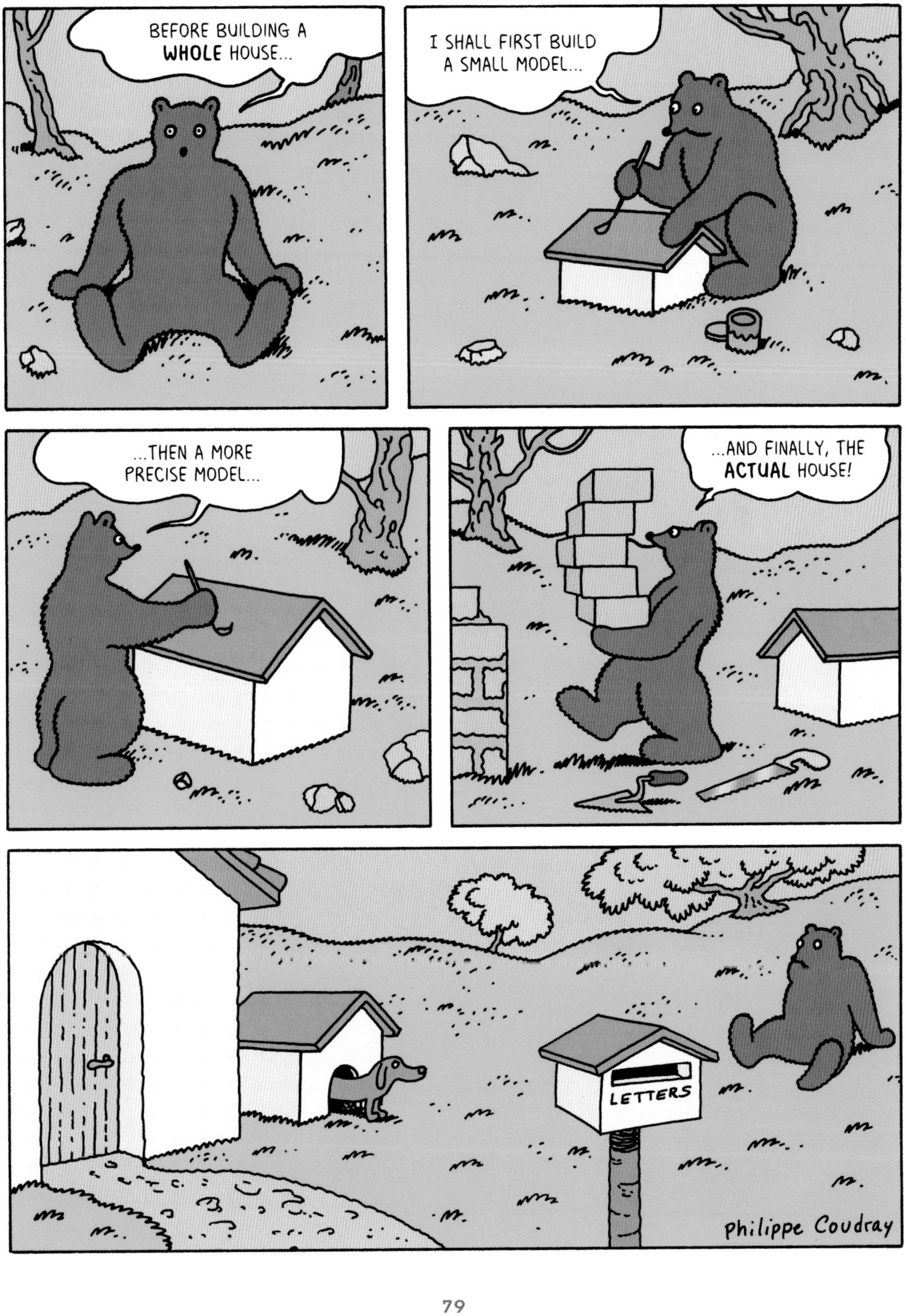
BEFORE BUILDING A **WHOLE** HOUSE...
I SHALL FIRST BUILD A SMALL MODEL...
...THEN A MORE PRECISE MODEL...
...AND FINALLY, THE **ACTUAL** HOUSE!
LETTERS
Philippe Coudray

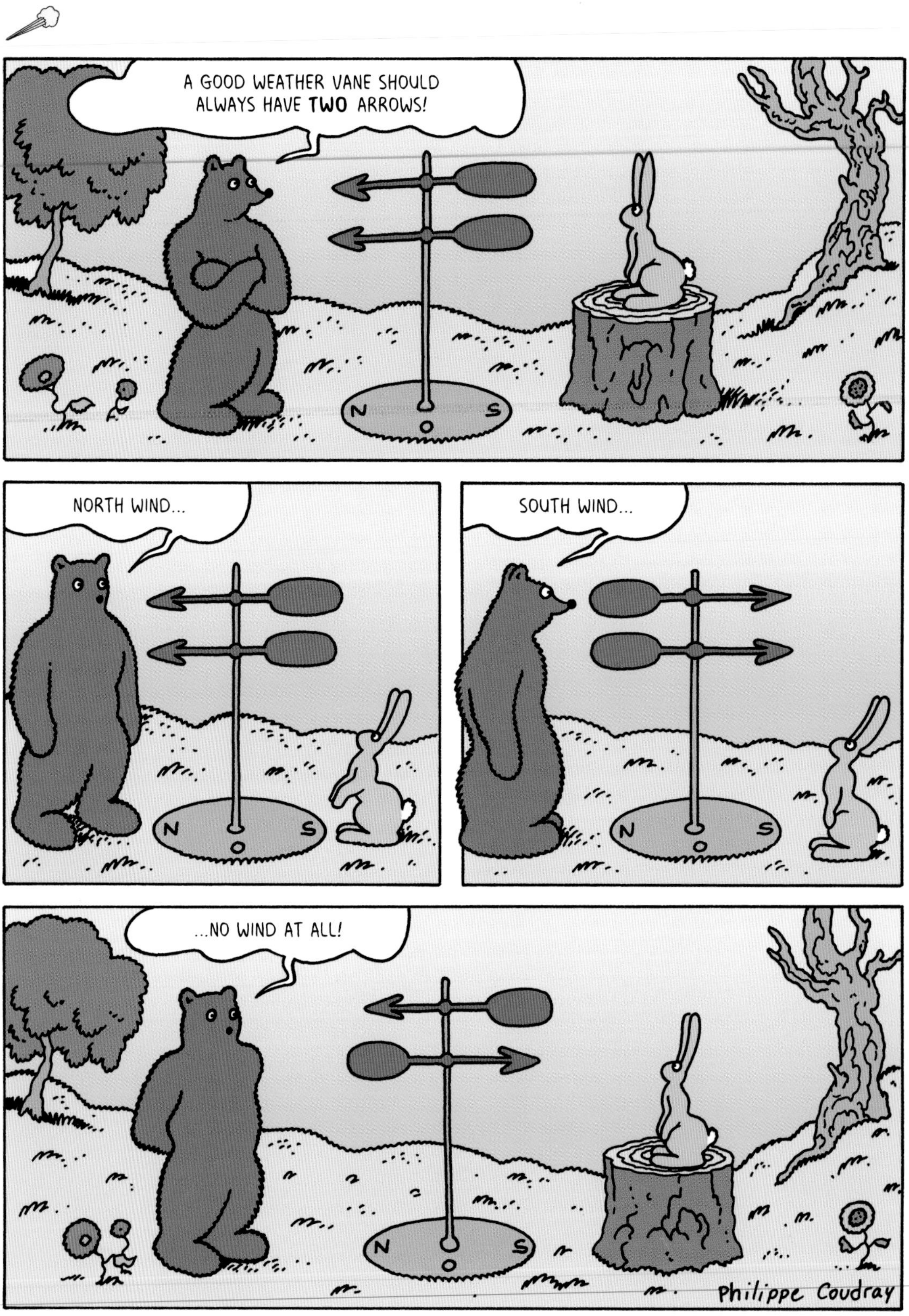
A GOOD WEATHER VANE SHOULD ALWAYS HAVE **TWO** ARROWS!
N
O
S
NORTH WIND...
N
O
S
SOUTH WIND...
N
O
S
...NO WIND AT ALL!
N
O
S
Philippe Coudray

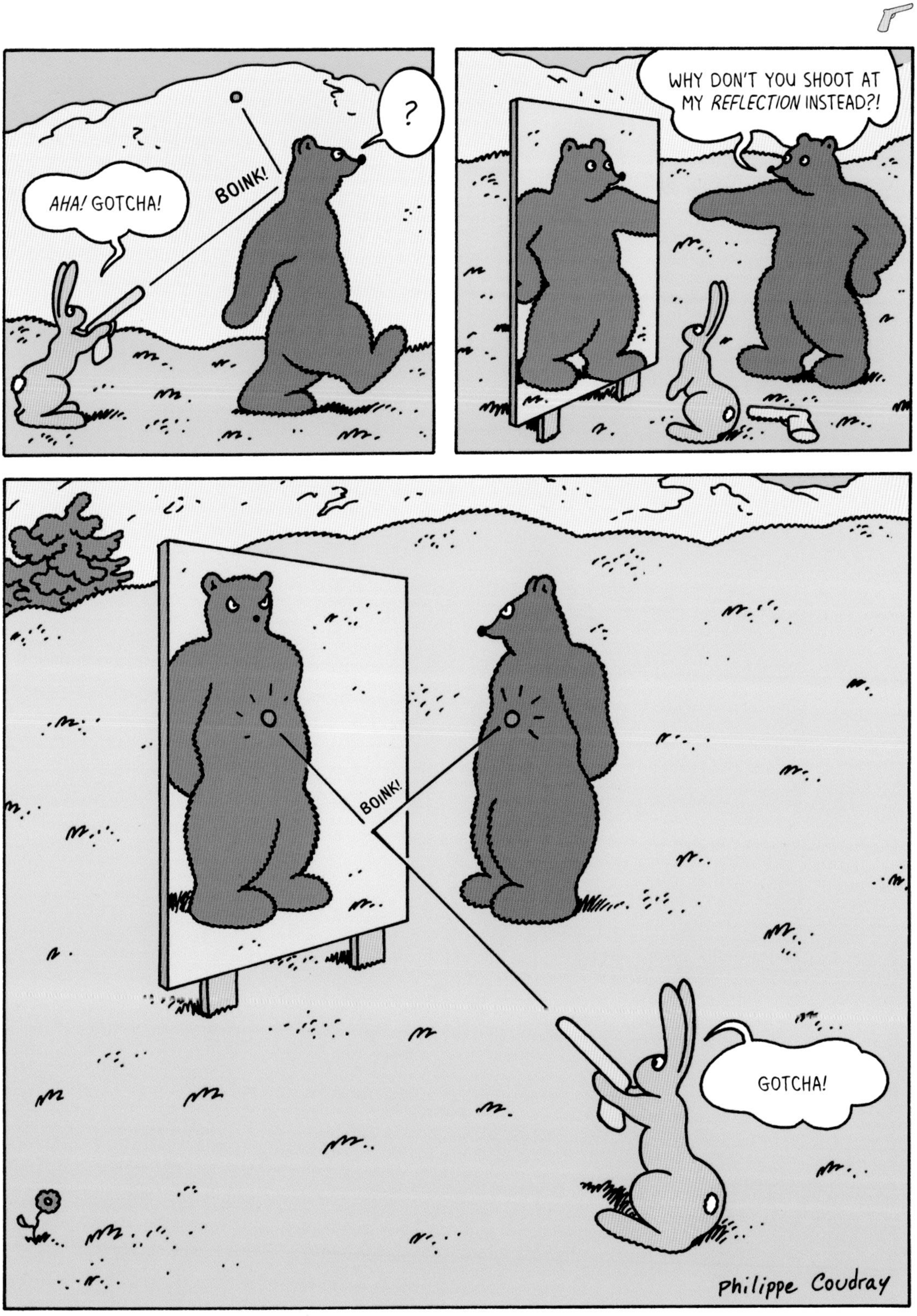
BOINK!
?
AHA! GOTCHA!
WHY DON'T YOU SHOOT AT MY REFLECTION INSTEAD?!
BOINK!
GOTCHA!
Philippe Coudray

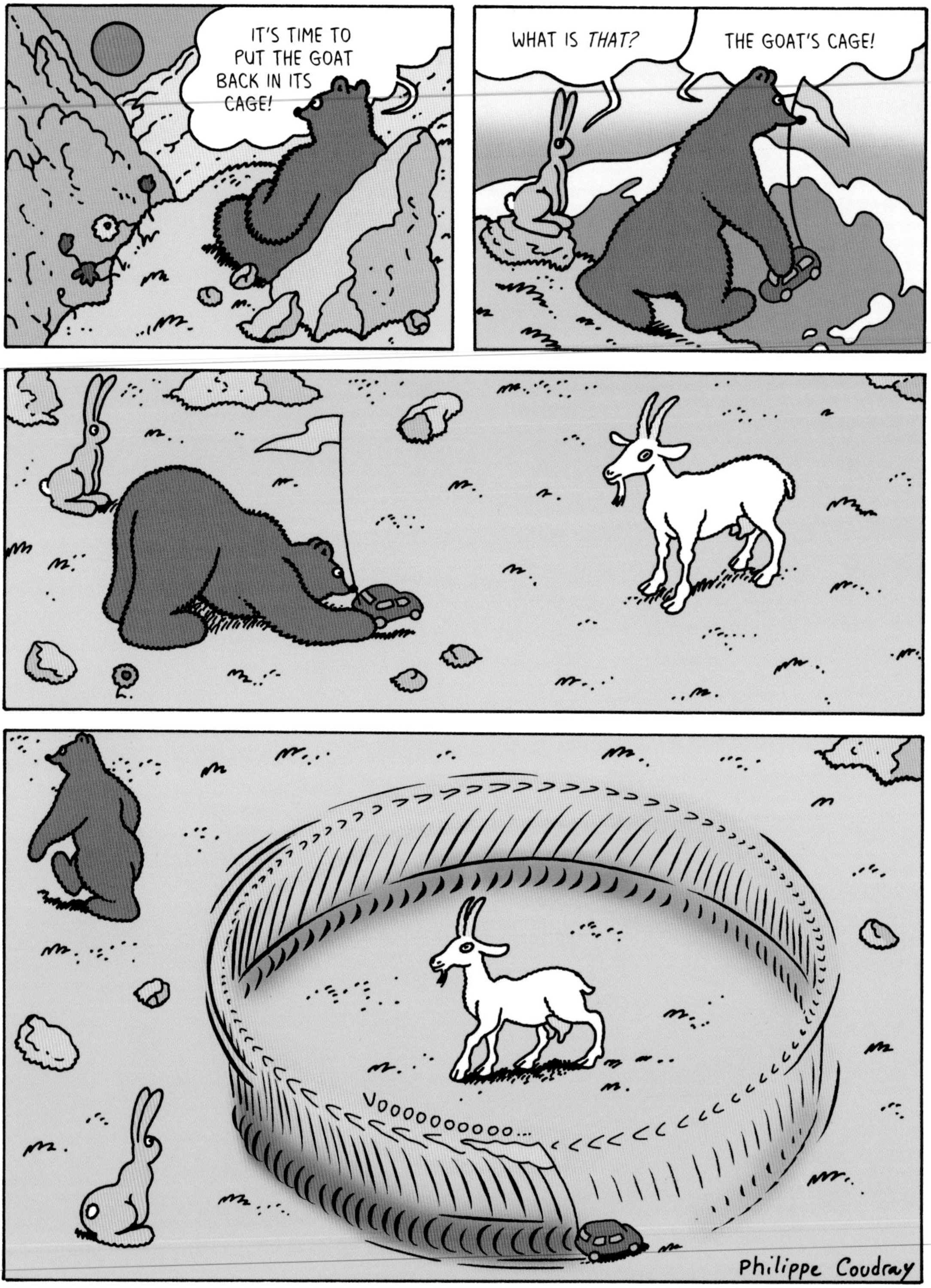
IT'S TIME TO PUT THE GOAT BACK IN ITS CAGE!
WHAT IS *THAT?*
THE GOAT'S CAGE!
Voooooooooo...
Philippe Coudray

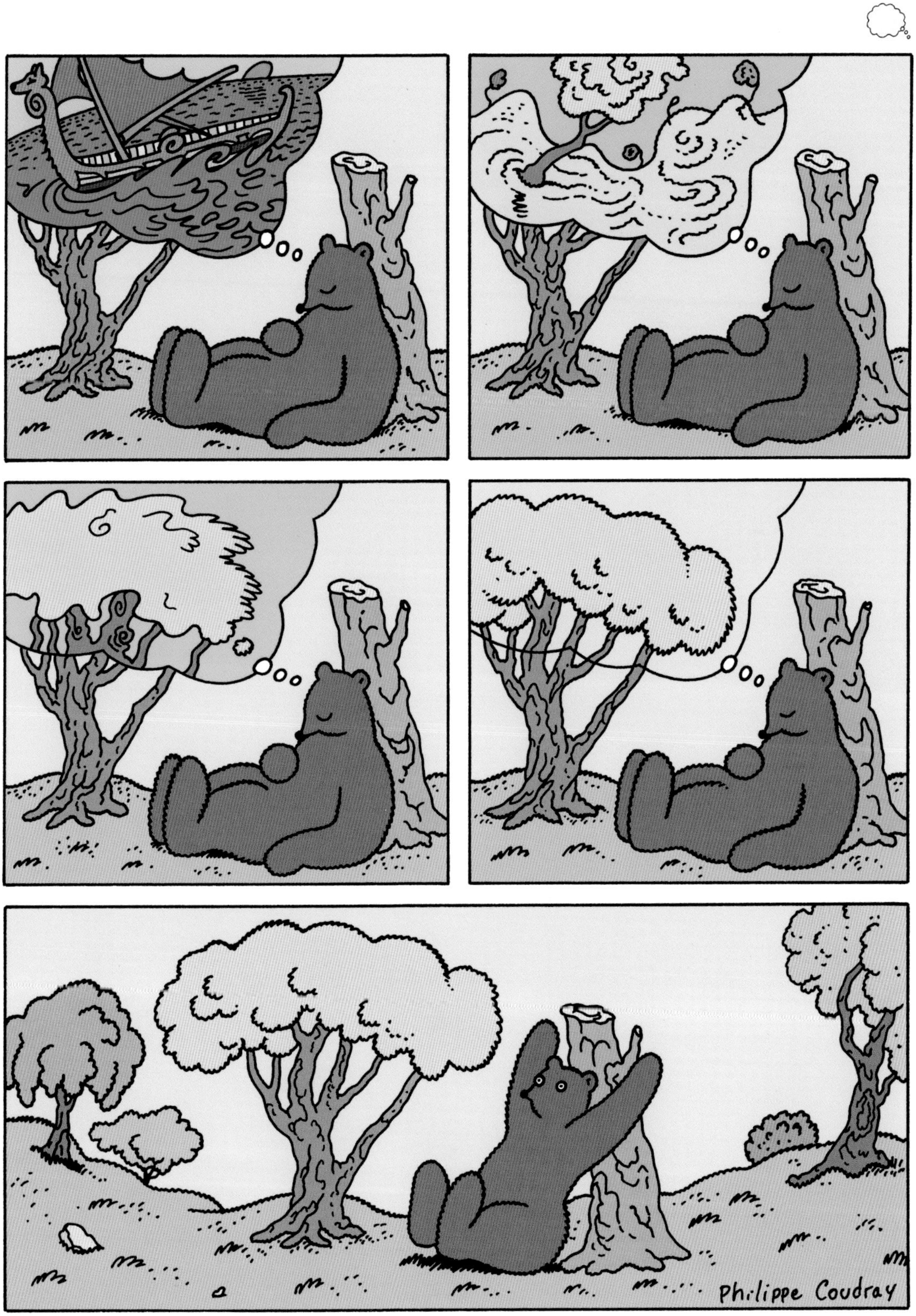
Philippe Coudray

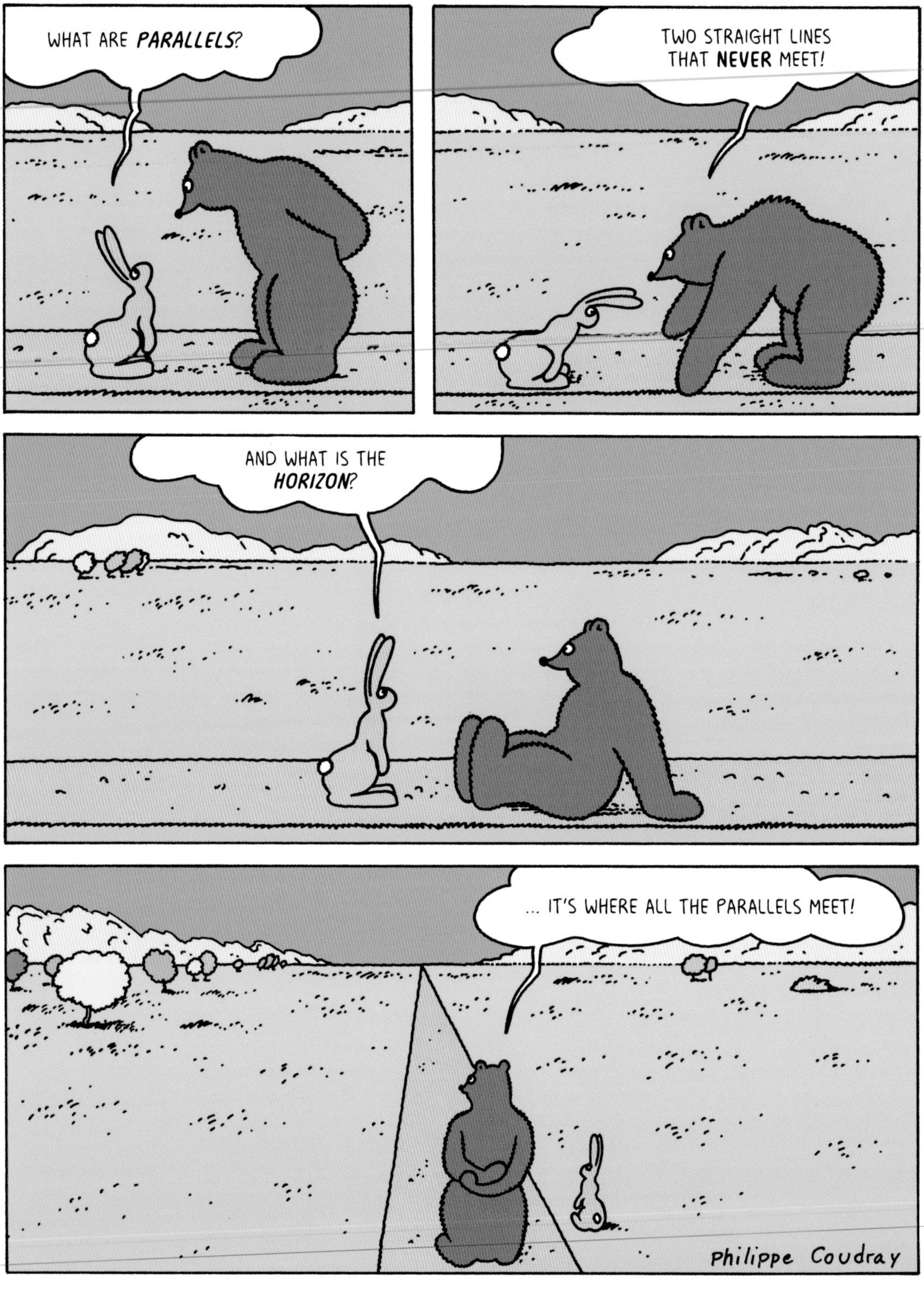
WHAT ARE PARALLELS?
TWO STRAIGHT LINES THAT NEVER MEET!
AND WHAT IS THE HORIZON?
... IT'S WHERE ALL THE PARALLELS MEET!
Philippe Coudray

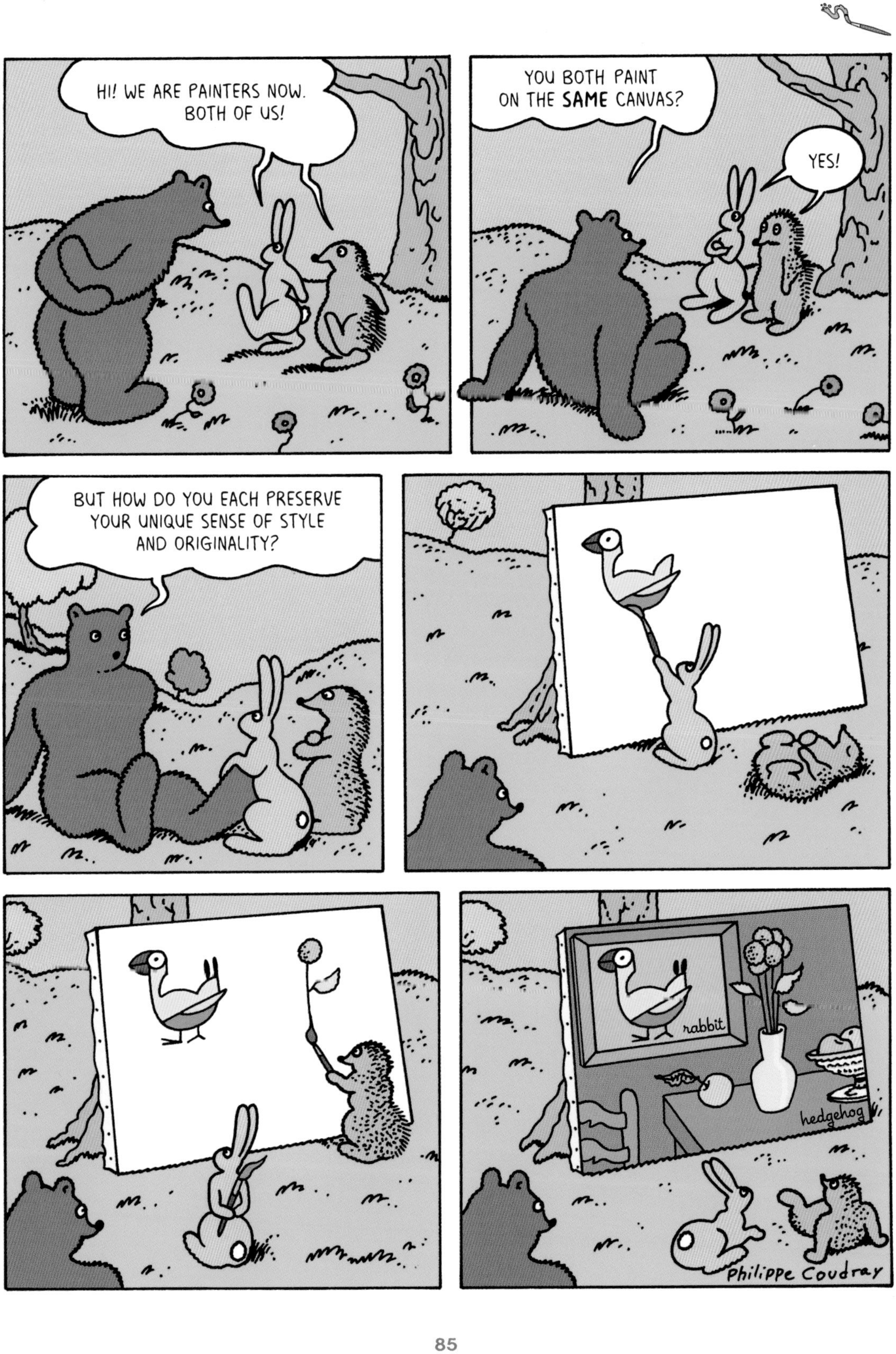
HI! WE ARE PAINTERS NOW. BOTH OF US!
YOU BOTH PAINT ON THE SAME CANVAS?
YES!
BUT HOW DO YOU EACH PRESERVE YOUR UNIQUE SENSE OF STYLE AND ORIGINALITY?
rabbit
hedgehog
Philippe Coudray

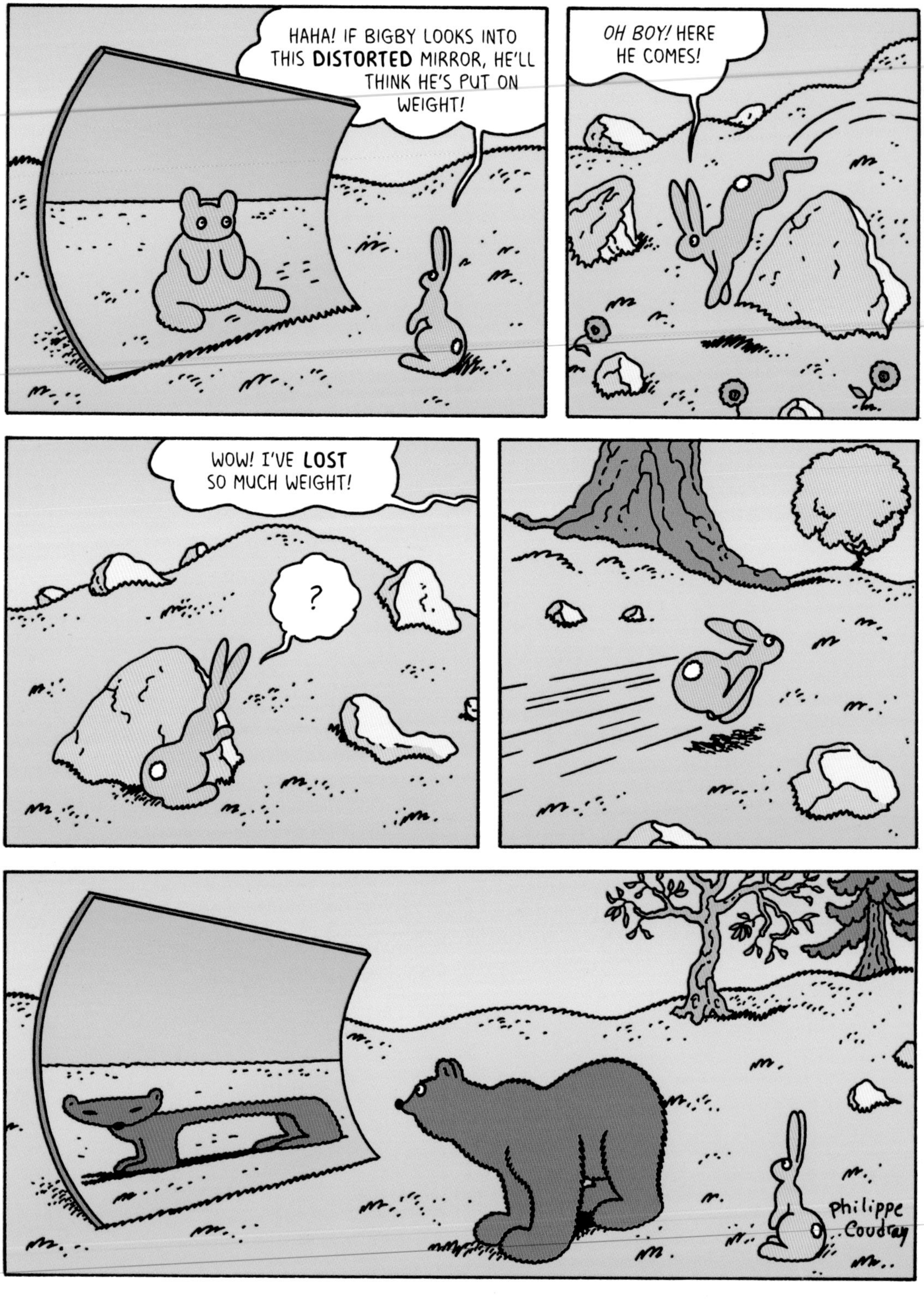
HAHA! IF BIGBY LOOKS INTO THIS **DISTORTED** MIRROR, HE'LL THINK HE'S PUT ON WEIGHT!
OH BOY! HERE HE COMES!
WOW! I'VE **LOST** SO MUCH WEIGHT!
?
Philippe Coudray

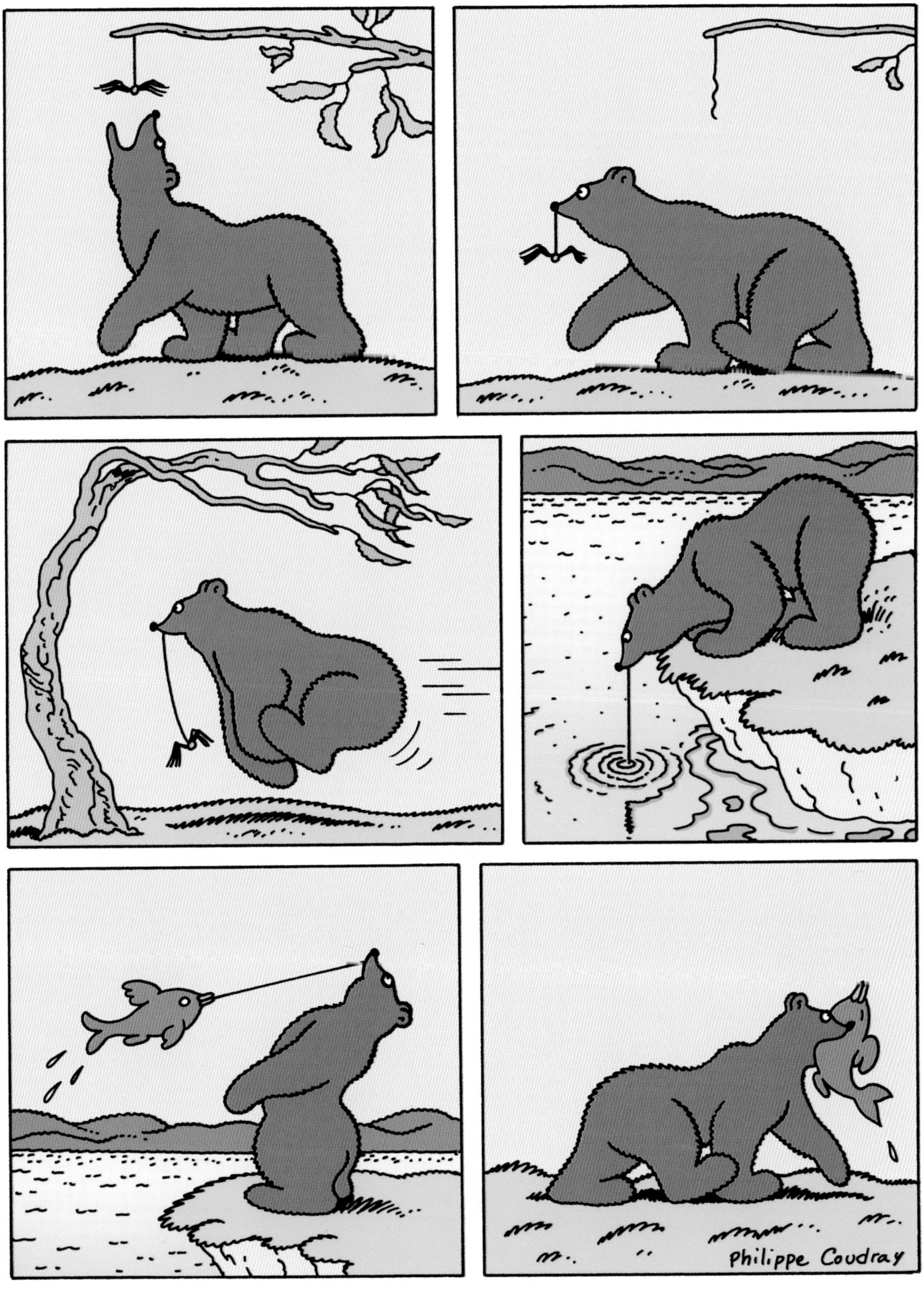
Philippe Coudray

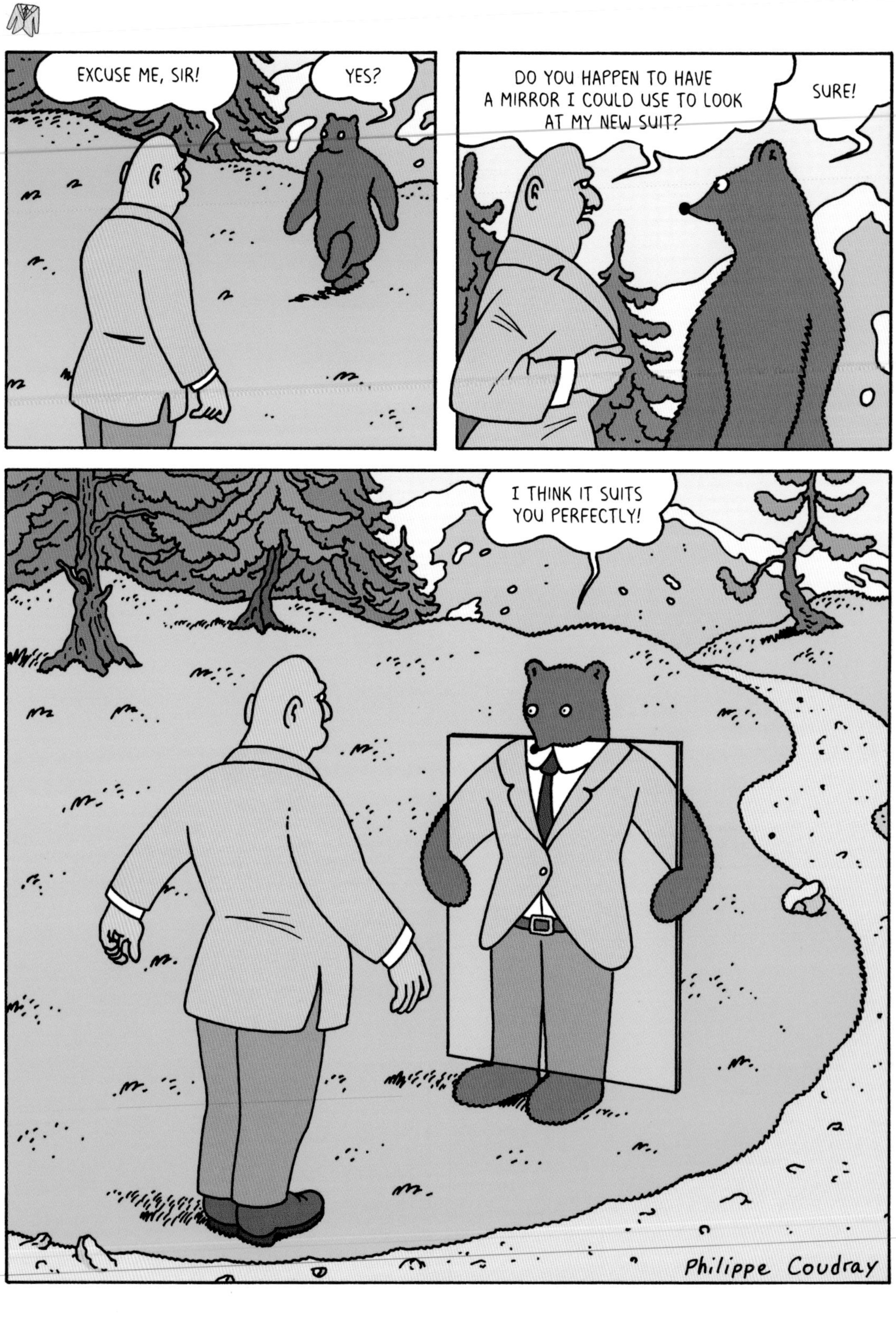
EXCUSE ME, SIR!
YES?
DO YOU HAPPEN TO HAVE A MIRROR I COULD USE TO LOOK AT MY NEW SUIT?
SURE!
I THINK IT SUITS YOU PERFECTLY!
Philippe Coudray

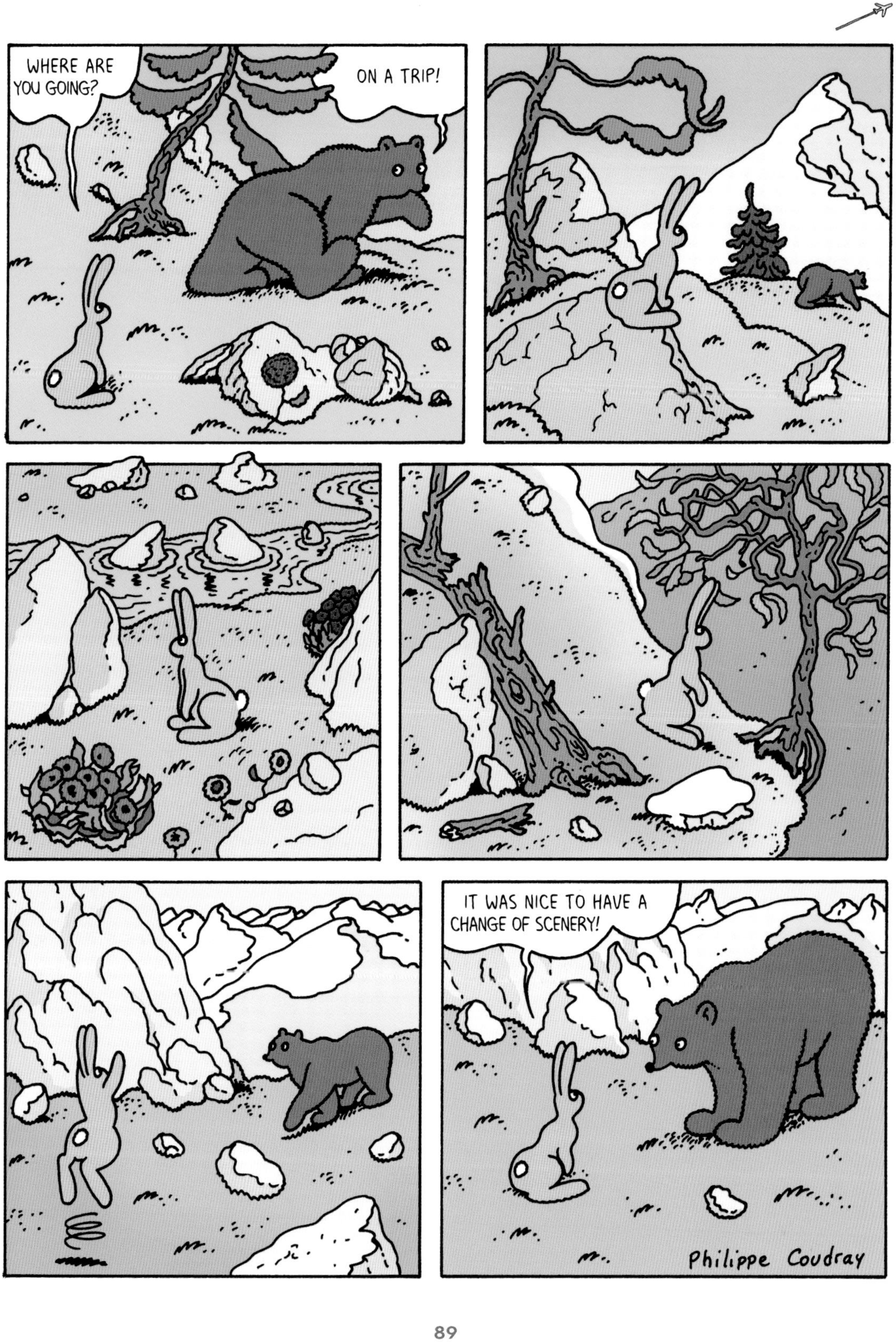
WHERE ARE YOU GOING?
ON A TRIP!
IT WAS NICE TO HAVE A CHANGE OF SCENERY!
Philippe Coudray

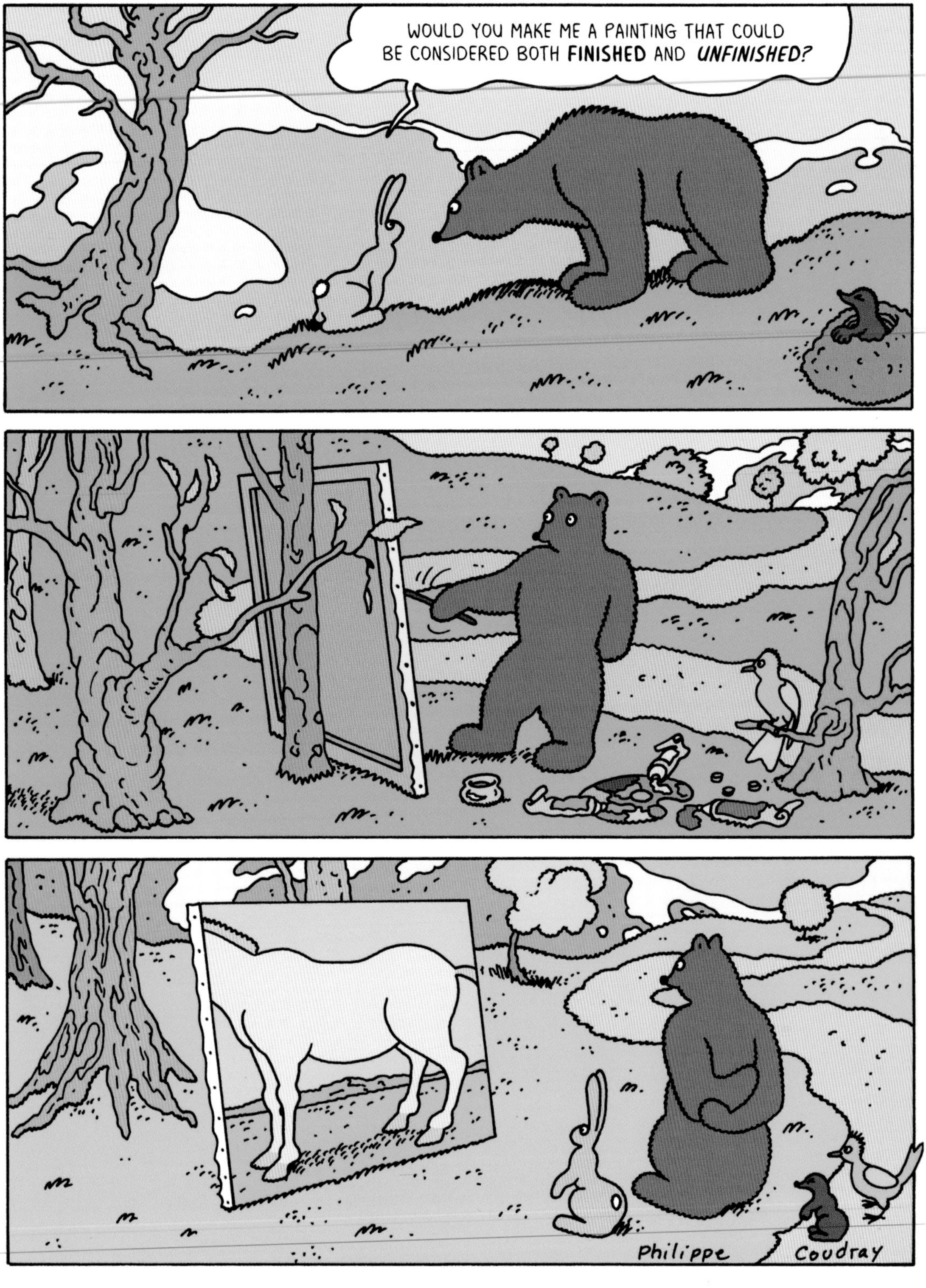
WOULD YOU MAKE ME A PAINTING THAT COULD BE CONSIDERED BOTH **FINISHED** AND ***UNFINISHED?***
Philippe Coudray

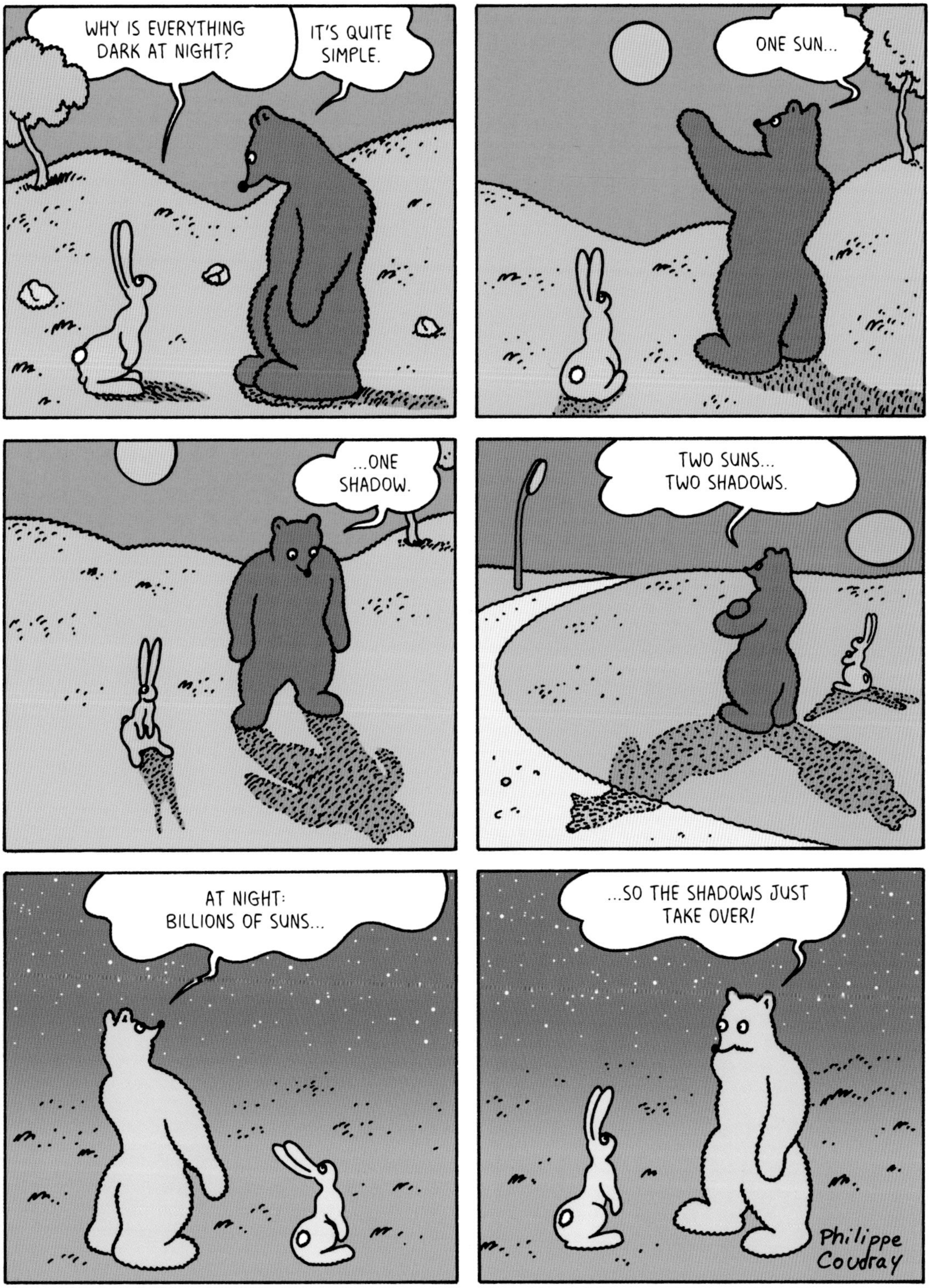
WHY IS EVERYTHING DARK AT NIGHT?
IT'S QUITE SIMPLE.
ONE SUN...
...ONE SHADOW.
TWO SUNS... TWO SHADOWS.
AT NIGHT: BILLIONS OF SUNS...
...SO THE SHADOWS JUST TAKE OVER!
Philippe Coudray

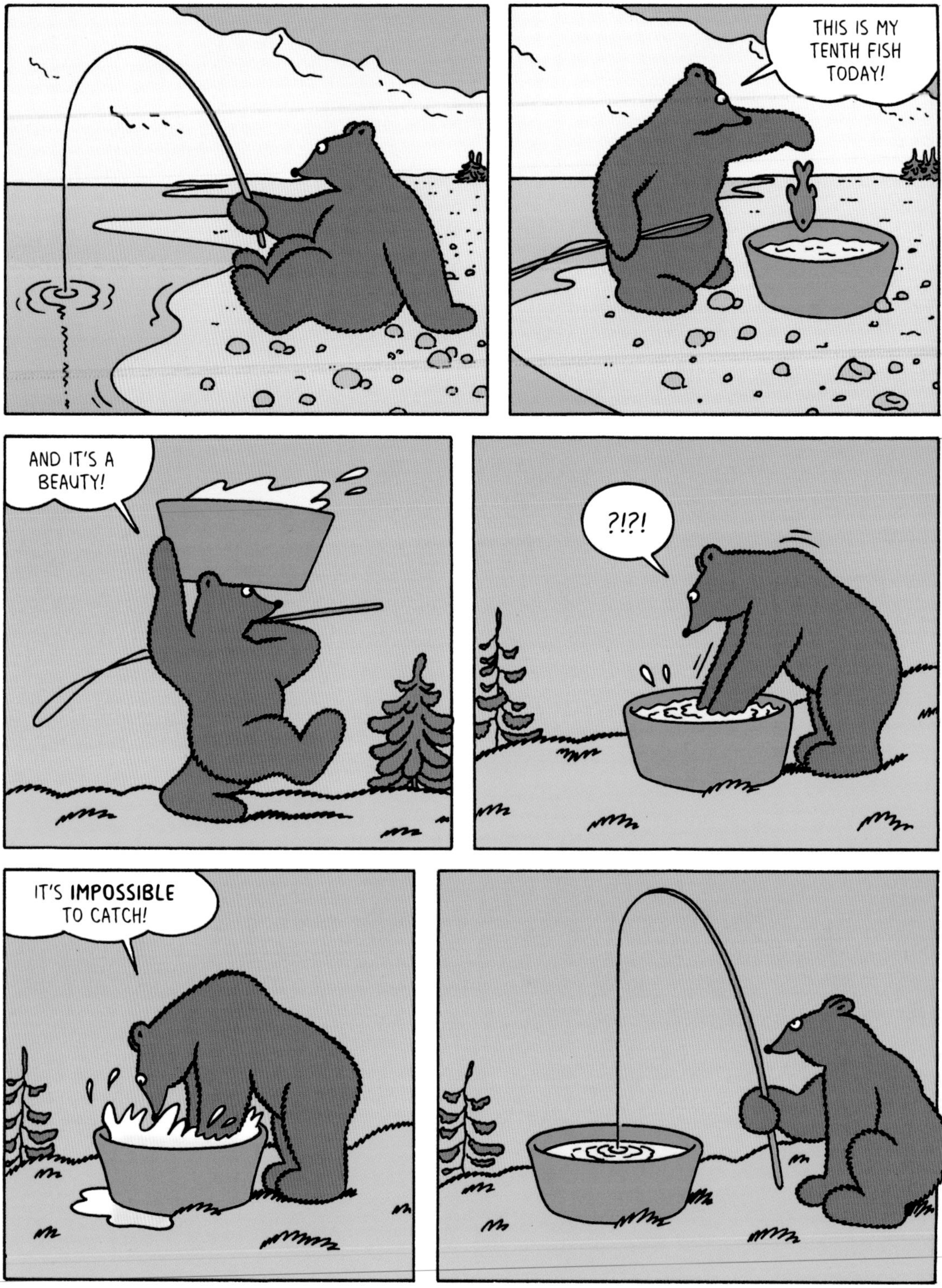
THIS IS MY TENTH FISH TODAY!
AND IT'S A BEAUTY!
?!?!
IT'S **IMPOSSIBLE** TO CATCH!

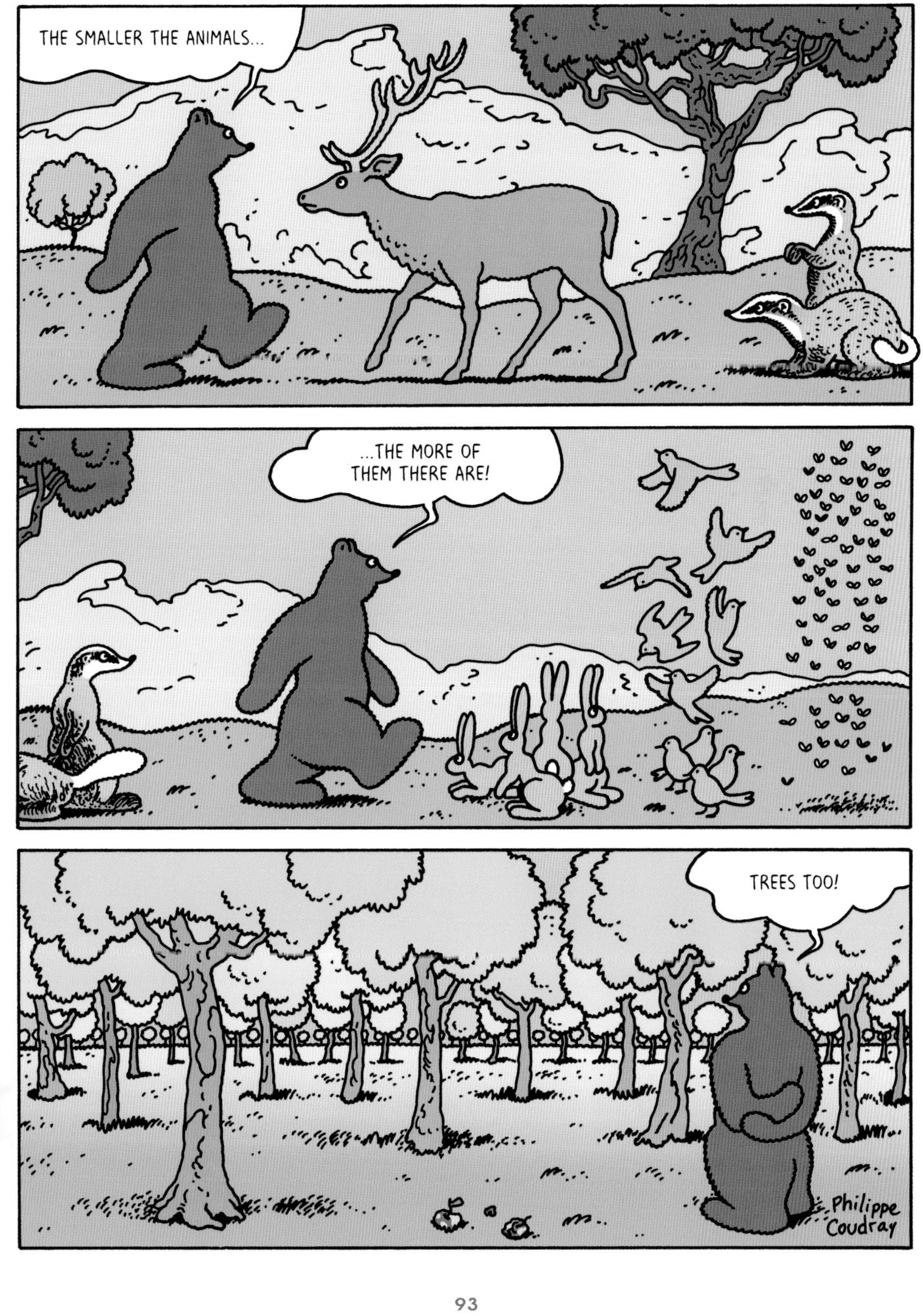
THE SMALLER THE ANIMALS...
...THE MORE OF THEM THERE ARE!
TREES TOO!
Philippe Coudray

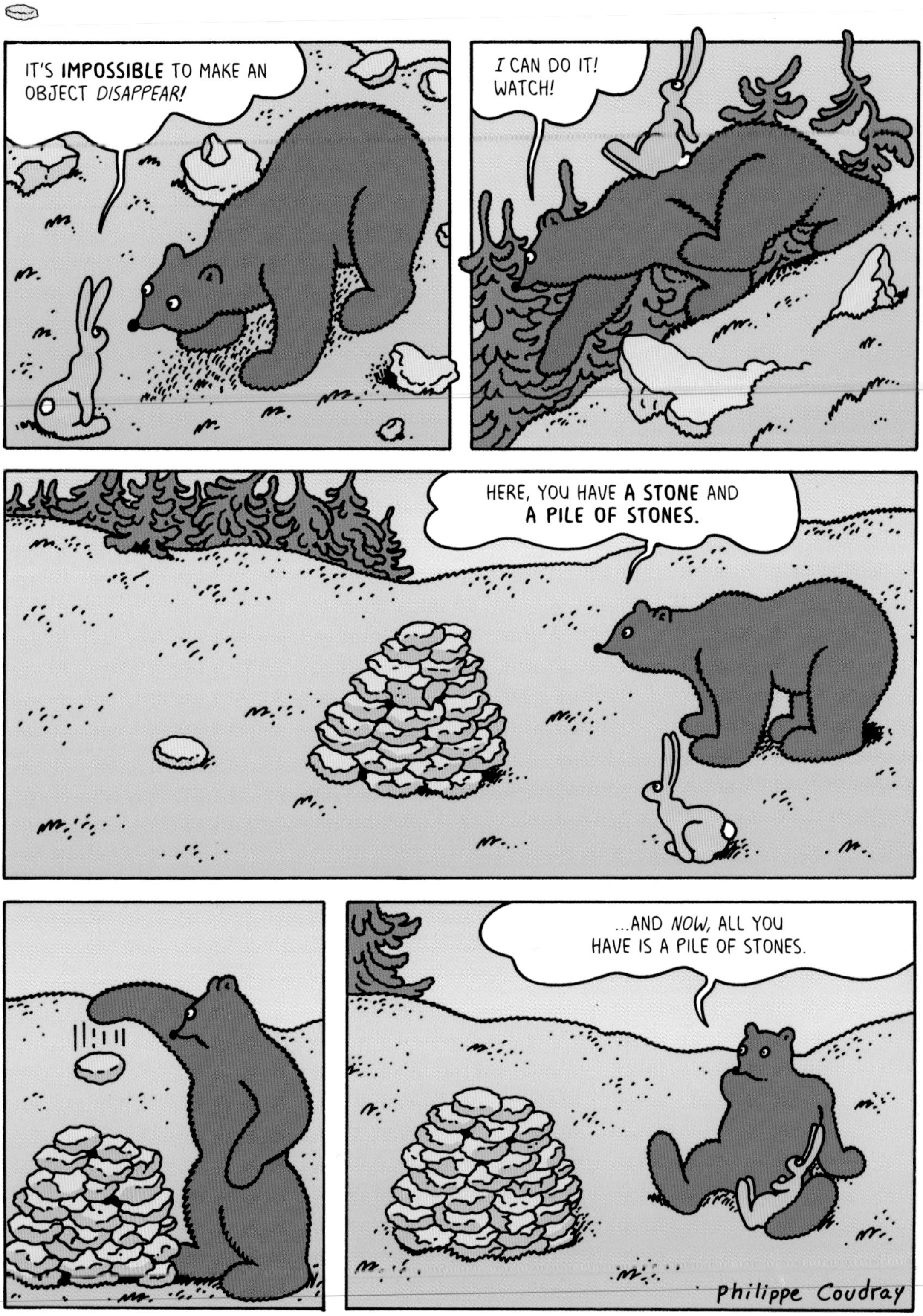
IT'S **IMPOSSIBLE** TO MAKE AN OBJECT *DISAPPEAR!*
I CAN DO IT! WATCH!
HERE, YOU HAVE **A STONE** AND **A PILE OF STONES.**
...AND *NOW,* ALL YOU HAVE IS A PILE OF STONES.
Philippe Coudray

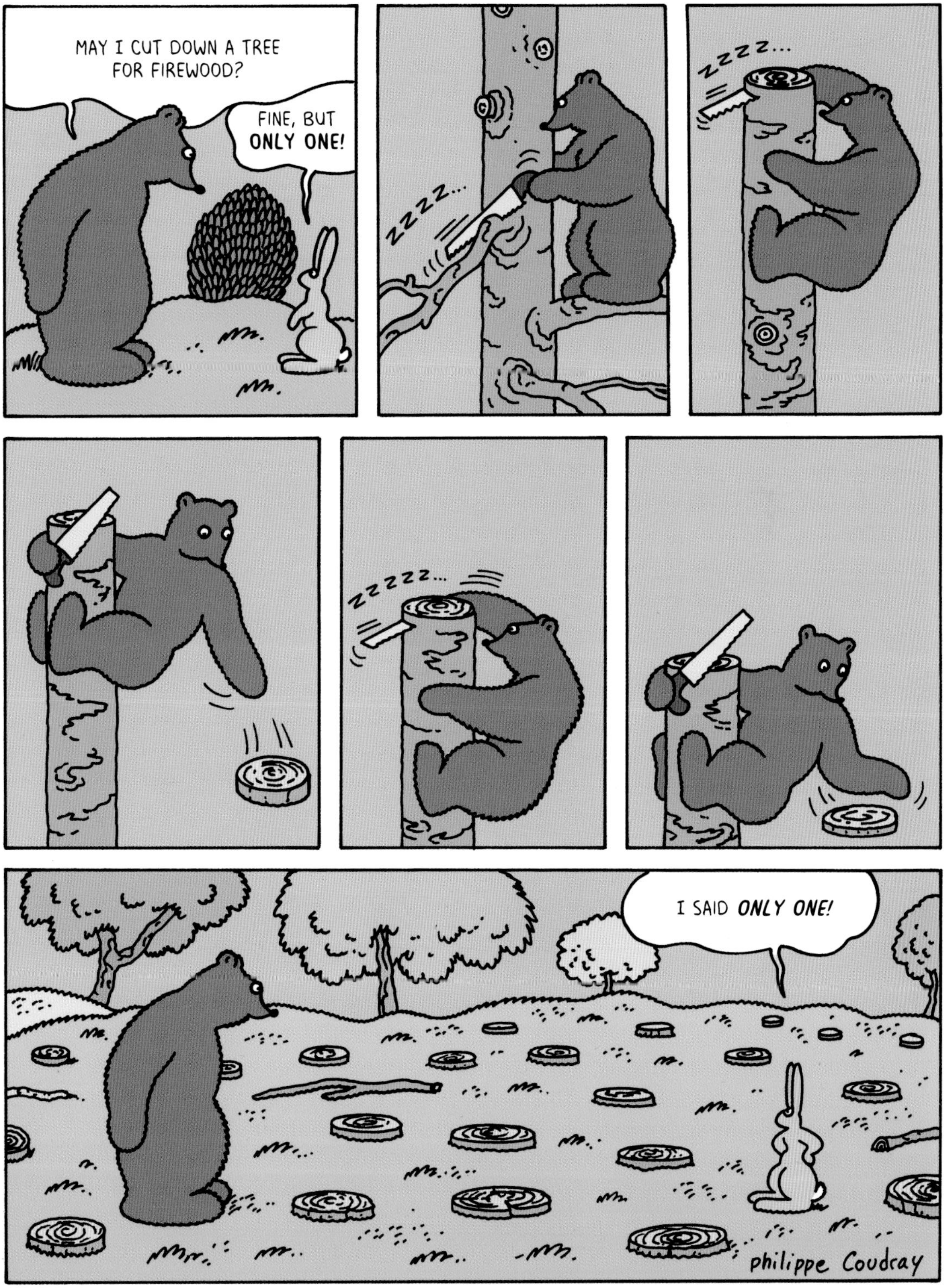
MAY I CUT DOWN A TREE FOR FIREWOOD?
FINE, BUT **ONLY ONE!**
ZZZZ...
ZZZZ...
ZZZZZ...
I SAID ***ONLY ONE!***
philippe Coudray

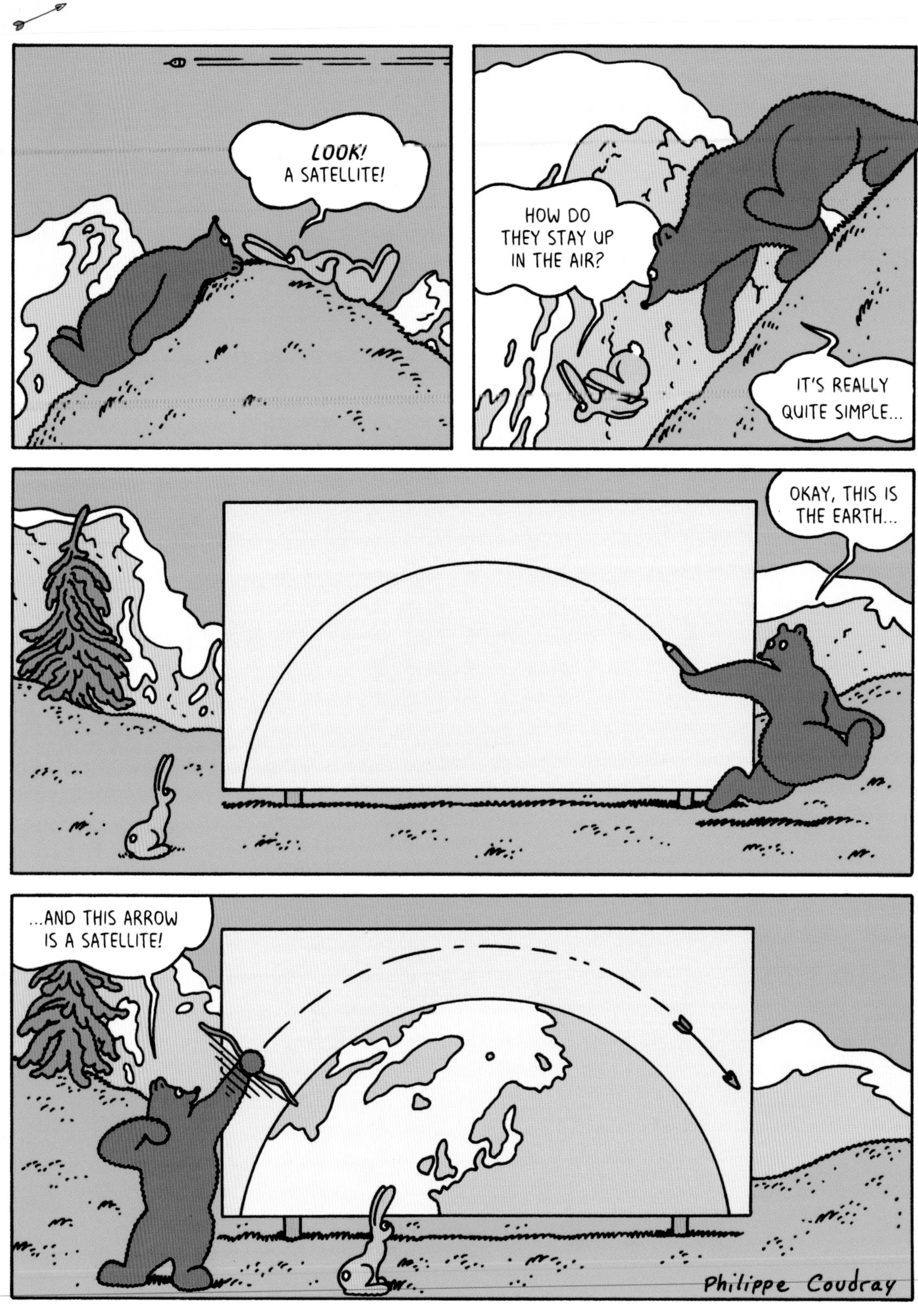
LOOK!
A SATELLITE!
HOW DO THEY STAY UP IN THE AIR?
IT'S REALLY QUITE SIMPLE...
OKAY, THIS IS THE EARTH...
...AND THIS ARROW IS A SATELLITE!
Philippe Coudray

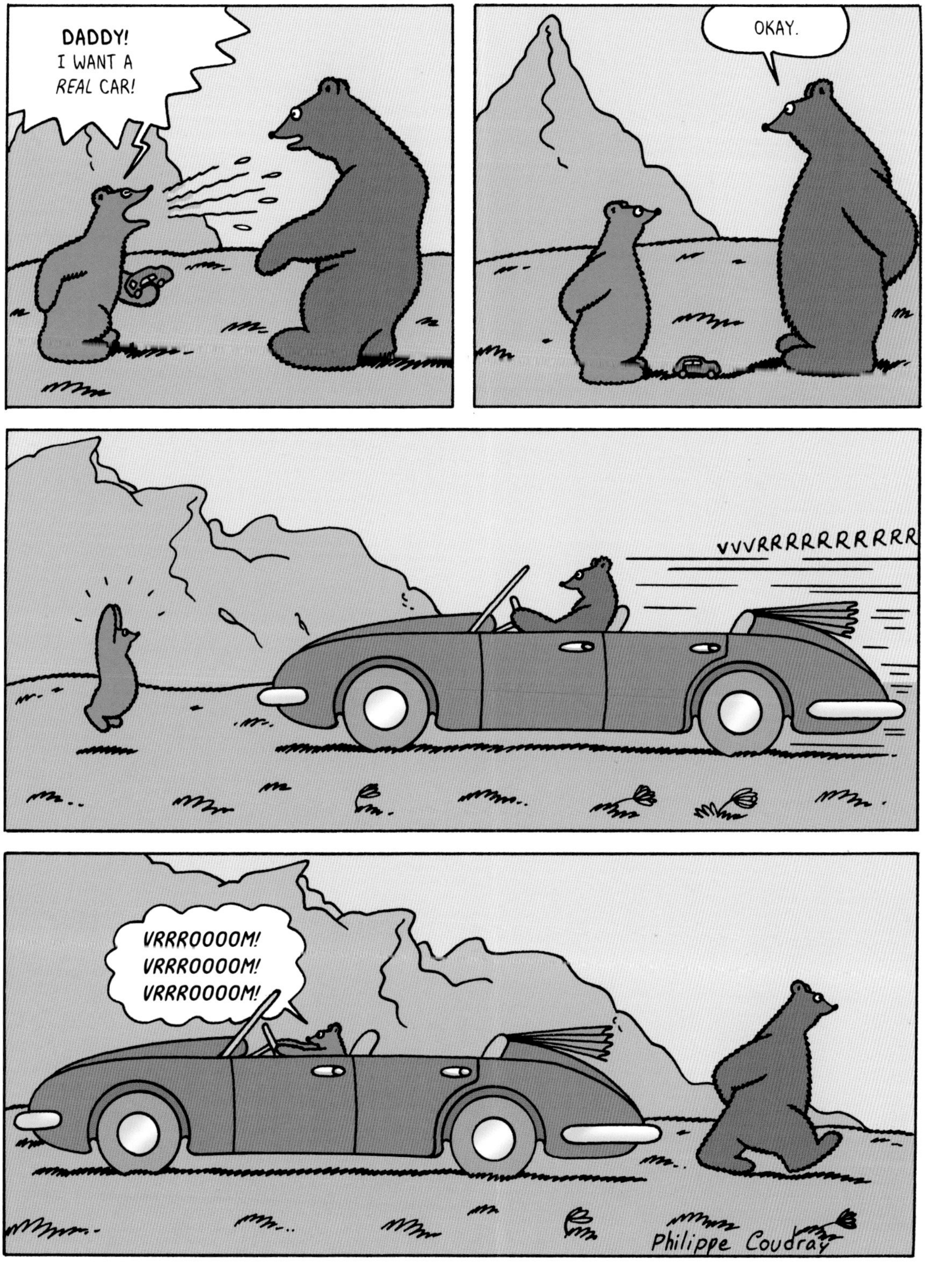

DADDY! I WANT A REAL CAR!
OKAY.
VVVRRRRRRRRRR
VRRROOOOM! VRRROOOOM! VRRROOOOM!
Philippe Coudray

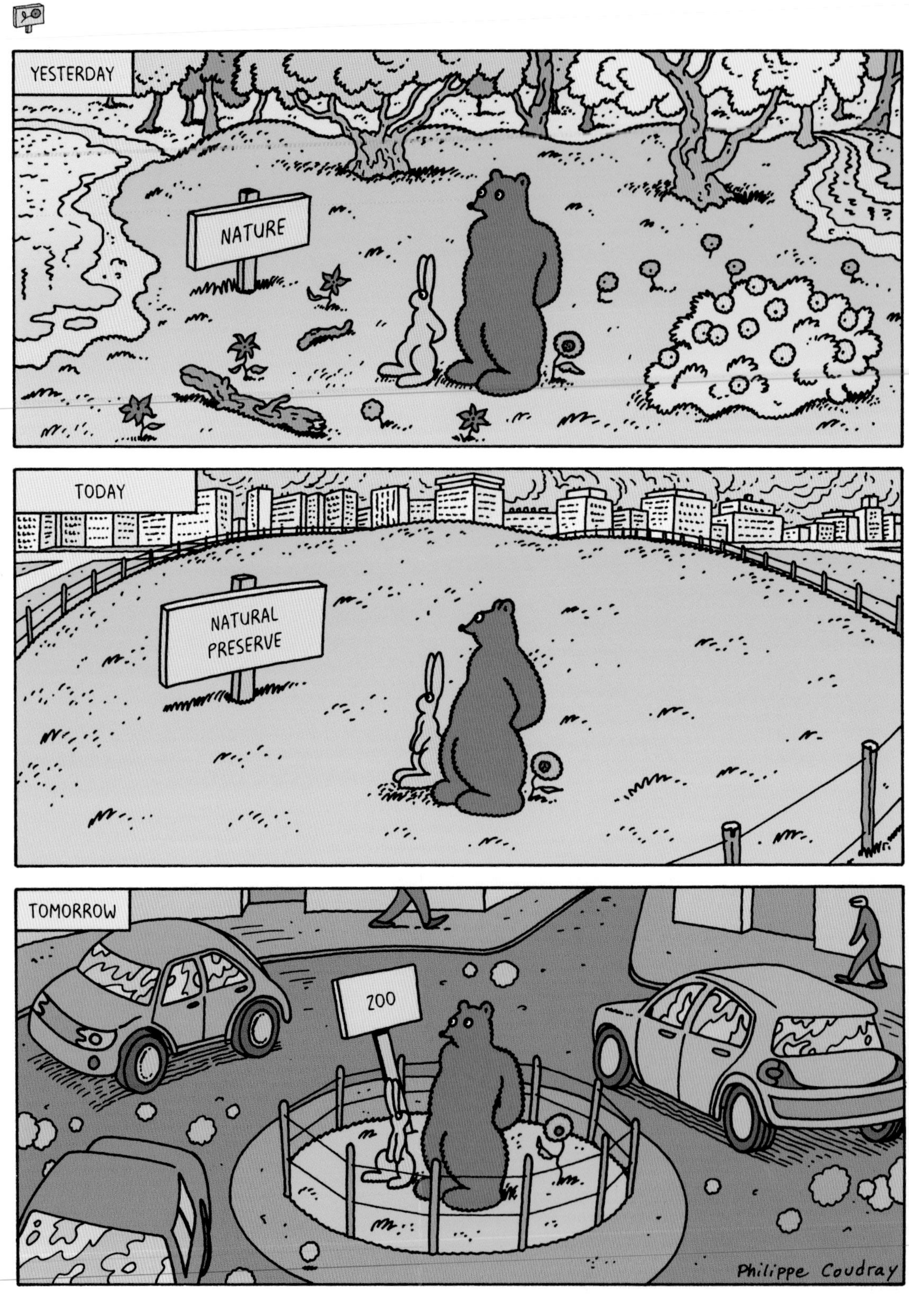

YESTERDAY
NATURE
TODAY
NATURAL PRESERVE
TOMORROW
ZOO
Philippe Coudray

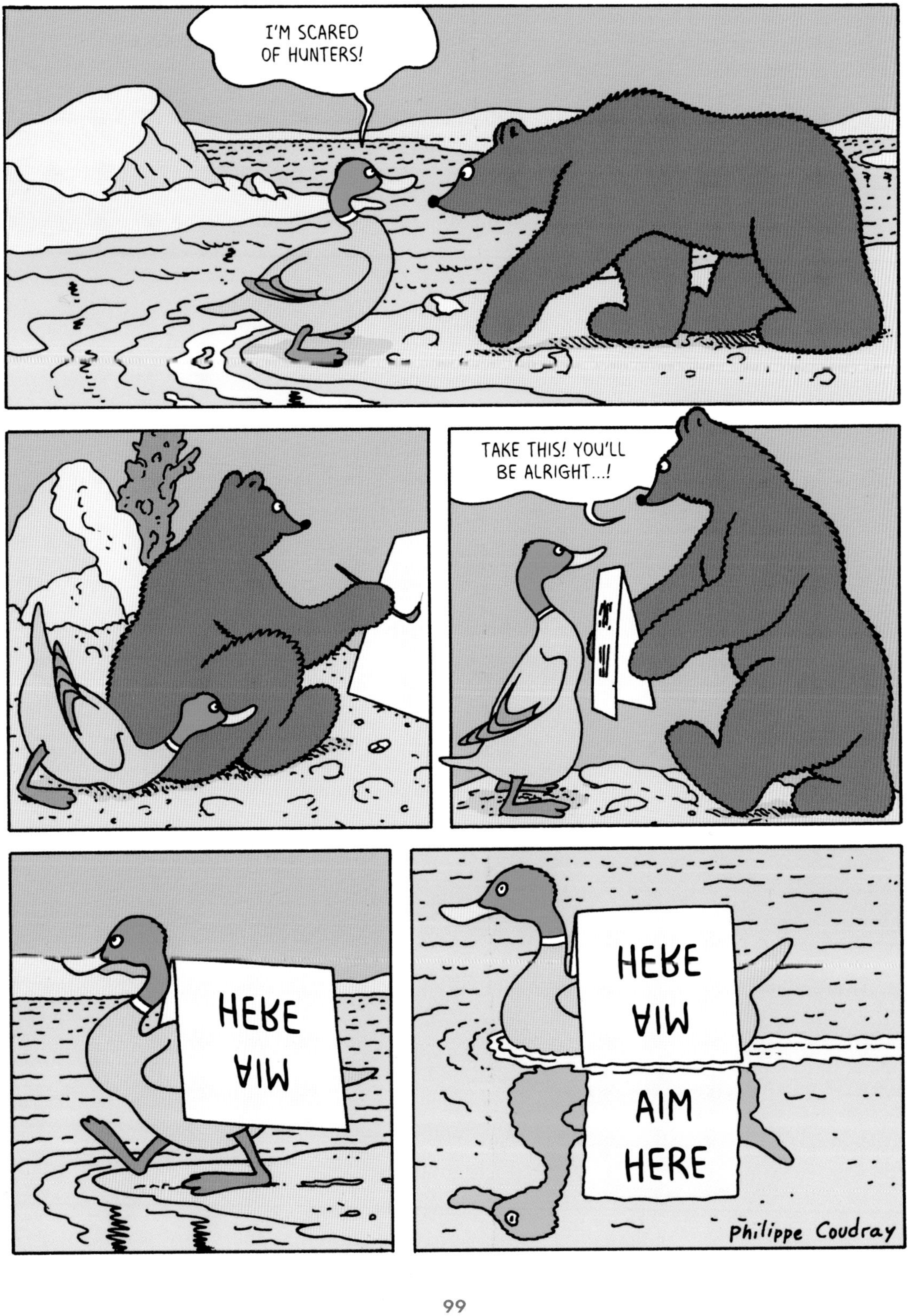
I'M SCARED OF HUNTERS!
TAKE THIS! YOU'LL BE ALRIGHT...!
AIM
HERE
Philippe Coudray

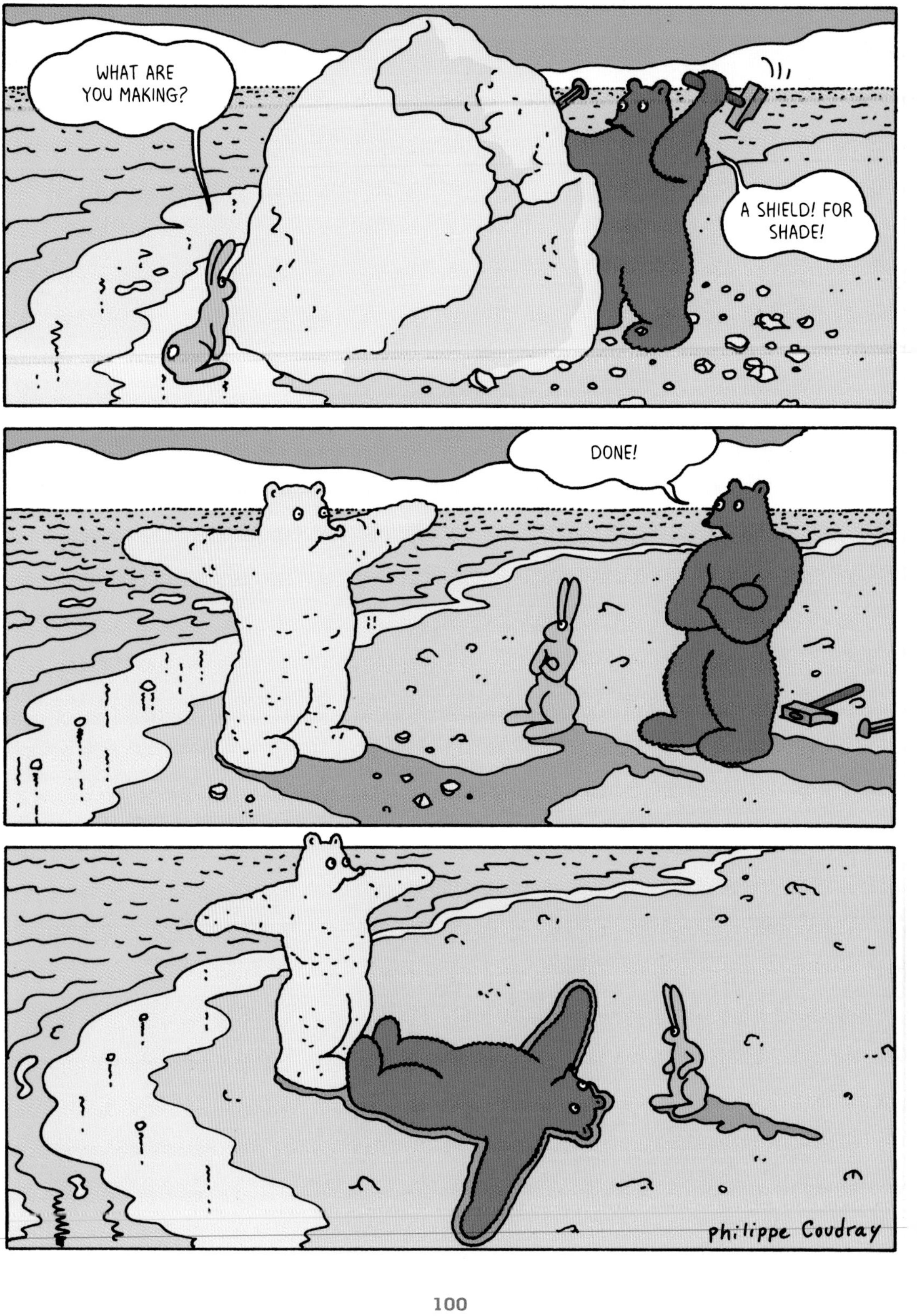
WHAT ARE YOU MAKING?
A SHIELD! FOR SHADE!
DONE!
philippe Coudray

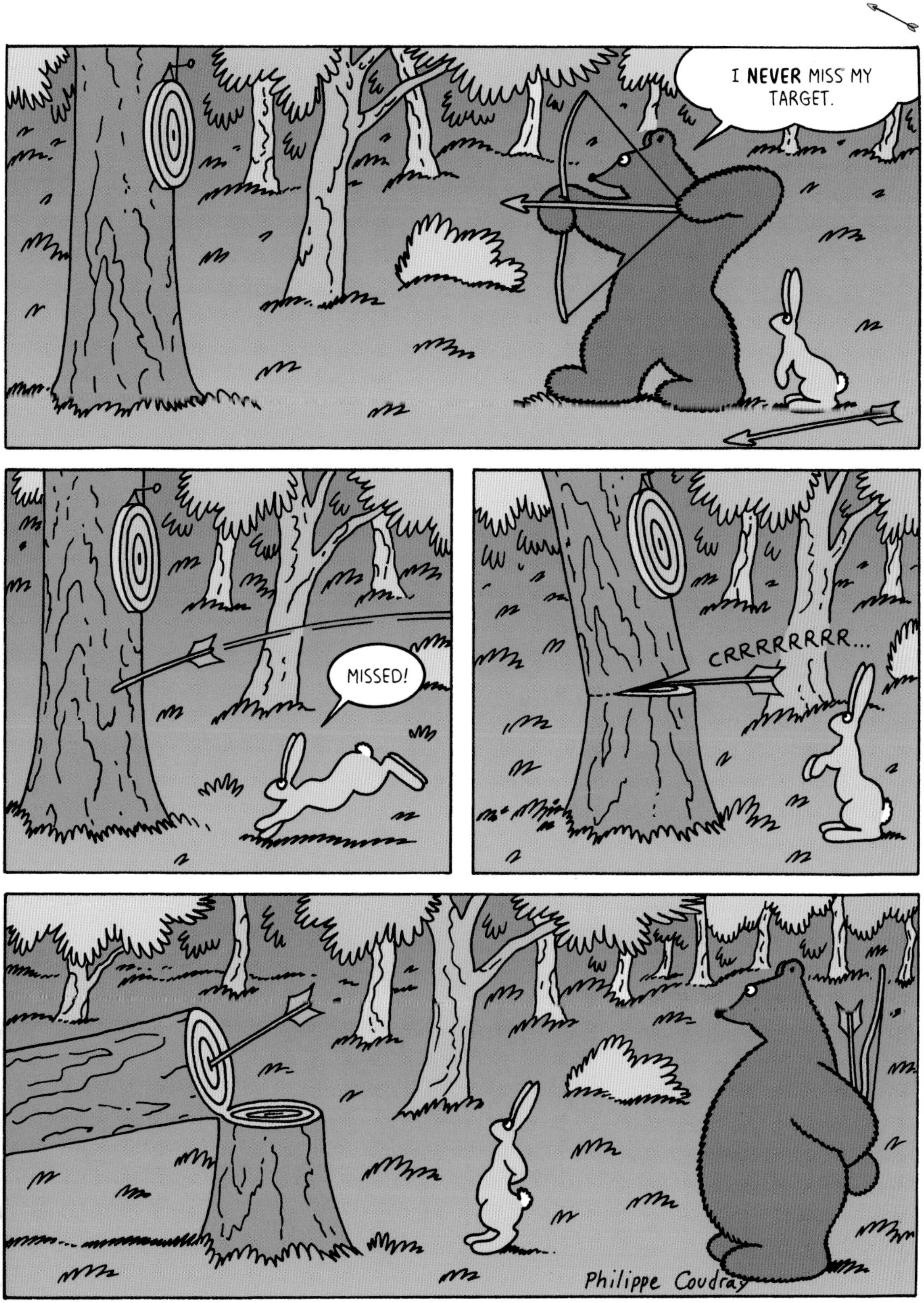
I **NEVER** MISS MY TARGET.
MISSED!
CRRRRRRRR...
Philippe Coudray

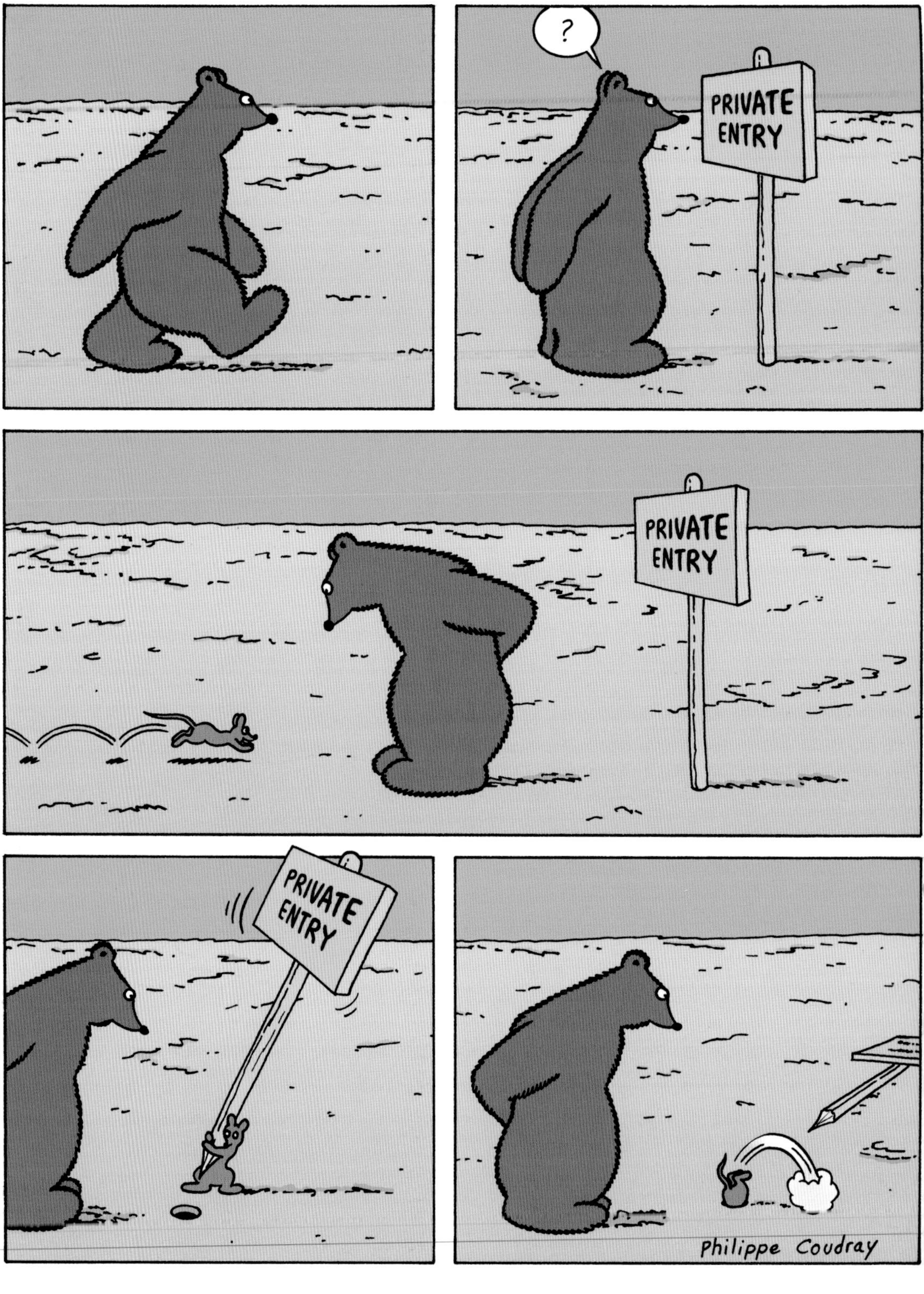
?
PRIVATE ENTRY
PRIVATE ENTRY
PRIVATE ENTRY
Philippe Coudray